6/21

GONE MISSING IN HARLEM

Gone Missing in Harlem

A Novel

KARLA FC HOLLOWAY

TRIQUARTERLY BOOKS/NORTHWESTERN UNIVERSITY PRESS

EVANSTON, ILLINOIS

TriQuarterly Books
Northwestern University Press
www.nupress.northwestern.edu

Printed in the United States of America

10 9 8 7 6 5 4 3 2 1

Library of Congress Cataloging-in-Publication Data

Names: Holloway, Karla F. C., 1949– author.
Title: Gone missing in Harlem : a novel / Karla FC Holloway.
Description: Evanston, Illinois : TriQuarterly Books/Northwestern University Press,
    2021.
Identifiers: LCCN 2020047147 | ISBN 9780810143531 (paperback) | ISBN
    9780810143548 (ebook)
Subjects: LCSH: Kidnapping—New York (State)—New York—Fiction. | African
    American police—New York (State)—New York—Fiction. | African Americans—
    New York (State)—New York—Social conditions—Fiction. | Harlem (New York,
    N.Y.)—Fiction. | LCGFT: Detective and mystery fiction.
Classification: LCC PS3608.O49417 G66 2021 | DDC 813/.6—dc23
LC record available at https://lccn.loc.gov/2020047147

This book is dedicated to my grandson,
Jacobo Xavier Arce-Holloway,
because we like to read books together and make worlds from our words.

Contents

Incident

My Baby Gone?

BABY CHLOE WAS ONLY ALONE FOR A SNATCH OF A MOMENT—WHICH some said was just long enough for exactly that—when her mother went inside Chasen's Grocery to pay for the apples she'd selected from the front window bin. It was mid autumn. Some leaves had already turned, distancing themselves from summer's green. A quiet morning light scattered through the leafy filter of the chestnut's canopy at the corner and unabashedly took up the gilded promise of the next season's colors. Despite the disarray to come, the day would be brisk and bright. Somebody, likely the boy Chasen hired to do the toting from the basement storage and sweep floors inside and at the store's front door, had meticulously stacked the apples into a golden, then green, and then deep crimson leading to striated shades of red pyramid that rose to a peak right under the window. A gilded and black-edged calligraphy scrolled the grocer's name across the glass. A mix of other produce—pears, carrots, and potatoes, red and yellow onions both, latticed baskets of tomatoes still attached to their tangle of vines, and mounds of string beans ready to be grabbed up by handfuls lay in a haphazard scatter across a hodgepodge of wooden crates. Only the apples were arranged, daring someone to break into the rising display. Selma Mosby did exactly that.

With each grasp of the round firm fruit, she got closer to her memory of skillet-fried apples simmered down into a buttery sweet nectar with

3

more than enough vanilla and nutmeg and cinnamon sprinkled through. Selma thought that if she repeated the childhood memory exactly right, she might come closer to being cherished like her brother June Bug had been. Then, when her mother came in the door of their small kitchenette, pulled off her hat, and hooked the thin felt cloche behind the door, she'd look over to the stove. The apples would have already simmered down to thick juices and tender slices, and DeLilah would have smelled them even before she got to their door because it would be hard to miss the sharp sweetness of cinnamon and nutmeg slicing through the grimy stairwell's stale air. But it would still be a surprise that it was her own household offering up the memory. And even more startling that Selma had peeled the apples, sliced them good and thin, and took the time to pull out the iron skillet she'd shoved up under the stove because it would only be out if there was a reason to cook, and these days it was hard to find anything close to reason. But her daughter had imagined the entire scene, right down to how everything could come together right on time, and then, with everything in place like it used to be when her brother still lived with them, it might be her mother's lips would edge upwards into at least a slight smile. And after that how she maybe could reach over and cup her daughter's cheek—even if it was just briefly—before she went behind the door to take down her at-home apron, wrap it round her waist, and pull out the flour tin to make up dough for fried pies.

Selma had the moment fully fleshed out in what was left of her mind when she tried to maneuver the baby's flashy modern pram into the grocery; but its wide wheel carriage couldn't make it down the aisle. So she backed the buggy out of the door and left it lined up against the bin that held the yams. It wouldn't take long to ring up the apples and pull some stick cinnamon from the counter jar. She wouldn't be gone more than a minute.

That much was correct. Selma was not gone for long at all. But the same would not be true for Baby Chloe.

The not-much-older-than-a-girl-herownself left her daughter's carriage outside and stepped back into the small neighborhood gathered inside Chasen's. She didn't notice the white man on the corner leaned against the streetlamp pretending to read a folded newspaper. A burlap sack was rolled and tucked up under his arm. He was probably no older than thirty, even though his pockmarked cheeks made him look older. He

4

had tortoise-shelled horn-rims and wore a brown fedora. And more often than looking down at the paper, he looked up and around, surveying the street, and especially watching the grocery store on the corner.

A few kids from the elementary school clustered near the counter. They took turns leaning over the candy cabinet, runny noses and sweaty fingers pressed against the glass, doing the arithmetic they'd just learned until they could figure what selection would get them the most Mary Janes and still have enough left for some Necco Wafers to cut the taste of the caramel. Or a twisted licorice stick, red if you were a girl, but the boys liked black so they could scrunch it up between their nose and upper lip like mustaches. The girls thought the boys were nasty and told them so.

Ada Chasen had a rule that candy bagged was candy bought and would not be put back even for a "Please, ma'am, I changed my mind. Can I have that one there?" pointing to an afterthought that now seemed the better deal. If she hadn't dropped the fluffy red-and-white peppermint pillow into the bag, she'd put it back. But if her pinchers had let go of the candy and it had already dropped into the bag, they had to make do with what they had chosen. It took time, and one of the things about Chasen's is that it was okay for them to think about it. Mr. Chasen waited for his wife to finish at the cash register, until each little one had a bag of candy they could grasp and share (or not), and then he weighed Selma's apples, counted out the cinnamon sticks, and took her quarter. He asked after her baby, with only the edge of his disappointment framing the question. He was concerned as to how she had been making do. He'd known Selma since she was a baby. He remembered her brother Percy, his disappointment still fresh of how he'd turned down an offer to work at the grocery, which Chasen only made because he saw how he was leaning toward a gang of kids whose decisions were bound to lead to whatever kind of trouble it was that made his mama send him off. At least he figured the mother had directed the sudden leave-taking. But DeLilah Mosby was so hushed mouth herownself, it didn't do too much good to do more than be pleasant and welcoming to her and her girl, Selma. Chasen watched her, though, and had an opinion like he had about most of the neighborhood kids who came in. He'd picked out Selma as a girl who would make her way to something fine. She was steady and quiet. Her mother was watchful. She carried her books cover out instead of hiding them in the crook of her arms as if she were ashamed of being bookish. She asked them questions about Germany and was really curious about the map he kept in the back of the store. As far as he was concerned, curiosity was the one certain characteristic of being a fine human being. But this time, when or if she answered his kindly inquiry about the baby, he didn't hear her because she had already turned away from the counter, her purchase complete and her dream of what the cooked apples might accomplish for her filling out its blurred edges. She needed to be her mama's baby girl again. So Selma wasn't paying her one bit of attention when Mrs. Ada Chasen followed her out in order to get a peek at her newborn. The grocer's wife watched while Selma bent over to place the brown paper bag into the pram. Neither of them stopped to notice the street's unusual quiet, even the white man had disappeared from his vigil at the lamppost. Selma laid the lumpy bag right on the baby's blanket, folding the top over on itself so the apples wouldn't tumble out. But it wouldn't have mattered if they had. There was nothing else there. No not-yet-turned-dusky-cheeked child, no grasping-fingers baby, no rose-lipped infant. With Mrs. Chasen standing next to her, trying desperately to understand why she saw nothing in the buggy but a bulging brown paper bag full of apples, Selma looked up and then over at the elderly woman and finally took in her worried look. She twisted sharply from one side to the other, and not seeing what was expected, took in some air (the last full and deep and deliberate breath she remembered) and said what she did. Mrs. Chasen's wail nearly drowned out Selma's soft questions. *"Is?"* She whispered her confusion. *"My baby gone? My baby gone missing?"*

PART I

The War Years
and
A Renaissance

1

Your Money or Your Life

HIS MOTHER AND SISTER STILL CALLED HIM JUNE BUG BUT HIS NAME was Percy Harrison Mosby, and he left Harlem when the gamblers that he'd gone and gotten himself entangled with took him over the edge. His way with numbers was prescient if not downright odd. He could see them multiplied, divided, subtracted, and added in his head. He could tell you the sum of something, divide it by all the boys in his gang, and even make fractions for who got what—at the same time he adjusted for the content of each boy's contribution. Percy could do it quickly and be so right that nobody dared to question him. Except his mother always told him "sometimes you so right you just dead right." And that was where he was now. Just like his mama warned. Sidled up and way too close to dead. It was past time to get going.

Percy was a slender boy with an oval-shaped head and deep-set brown eyes that were nearly covered by more than his share of long dark lashes. You could see his high cheekbones when he grinned, which was worth waiting for because the playful mix between mischievous and sweet-tempered was sheer good fortune to anyone on the receiving end. Despite his good looks, nobody would ever accuse him of being braggadocious or having uppity ways. He was quiet and unassuming. Whatever it was that was going on with Percy Mosby happened mostly in his head. Even at home he wasn't known for much more than a "Nope" or "Yes, ma'am." There was his clear kindness and dependably compassionate attention, but you had to be close to him to know it was there. Once he reached his teen years and began to stretch out, what made folks take some notice of him was that he brought them to mind of his Daddy Iredell. Not only in manner, but also his looks. He leaned toward a kind of tall and lanky that made his walk more a graceful ambling than the brash swagger of his age-mates. Folks called attention to how he walked with the same kind of ease that Iredell had and that made them take notice of how he shared the same features as his daddy. His sharply chiseled chin, his bright chestnut shimmer, and his angled ridge of cheekbones all looked to be straight from his daddy. Percy's face was narrow, but it still had room enough for a dimpling that came on easy when he laughed. That and his full-on smile, as broad and kind as it was sincere and interested, earned him more forgiveness than he was usually due being that he did have some prankish ways. Nevertheless, despite how much he loved his daddy, when folks remarked on their resemblance, it gave him no pleasure. In fact, it was not at all a comfort for Percy to hear how he was growing to look more and more like Iredell; it was just another reminder that his daddy was dead.

And anyways, in all the ways that Iredell had been loud and generous and gregarious—the kind of man folks entered a room asking, "Where Iredell at?" before they even took off their cap or let somebody offer them something to drink—Percy was unobtrusive and quiet. Not so much that folks could say *still waters*. But the kind of quiet that made his mama anxious. The kind that led to the wrong folks noticing him despite and—to be truthful about it—because of his silences. Percy could blend in like a chameleon and be just another colored boy on a street corner or lolling about on the edges of a room; or—what he did most days—sit so quiet you barely knew he was perched at the corner table in the nearly empty apartment, his long legs splayed to either side and his head bent down, attentive to a fault to whatever was his given task while Boss beat a customer into giving up the money he owed.

Boss was just another of the white men who stalked Harlem looking for folks who would do what they wouldn't; who could go up in the tenements and get the one they was looking for without their having to do anything other than stand outside and wait. White men hanging out on the streets were worth maybe a second glance. But Harlem's colored boys measured the community's rhythms, moved with ease inside the safety of shared stairwells, and could lean for days up against front-stoop railings without anybody asking them anything more than *How do?*

Inside, Harlem's families kept their kind of outdoors. Used to screens, some even left early morning doors open to let the air pass through or propped them again in late afternoons to welcome children coming in from school or back from an errand. *You still out there on them steps. Come on up here and put my things in the icebox. Ain't nobody in this house got all day!* Open doors let occupied mamas stay abreast of stairwell shouted stories of "what had happened when . . ." and still keep to their ironing—which they would've brought out there too, if they could. Inside-the-tenements kept to its own rules, and one thing white folks knew was that it was no space for them. If you wanted to hear doors slamming shut, let a white man head up the stairs. Or the mutual insurance man. No difference. Don't nobody want from them. But that's why Boss did his business by sending boys like Percy in for whom or whatever he wanted while he watched—usually from right across the street.

Boss could have been unremarkable except for his horn-rimmed glasses, pockmarked cheeks, and the way he always wore the same brown fedora pulled down over his eyes, and how he kept a watch fob dangling from his inside pocket, making it easy for folks to say "you know the one—pale on the side of gray, pocket watch, gimp-legged, brown fedora . . ." The gimp came from what he told Percy was the first and last mistake he would ever make. Somebody took a shot at him instead of turning over the money he was owed. The lesson he took from that (and the one that he shared with Percy) was that the only way you carried a gun was with plans that you would be the first and only one to use it. He carried one up under a shoulder holster. Percy had never seen it. Until now.

Boss chose Percy from a bunch of kids, all eager to get "on payroll," as he described it. Percy got picked because he didn't let on he was interested; he just listened and watched, noticing how the man kept his hands clenched for the entire time. He instinctively understood Boss was holding a fixed posture and how he deliberately kept to one pitch. He didn't waste words—something Percy easily understood since he wasn't much for conversation hisownself.

On the day things went wrong, it was really closer to night. Almost dusk-dark. If you looked back over your shoulder just before you entered the unoccupied building, you could see the phosphorescent wake from the Harlem River churn a luminous watery bilge from a passing barge. There would soon be a full moon, but its glow mattered less than the electric Bishop's Crook lamps flickering on at street corners up and down the river drive. Boss used one of the building's empty apartments for his office. Used to be shops on the first floor until they got burned out. The second floor and iron stairwell behind the building were okay, if you knew how to navigate them. Through the passway back to the rear and two flights up. He kept one eye on the failing daylight and the other on his pocket watch, but mostly he depended on twilight's slow filter, when the certainty of lingering shadows helped him navigate the job's necessities.

Percy was aware of each stage of the shakedown happening across the room. He didn't need to watch; he knew its pattern. This one was worse than usual not only because the man had no words, none of the stuttered excuses or "Hey, man" explanations ... but the pitiful whimpering from somebody who knew he had no means of escape, no plea, no explanation that might suffice. The man came in ahead of Boss, stumbling over the threshold and already bent over from the fist that Boss jammed deep into his kidney on their way up the back stairs. He looked around, as much for an exit as anything else; but also to get his bearings. Boss kept the room empty precisely because of the disorientation it accomplished. He followed the guy in and slammed the door more for effect than necessity. Percy was positioned in the far corner. He sat on a high stool behind a desk. There was nothing else in the room. The windows were shuttered closed. The man would wonder whether Percy could help. Whether his being there was a reason to think there was a chance three of them might eventually leave the room, even if he'd carry some deep bruises and likely broken ribs. But because Percy didn't look up at all, the man knew he was on his own. "Why you making it hard like this?" Boss didn't even bother to ask like he wanted or expected an answer. The man was already shrinking back, covering his privates like they were what was in danger. Percy could've felt sorry for him if he paid attention; but his job was to wait for the money so he could count it, get his share, and head out. He was still counting and stacking from the last transaction, focused on deciding whether he wanted to arrange the coins and bills into piles that reflected denominations and sizes (pennies before or after the dimes?). He wouldn't allow himself to be distracted by the whimpering and, truthfully, he could not have said later whether the man was pleading or not. His instructions were simple—the kind of direction he understood best and that suited him to the job. He was to sit, keep his eyes down and away, wait for the money, count it, and then signal the result. Nobody needed to notice him, much less remember him. His usefulness certainly came in his discretion, but also and especially in what he could do quickly and unerringly. Everything depended on his disinterest.

It wasn't a problem. Percy was perfectly satisfied keeping to his place at the desk. He appreciated its workmanship. He ran his hands over its carefully tooled surface, lingering at the joints (all dovetailed), exploring hinges that held a hidden slip-shelf. The cubbies had wooden slats where different denominations of bills could be stacked. The edges of his fingers slid against the wood each time he added a bill, and he listened for the dull drop of coins down into crescent-edged slots, crafted to handle loose change. He leaned into the desk, his legs spread wide. In ordinary encounters, Percy counted whatever money the men, sometimes boys, pulled out from clenched paper bags—or sometimes a sock, or the inside of a hatband, even the underside of a cap—and reluctantly handed over to Boss. When bills hit the table with a thud, or sometimes a slap (those times there was usually something still due), Percy counted and stacked efficiently and quickly enough to keep the exchange on the other side of the room from getting to the point where the man who came with a payment was useless. "Now, why you have to make me wait like that? This thing here didn't need to be difficult." By that time a slow smile would spread across the colored man's face, mostly from the relief of knowing he'd see the other side of the door again. But when the money wasn't forthcoming, or, worse, when it was short and had been offered as what was due, strategic slaps and punches echoed across the otherwise empty room. Even the groans and grunts when somebody's air got knocked out, or a thump when they hit the wall, didn't interrupt the boy. Percy kept on with his counting. The sooner he got done the sooner he could take his share and get out.

If the amount was okay, he signaled with a circle of his thumb and first finger. If it was not, a shake of his head was all that was necessary. He never quite understood why it took more than one go-round to make somebody give up what they had. It was like they said in the movie that was all the rage: *Your money or your life.* Most folks gave up long before the equation shifted to their disadvantage. When Percy signaled that things did not add up the way they were supposed to, it didn't take long for the rest of the money to show up. They usually tried some kind of humor:

"Oh, I done forgot this here," sheepishly handing over another pile of bills. Or else they were angry when they bent over to get it out from the inside and underneath a shoe sole or from the slip pocket of a jacket. Sadly, the only thing that really bothered Percy about those encounters was the way they started and then ended so quickly that he rarely had time to finish collecting the bills into neat and denominationally similar stacks and the coins into towers. He'd made a self-serving decision early on that if folks was stupid enough to get themselves into the kind of fix that they ended up in a dead-end room being pummeled for money by a white stiff, well, that was the error of their ways. That last part was something his mother would have said.

This encounter was already different enough for Percy to notice the change in rhythm. The irritation that showed in Boss's voice was disorienting. He didn't like change. Percy had been through the ritual enough times to notice the shift. The room was thick and dense with an anger that filled the space and made him breathe deep. The air felt thin and spare. He'd just indicated the amount was short, and this time he happened to look up just in time to see Boss pull the pistol from inside his jacket and shoot the man right between his eyes. Percy watched the blood splatter and its spray. The man's body hit the floor—and would have hit the back wall hard had his feet not crumpled when the force of the bullet thrust him backwards. One thing that was clear was there was no space between the bullet piercing his skull and the man being dead. *Your money or your life.* Boss stepped back and put the gun into his holster. Then he turned, shaking his head while he crossed over to where Percy sat. It took no more than five long strides. He leaned over Percy's desk and pressed a blunt and stubby finger onto the boy's lips. The touch made the gesture worse. His head tilted back, gesturing to the scene on the other side of the room. Boss counted out the bills that Percy had stacked on his desk. Then he pushed a short stack back toward June Bug. "Here you go, boy. This one earned you a bonus." He jerked the rest of the bills out of their compartments, completely disregarding the careful organization Percy had accomplished. Stacked coin towers toppled while Boss swept everything into his leather pouch and then slid the sack into the inside pocket of his jacket. He mumbled, but it was clear enough to hear. "Nothing here worth remembering. Am I right?" Percy offered the same gesture he'd used to signal the money was accounted for. "You get on home." Boss was striding toward the door, but Percy heard his last words with a clarity that was absolutely intentional. ". . . back to your mama's down on 129th." Lilah made him repeat that line when he finally relented and told her the whole story.

The door closed. Percy listened until the footsteps sounded down the two full flights of stairs. Blood was beginning to stream across the floor and seep into the floorboards. It would soon congeal behind the man's head. He wiped the back of his hand across his lips, trying to remove the impress from Boss's finger. He pulled his eyes away from the body slumped on the other side of the room and stared for a while at his desk. His hands gripped the edges so tightly that his knuckles ached long after this moment had passed. It was quiet. The room's silence melted into a fresh scent of iron, rust, and cinder. The dark that drifted through the room was saturated with a sharp, rank odor of blood that brought him back to a necessary alertness.

Just that quickly, Percy was no longer the street kid whose long and limber style reminded folks of his daddy. He was alone and scared and didn't feel like "almost a full growed man" at all—which was what they had taken to calling him at church. Especially since he had helped his family become financial with a monthly contribution to the building fund. His mama could finally join her birthday club, and he felt good and grown in helping her take her place alongside the church elders. But right now, Percy was feeling more like her baby boy. So it was her June Bug who came running home and her June Bug who folded himself into his mother's arms and told her what it was he had been up to and where the extra money for church and groceries and enough to give his baby sister an allowance had come from.

After she composed herself and pulled her hands from her apron and managed to take his face into her hands until he looked her straight in her eyes, Lilah didn't say much more than "Well, then, son, you got to go." She didn't say "again," and didn't say anything about how the last time the whole family was rushed out of a place without time to think of much more than getting gone, it was because of what her boy had done. She pushed past her memory and fear—because either or both would have disabled her—and helped him pack up. They waited together up under the kitchen window, leaned against the sink and not saying much of anything at all until the night was near enough to day so he could slip down to Penn Station unnoticed and catch the train back home. "Maybe you can find something for you that won't . . ."

"But, Ma. I don't remember nothing about home. What you want me to do there? I don't know nobody!"

Lilah sighed over his neediness: "It's not what you know or remember. It's what is yours because you my son and your daddy's. You your sister's brother and my June Bug. You can't lose track of that. Scared ain't a stop sign. Sometimes being scared is the way you learn which way to go." She struggled to tell him something he would remember, something he could use. "When we came up here, when you was just a boy and before Baby Sister was born, I was scared. I didn't know nothing about this place here. But your daddy helped me to learn it. Helped me figure out how I belonged to be here just like anybody else. Helped me find my place. That's what you take back home. Take your place. And after you do that, then make you a plan. Iredell, he always had him a plan. You more like him than me. Make you a plan." He leaned into her arms and sank back against her chest. He sighed and muttered and even sobbed some.

"There ain't nothing in those parts for me."

"Boy, ain't nothing *but* you in those parts. That's home. When you go back home, it's already somewhere you belong. That's the first thing. The second thing—whenever you figure out what it is—will come soon enough. You just got to notice it when it does." She didn't think she was making sense or being helpful. But it didn't much matter. What he needed now was her voice. Its calm and rhythm. Its deep tones. Some assurance. Blessing. It almost didn't make any difference what she said. It was how she made him feel. Some memory that he could take with him and bring out when there would be a need he couldn't address.

Back when his daddy died, Lilah had no time to tell Iredell the things she wanted him to know for sure about how she loved him and always would, how what he had taught her about claiming a place in the world would surely come to some good, how she would raise the children to remember him. She told her son some of what she would have wanted his daddy to know and especially what she wished she had heard from him. "You remember me every day you gone. And Baby Girl too. We the ones who will love you no matter what." Later, she was grateful she had said something to him about love because when you are frightened for a child, it's more usual to speak from fear rather than love. And act that way too.

Before the streetlights blinked out or the city awoke, she nudged him awake and said, with more forcefulness and less sorrow than she was feeling, that it was time for him to get on going. He crept over to the sofa, where Selma Althea slept. Every night she curled into the space between the seat cushions and the worn back until it was almost impossible to distinguish her from the cushions. But he could. Percy leaned over and whispered to her. He held his mother close—or she held him until there was nothing to do but shut the door behind him, then cross back over to the window to watch him disappear down the street. *He walks like Iredell,* Lilah thought. She twisted the wedding band on her finger. Percy crossed the street in long strides, not running but purposeful. It was near light. The sun's scarlet streaks hit the horizon and promised to lift the gloom. But now, between dawn and day, the streets looked grim and dangerous.

He made it to Penn Station just before the city began its stretch into morning. His hands stuffed into his pockets, his cap pulled down nearly over his eyes in order to give him the look of just any kid rather than the boy somebody might decide to come looking for. Percy waited for the train headed home to swept dirt roads instead of the steaming tar that spread out over cobbled stones that had been in place since the early days. He crept against the tracery of iron girders and glass porticos on his way down to the platforms, seeking the safety of the shadows that fell from the steel pillars.

Upstairs and beyond the train station's glass doors, the light slowly shifted as the quiet creep of day slipped across brick walls, leaving a soft shimmer on the curbs. Wet from the swish of water trucks, the sidewalks and slick pavement glistened, masking rank night odors. Creaky rolls of iron gateways pushed back from storefronts, brooms whisked through leftover puddles, sweeping silt and soot off curbs down into the gutters. It was a symphony: the swish of brooms, watery dribbles into metal gutters, the clop of horse-drawn wagons, and newly sputtering gasoline-fueled engines in trucks packed with the city's necessities—meat to be flayed by the butchers, ice to be stacked into basement holding rooms, bottles and boxes and crates that would be sorted through, carted up to butcher shops and groceries, and unpacked in order to line the long bins dividing the aisles at the five-and-dime. The city came awake in trembling syncopation. And yes, part of its rhythm was the now-distant chugging engine of the train that just left the station and carried a boy who would strive to become at least as forward-looking as he was now forlorn.

2

Just Us Women

SELMA WOKE FOR SCHOOL, BUT THERE WAS NO CEREAL STEAMING FROM a bowl on the kitchen table. A battered saucepan held remains of burned crust. Earlier, despite the night's painful unfolding, Lilah tried to keep to her morning breakfast ritual, shuffling mechanically through its tasks; but when she turned away from the stove to set the table, she moved three cereal bowls from the cabinet to the table's stained oilcloth. She set three jelly glasses and three spoons from the drain to the right of each bowl. She even reached back and to the side of the cupboard for another bowl after noticing the cracked rim of the one on the table. But then DeLilah looked down at the three place settings and remembered between this moment and the one when Percy left. Her breath caught in the gap, bound by what had been and now. She was still for so long that when she finally had the wherewithal to turn to the stove and cut the flame, it was too late to save the cereal. The pan had absorbed the water, and the bottom was crusted brown. She reached out for the ladder-back chair and sat down at the table, fixing herself to stay put. Without moving from her seat, she leaned over and pushed the cloth hanging on a rail under the sink and stripped some root from the paper sack she kept there. She placed its pieces into a small strainer and laid the tarnished silver sieve across the chipped edge of what used to be a fine china teacup. A faded trail of violets circled the rim of its barely gilded

18

edge, ready for its hot steeping. But the water in the kettle had already boiled away.

Selma saw her mother in her seat, her hands moving rhythmically underneath her apron. DeLilah was fully closed to any morning chatter. So her daughter moved the kettle to the sink, leaning into the hot steam that rose when she turned the tap to cool it down. She buttered a piece of white bread and sprinkled it with sugar. There was just enough milk left in the last bottle in the icebox to mix with a bit of tap water and add to the charred edges of semolina rescued from the stovetop. She scraped what she could into her bowl, mixed it with the watery milk, and added more sugar. When she finished, she rinsed her bowl and the spoon and left them on the drain. She placed the empty bottle alongside the others in the rack by the door—the milkman would not come for two days. Selma kissed her mother, lingering long enough to take in her scent from the splash of lilac powder that she and June Bug had given her for her birthday. She tried to reach down for her hands, to give her mother at least a squeeze—and especially and maybe to get one too—but Lilah's hands were buried deep in her apron pockets and she wouldn't budge.

Selma remembered more than she would say about her brother's good-bye. She'd heard his late-night confession, her mother's decision, and she'd felt his good-bye. In fact, she'd reached up to touch his cheek when Percy leaned over and whispered to her. She knew exactly what he said. Because of what would happen to her later, she never had the time to wonder over whether her brother had even felt her touch when he bent toward her ear. Her mother's stillness seemed correct and even instructive given the weight of the night. So Selma made the morning as ordinary as she could, leaving for school with whatever longing she had unspoken. The nighttime whispers—mother, son, and brother—disappeared into a throaty susurrus. There were no forehead kisses that June Bug swiped off as soon as they were planted, no recitation in unison to "have a happy wonderful day" as if it were promise, no "yes, ma'am," when their mother reminded them to "keep to yourselves" as if it were, or could be, protection.

Those morning rituals fell away as quickly as Percy disappeared down the street, taking with him his mother's heart and, eventually, his sister's voice. In fact, Selma's own silence, the one that came to characterize what folks came to call her "malady" after her baby went missing, actually started long before the thing that seemed to finish her.

On that morning and then later, as a matter of habit, DeLilah felt little but her own pain. And when that began to wane or at least when it seemed less keen and not quite as raw, the loss of that hurt felt so isolate and so personal that she marked the memory. She took to wearing dark slips under her dresses and washed them separately so the rusty stains from the tracks she etched into her thighs would not ruin the rest of her wash. Certainly it could have been that she gathered every bit of her daughter's own loneliness, as well as her budding brilliance, her curiosity and loveliness, into a focus that would nurture them both. It could have been that she found ways to clasp rather than relinquish her girl child. But Selma was neither her mother's solace nor focus. If anything, her bright and beautiful daughter was a reminder of who was absent. "Just us women . . . Just us women left," Lilah pronounced, even though Selma was only a girl whose womanhood would soon be forced rather than chosen.

That first morning, after her lapse, setting the table as if Percy were still there, and after Selma had gotten her own breakfast and seen herownself off to school, Lilah sat motionless at the kitchen table until the sun was high enough to cast his shadow at the door.

Hey, girl. And then: *It feels like trouble up in here.*

Lilah didn't even look up. She knew he would come. Her heart had called him and she knew that with some patience, and perhaps some imagination, he would answer. She was wondering if it was all right. If there was something wrong in her wanting him fiercely enough for this to happen. She missed him so deeply and so thoroughly that her grief took shape. For the moment, it seemed to be enough.

Her hands clasped tight, and then loosened under the drab apron she wore on her Thursdays when her work would be for her own house and her own children instead of the bright white and stiffly starched piece of an apron she wore for the tasks that took up her time working for her Manhattan white folks. She looked down at her Bible that lay open on the paint-worn table and saw it was on Jeremiah. But it was no balm for her. The tissue-thin papers barely made a sound as she turned the pages and waited for him to have his say. Surely there was something to say. Some direction if not devotion. His silence forced her own words.

"He gone," she said. "For good, I 'spect."

What kinda gone we talking about? He shifted with the sun and leaned against the door's casing.

"The kind where I packed and sent him off. The kind where he had to leave. And the kind that saved him from white folks' kind of trouble." She paused and let her breathing slow. Then she said, "The kind like the last time." And then she told what she knew. Their whispers saturated the room, back and forth, until the clouds of silvery dust flew upwards and danced the rhythm in their words. "So I sent him back home, before they could get hold to him." Her story went quiet and settled between them.

I see. She watched the sunlit specks of dust drift through and across the space between them. They took their time. *Seems like you did what you had to do.* Lilah turned another page, not sure if she should look for solace in the book or to that memory lingering in her doorway. Her puzzlement provoked. *Didn't I always say that once you birth a boy, the rest of the time is you getting ready for them to take off? A boy—they's always fixing to leave, or get put out, or do something that makes us have to do something to them for their own good. It's a fine hurt when it comes to that. But more times than not—*

"I know. I know you right," Lilah interrupted. "I knew that when you left me. Even though if you or anybody had known to tell me that it would be me and her left here"—she gestured toward the couch where Selma slept, thinking she could probably make over the cot to her that June Bug slept on now he was gone. Tattered antimacassars draped tenderly across worn side arms. She let the thought drift before she spoke again. When she did, her voice filtered through the light. "Seems like I already spent most of my life tryin to figure out what this would be like." His hands were in his pockets, and she wondered briefly if anything was in there. "Ever since we come up here, when we was pushed to leave before we was ready because of him." She glanced sideways like an accusation, or an ask. "You could've hushed him. I always thought that. Made him just hush. A swat across the butt. Or upside his head. Something that would've stopped the sound."

You sure that's what you wanted?

She didn't know what question he was answering so she kept on talking. "Ever since you went, I spent my days figuring out how it was going to be when I lose him. Already lost you. Losing him had to come next."

You forgetting our baby girl? She here. She need you.

She wanted to ask how he would know about Selma. Or know the worries that came with a girl. Selma wasn't born when Iredell died. She was barely a rounding plump beneath her breasts. An occasional kick. Even hiccups. A flutter that seemed like a promise, or perhaps a threat. But she wasn't here. Like he—like she was now. She thought he might could use some reminding of that, but it sounded mean and that wasn't her intent. She was looking for some understanding. A loving kindness. So instead she said, "Girls is different. They don't go. They just empty you out while you standing right beside them. A different kinda losing. Right now, Baby Girl doing good. She in school. She do what all I say. She know her lesson. She not making me fearful of what's next or waiting round for something to go awry." She wanted to say "not yet," but she already felt assaulted by time so she let it lie.

One of his legs slowly crossed the other. She could see a worn piece of leather barely attached to his gritty sole and wondered where it was he had been walking. Was that graveyard dirt trailed across her floors? She thought about the broom they kept to the side of the icebox.

"A son means figuring out how to keep him long as we can and struggling not to let fear be the thing he knows better than love."

You right, she heard him say. *You always right about love.* Her eyes spilled over, and Lilah wept without consolation. His shadow was still, but it shimmered. "He was my baby boy," she sobbed. "All's I did was to help him leave me. Again. Just like I helped you to go wherever it was you went." She gulped the last words more than spoke them.

Did he say, *Girl, you done moved from grief to foolishness?* Did she hear: *What do that mean "Just like you"?* His words were almost too fast for her to catch their whispers. *I got the flu and you held me.* She remembered his tissue-dry skin. The scaly flakes that peeled off his palms. *My body was wracked beyond pain and you soothed me.* She could feel his head settled into the hollow of her chest. And she remembered its vanishing heft, already challenged by his illness. *I nearly coughed out my insides, and you wiped my mouth and gave me sassafras.* She smelled the root now, its sweet scent spilled out from her violets cup.

Step away from that grief and settle on how you done had us both. My gone ain't like his. Every good-bye ain't gone. June Bug, he'll get back some kinda ways. Ain't nothing that fearful to keep him gone forever. You got to hold on to some kinda hope. She sighed. *And too* . . . Yes. She heard him. He always was saying "and too" instead of something like "also." *And too, we got Baby Girl. She gonna need her mama to be there for her. Keeping watch. Maybe you could settle on her.* Did he say *could* or *should*?

Lilah had no idea the sun had slipped to the other corner of the room until she looked up and across the small foyer for his shadow and only saw its dimmed outline, or her memory of it. But she heard *settle on her* clear—almost like it was an echo. She laid her head down and wept. An edge of sunlight cradled the worn corner where the legs met the table's edge, and her hand reached out for its warmth. Perhaps she felt something brush against her fingertips. She wanted the embrace and stretched out her hand only to find and then hold on to the edge of the table . . . tightly at first, until she went limp with sleep. She needed more than a sliver of sun. But knowing those days had passed, she surrendered to what warmth there was left from the light.

Midafternoon her lithe-limbed daughter cautiously turned their doorknob and peeked in, not knowing what she might find and worried what she would. She sighed—perhaps from relief, but perhaps not when she saw her mother still at the kitchen table. One of her hands was splayed across the open Bible and the other stretched out across the table. Selma took the throw from the sofa and laid it across her mother's shoulders. Then she quietly pulled out the other chair and sat across the small table from her sleeping mother and did her schoolwork. First a page of numbers. She diagrammed five sentences. Then read through her civics lesson, answering the questions at the end of the section. She mouthed the words so she wouldn't wake her mother. Lilah coughed quietly, turned her head so that it rested on her arm, and sighed herself back to sleep. Selma took the kettle from the sink where she'd left it that morning and filled it with hot water. She sat at the table, looked out the window at the pattern of bricks on the far wall, watched the sunlight slip from one row to the other until it was gone, and waited for her mother to awaken.

3

Peculiar Since Day One

DELILAH HARRISON SPENT HER DAYS WAITING FOR IREDELL MOSBY TO return from the war. The train station was packed with colored soldiers wearing their uniforms like a provocation and moving with an ease they had not had when they left. Some swaggered down the platform. But others limped or were carried on gurneys and struggled to raise up and into relieved embraces of parents or girlfriends or brothers or sisters. Lilah spotted Iredell from way down, as soon as he stepped away from the car. He'd fixed his eyes straight on until she emerged from the crowd, and when she did, he came toward her like she was the only one there. He picked her up and whispered his plans for them: "In no less than a half hour, baby girl, you gonna be . . . and I'ma be looking for everything I missed. And then . . ." He whispered what would be first, and Lilah shushed him. His mother was standing right there, holding on to Percy. He grinned in a way that let her know that every part of him, head and heart both, were home. "But right now? Right this minute? I need to see my son. Where's our boy baby?" She felt the warmth of his return and the protection of his savvy.

He said "our," she thought. Loud enough for all the folks primed for rumor and ruin to hear. *He done saved me right and here and now with his words.* She turned to where his mother stood holding their baby, and the smile she shared with her stitched them together like kin.

"He right here," Gran'mam said, holding out the squiggling almost one-year-old. She tried to say it with all the fullness he had just placed in her heart. His mother seemed to relax in handing him over. "Meet your baby boy." Lilah exhaled.

"Percy Harrison Mosby, this here your daddy."

Iredell's hands sank into his son's dark-as-night and tight-as-rope curls and then moved them across his head, tracing the folds of his perfect ears, their coffee-colored tips, and stroked the back of his fingers across their baby's chin. He stopped when Percy reached up and grabbed his finger. "Hey, hey, lil June Bug." His son's chubby grasp was enough to make him sigh long and deep as if it were the first time in a long time that he'd taken in some air that could do him some good. Iredell held on to the baby, and Lilah slipped her hand through his. His mother held on to his other arm. They left together, Iredell between them, like a real family. The thought caught her happiness short. *What wouldn't be real? Why would I even think that?* But then Percy did a deep little growl and set off a stream of babble that made Iredell laugh so she did too, pushing away the kind of worrisome thinking that was wont to stay with her like a quiet but persistent hum, just beneath the surface. She had to work harder than she ought to keep it at bay. *He deserves more than my fearfulness.* She fought against her instincts. Iredell was going to need her fully present if what she'd come to notice about the men come back home—their skittishness and daring, their easy challenges and face-front uniformed boldness— was in him even a little. Every bit of this kinda acting out was a danger.

Sedalia's men returned to places grown used to their absence. Their insistent, explicit presence startled white folks, and some colored too. They walked, moved, even cropped with a righteous assertiveness they certainly hadn't had when they went off to war. Their bearing was a conversation for hushed whispering amongst black folks, and it riled the whites. Coloreds worried that their already-precarious places would be more at risk by a straight-on look, or really anything that suggested something other than they knew their place. Lilah had to work at disallowing anything with Iredell that might endanger their family. He was given to strength while she cultivated caution.

They were busy setting up their household, and especially getting ready for their church wedding. She wouldn't tolerate any more gossipy, meanspirited talk about her having that baby outside the bounds of the Lord's blessing. None of that mattered now. Not another measure of what folks had been saying; not a whiff of their self-righteous harrumphs or how they would slide away from her to farther down the pew in order to set some distance between their holiness and her and her baby. None of their overly dramatic flutter of funeral home fans when she reached to the back of the pew for the hymnal would shatter her now. Not even the inquisitions after service in the church hall could shadow her joy. "You think he look anything at all like his daddy's people?" Without Iredell being there to claim his son, it was easy to focus on how there had been a time when Augustus Billingsley was the man folks linked to Lilah. After Iredell went off to training and then got sent overseas, and especially after the baby came, it focused everything that had been left unsaid about whom she was courting available for gossip. It didn't help that Billingsley did his best to insinuate the two had the relationship gossiped about. Iredell's absence and her insistence that "You mean Iredell" when people asked after the baby's daddy seemed to service the rumor rather than correct it. Augustus didn't do anything to stop the speculation because he was still mad that she hadn't chosen him. He hung around town just waiting to see her, sidling up to her in Bassett's store, grabbing her wrist or her waist as if there was something that intimate between them. It was not only his anger and envy, but some want that motivated his ugly ways. DeLilah had spurned him, and so had the army. Augustus got called up alongside Iredell and the rest of the town's boys and men, but he didn't make it past the physical. While some came out of the storefront center headed straight for the bus that would take them to segregated barracks and segregated training over at Tuskegee, those who didn't make it through— too short, feebleness, syphilis, illiterate, or whatever—headed back to Sedalia without the army-issued fatigues, without a smart khaki duffel, with nothing other than the slow shuffle of embarrassment and failure. Their braggadocio about whom and how they'd shoot fell away as quickly as their imagined overseas victories. That lost potential irked Augustus as much as the comparison to Iredell because folks were already talking about Mrs. Mosby's boy like he was some kind of hero even though he was headed overseas to do no more than follow somebody's orders just like he followed them here. So it was as much spite as interest that made Augustus use the only way he had to manage the comparison by encouraging the rumor that DeLilah was still his girl. In fact, he helped it along. Even after the baby came, he didn't do enough, in Lilah's mind, to make clear that Percy wasn't his son. Couldn't be. They were never together like that; but the fact of that didn't give Gus reason to clarify matters. Which was why Iredell's mother was never fully sure—not until Percy's color came in alongside the clear imprint of the turtle-shaped birthmark on the baby's ankle (just like the mark on her son)—that Percy was absolutely Iredell's blood. That was helpful, but what finally set it all to rest was her son's return and how, around the same time, Augustus took up with one of the girls who was war widowed. It wasn't fully unreasonable to assume that the government pension her loss had earned assisted Gus's shift in interests. So by the time Iredell John Mosby followed Reverend Wade into Brown Chapel AME Church, his stature and pride emphasized with his starched and well-creased army dress uniform, he and DeLilah both had earned the approving nod of the church mothers. It helped, of course, that Iredell insisted on holding their son in his arms from the beginning of their nuptials through to the pronouncement by Reverend Wade. There were no more questions about the baby's daddy. The congregation shifted their demeanor from approbation to approval. Their spirit shifted to embrace.

When the piano started the chords of the wedding march, DeLilah was standing at the back of the church, centered in the framed arch of the ceremony doors—the ones opened only for weddings or burials (otherwise congregants entered through the smaller doors on either side of the ceremony entrance). A breeze took up the gauzy fabric of her dress and it billowed out, drifting back toward the churchyard that had been meticulously swept into old and remembered patterns—a quilt of textures like carefully cultivated fabric. At the fence, tall grasses grasped posts that separated the churchyard from the carefully tended burial grounds vigilantly kept at the ready to claim the community's men and women and some children too, given how dying was as ordinary and predictable as birthing. In this late-afternoon wedding, the divide of grasses took on the same rose-gold glow of evening that bathed the bride in its light long enough for Iredell to see her at the very moment her creamy dress took on the glisten from the near-to-setting sun and the almost-night sky.

Iredell held his son and watched Lilah walk the short distance from the open doors up to the pulpit. Her clutch of wildflowers—Queen Anne's lace, honeysuckle, and some pale-pink fence roses—were tied with an indigo string. Her first-Sunday dress was trimmed on every edge possible—the hem, the finish of each sleeve, the collar, and her waist—with meticulously shaped fringes of bright white lace. For the small congregation, Iredell's being there stood in the place of all of those who didn't come back as well as those who did but with less in body or mind. Folks came to embrace and share in the promise this sweet couple held—a glimpse, they hoped, of how things might could be mended and move from nowadays okay to even better tomorrows. They needed some way to think it could be that the war didn't fracture everything good about the men coming home or, for at least a brief ease from the grief in memories of the men whose bodies stayed, lost on some overseas beaches or buried in newly dug cemetery rows. Lilah standing there with Iredell holding their boy right up at the front of the church looking whole and joyful made up for a whole lot of folks gone missing.

The couple returned to cropping after the wedding, taking their place in Sedalia's colored community, helping it along as they could, but planning to leave as soon as they were able. Iredell had seen too much possibility to have the small town frame his potential. Going north was a version of the promise they'd invested in the family. When letters came back from others who'd found their way in Philadelphia or Detroit or especially in New York City, they read and cherished them before relinquishing them back to the basket at the back of the church, where the preacher gathered the correspondence so the community could learn as much as they could about what they needed to know. Iredell and Lilah pored over letters that gave shape to their dreams.

"See there, baby girl? Joe Lee say he's working up in the sky on a high bridge that brings together two New York shores! This one says his crew boys do buildings taller than the steeple on the church. That's for me. I'ma be up high, on one of them skyscraping."

"Skyscrapers," she said. Even while wondering, *How can that be?* She brushed the tips of her fingers across the word thinking that something that extraordinary deserved more attention. She said it again to give it the shape of her voice. "It says '*skyscrapers*.'" Together they read over letters from men who worked on suspension bridges and cables, and marveled at those who wrote how they walked across girders no wider than a floor-board plank to build walls with glass windows wider than their own front door. They made lists and counted days and practiced thrift. They prayed on weekdays and tithed on Sunday. They were cautious with their every-days and considerate of their community. They worked hard and lived as they should and controlled everything that was within their imaginations. They planned.

Despite Lilah and Iredell's every and fine efforts, it was their boy Percy who made it all fall apart, even though neither one of them would ever say aloud a single solitary word of blame. They couldn't attach that failure to him because to fold him into anything other than hopefulness would be a taint. And too, if she could have laid the blame anywhere, Lilah would've said it was all on Iredell. But he might've reminded her what she did to their boy at the moment he couldn't understand anything at all but her fear. And she would've had to go back to that place where her anger from being left and lost and left again stayed lit like a burning coal. All and any of that was too hard.

Percy was six and precocious. He hadn't learned, and his parents (so taken with his every word and every habit) had not taught him, the necessity of keeping his mouth shut in front of white folks. In fact, they may even have been complicit in preparing him for an up-north kind of living where being colored—at least in their vision of it—would mean a kind of freedom that wasn't ordinarily a part of their day-to-day. That was where Lilah would've laid her blame. In Iredell not reining him in and teaching him his place. In letting him be the kind of brash he'd practiced but suppressed in himself, out of his learned and fully reasonable wariness about white folks. In his plans, Percy's future would have a shape much different from his daddy's everyday. It would be without the kinds of constraints that narrowed their thinking and scaled them small. *Skyscrapers.* When Lilah first heard what their son had done, she repeated the word as if it were mantra or magic. *Skyscrapers.*

THE DESK THAT USUALLY SAT AT THE BACK OF BASSETT'S STORE HAD been dragged outside to the platform. Mule-drawn wagonloads of bagged cotton, husked and shelled, stretched out about eight to ten back. A group of colored boys stood at the ready to unload them, and Mr. Bassett sat behind the desk ready for the accounting. He wore his store apron and had his sleeves covered with cotton protectors that pulled up to the elbows and also down over his cuffs. But it was his spectacles that made it clear today was a different kind of day than the usual running of the store. Usually they just dangled from the chain around his neck, but on accounting days their thin wires bent across his large, hairy ears and, because accounting took time and the day was hot, rivulets of sweat continuously slid down his large bulbous nose, and he would stop, put down his pen so he didn't get ink on his face—which he usually did anyway—and push them back into place. His fingers were stained dark, and he constantly wiped his hands across the blotter until its stains transferred to everything he touched. He bent over his record book and spoke deliberately. With each man he spent considerable time going over the columns, especially the subtractions: labor and maintenance costs, the rental for their shack, the tax on their advance of materials and goods at the beginning of the season, the depreciation of everything from the cabin they leased—whether it was a shack, lean-to, or framed—to the land they tilled and planted. There wasn't much difference one from the other, except the number of children always added to more or less goods that wives and mothers and grandmothers put on the account books during the planting and growing seasons. Now that it was harvest, he wanted to make sure he had the right boy standing in front of him. "Lemme see, you Burrell, right?"

"Yassir. Mr. Bassett, sir. Whittaker. *Mister* Burrell Whittaker." The elderly farmer, used to being called a boy, but taking on some of the hubris of his returned sons, tried out what it was like feeling like a man, so he emphasized that he was a "mister" even though there was no way the white man would return the courtesy. In fact, he was fortunate that Bassett pretended not to hear it.

"Uh-huh. Like I said, 'Burrell.'" He pronounced it like it was one syllable 'Burl' instead of how folks who knew better said 'Burr-ell' and pronounced it with all the gravity his mother had intended when she chose her son's name. And then, taking his time (and everybody else's as well), he drew a stubby ink-stained finger down the columns, laid his wooden ruler across the row under the elderly man's name, and doled out what he determined was due. He slid the coins and some bills just halfway across the table and, then, as was his habit, waiting until Mr. Whittaker reached out to take his pay, Bassett slapped his large palm across a not-insignificant portion and pulled it away from the farmer. It was a performative flourish that helped to remind the men whose debt they were in. He accompanied his act with a well-practiced explanation, "But with your deficits, this here"—he pulled the money slowly away to make his point—"this here is what you owe me." This was his payday as much as theirs. Whittaker could not help but show his disappointment with what was left on the desk and spoke out.

"That's it? That's all I got coming to me, Mr. Bassett . . . ?" And then he added, "Sir?" It was plaintive and nearly pitiful. He already knew that there wasn't going to be any recount. But it did open the opportunity for Bassett's speech.

"Y'all understand it's market costs an' I ain't got no kinda control over how cotton goes up and comes back down." He was chewing tobacco, and his spittle and pronunciation made his words sound like short phlegmy bursts, but folks were clear enough about what he was saying. He did it every year. He looked away from the spittoon, which he'd missed. "It seems like for all y'all"—he surveyed the line of black men standing with the harnesses of their mules in hand, or the ones still perched on the seat of the wagons waiting their turn with the ledger on his desk. "It seems for all y'all—I'ma say it again an' loud 'cause I ain't in the biness of repeating myself for a group of niggers. So lissen up." Shoes dug into the ground, and folks turned sideways in order to keep their bearing. They couldn't leave; but being there came with a cost. "Boys, I'ma tell you we not getting much at all for our cotton. Just wasn't our season. And y'all's pickin habits . . . well, nobody but yourownselves to blame on that one. So don't be expecting much when it comes your turn up here. I'ma do my best by all y'all, but that's all I kin do." Somebody pulled at Whittaker's mule's harness, and his wagon moved away while another pulled up. The man got down, climbed the stairs to the platform to take his turn and have his accounting. This one had a kid with him. "You Mosby, right, boy?"

"Yessir. And this here's my son. His name Percy. Say good day to Mr. Bassett, son." He pushed his boy forward so Bassett would notice him. It may have been that nudge that began the unwinding. Percy could've easily felt it was like church and being nudged up to the minister for a pat on the head or an acknowledgment of how nicely he had said his piece when called up to the front with the rest of his class to speak the lesson the children had practiced in Sunday school.

"G'day, Mr. Bassett. How you?" Bassett grunted and began to read down the ledger of subtractions, pulling his stained fingers down and then across the page. He got to what Iredell Mosby was due and started counting out the coins and few bills. Mosby reached. Whittaker slapped and took back his share. Nobody expected a comment, certainly not after the white man's speech and especially, nobody close in line to that

31

encounter. But certainly no one at all anticipated a comment from a child. Much less a correction. But Percy Mosby spoke up and made a correction as well. Folks were shushed with the surprise of it all. Bassett's hands were fixed to slide the money away from Iredell when his boy interrupted the rhythm of the encounter.

"Oh, uh-uh. Naw. No, sir. That ain't right." He looked up at his daddy. "It's *Mister* Bassett, right, Daddy?" he asked, wanting to remember his manners. And then, before Iredell could respond, his childish voice carried across the platform and out into the yard. "Mr. Bassett? You ain't cal-ca-lated that right." Iredell could feel a thick silence settle around the weigh station. Percy had a loud squeaky voice, and folks could hear what he was saying and their worry congealed. But Percy took the quiet for listening. "No, sir. My daddy don't owe you no more money. But you owes him some!" And then he giggled. He was just seven and thought that it was funny the white man couldn't add any better. It was the giggle that finished them. "You owes my daddy 'cause you said cotton is coming in at five pennies more per bushel than you done wrote down there in your columns. I done it in my head what you got wrote down there." The men looked around, counting who was in the yard and who could hear and who was white. Percy chirped happily: "You wrong, Mr. Bassett. You charging my daddy like you wasn't getting a nickel more than you done wrote down for each one of our bushels we done unloaded and we got . . ." He told the man how many bushels. Multiplied it by twenty. Subtracted the fees, which he did not dispute. And then he reported the balance owed his father.

Iredell put his hands over his son's mouth and told him to hush. He looked frantically at the man behind the desk, whose large hairy ears were flushed red and whose mouth was dribbling tobacco. He was holding on to the ruler like it wasn't as big a stick as he wanted. "Mr. Bassett, sir . . . my boy, Percy . . . He . . . Umm . . . He addled. Yeah. That's what it is. My boy a bit different." And then, as if the idea was new to him and might be usable, expanded his fiction. "Been tetched all his days. Breaks our heart with what he says sometimes. We don' pay him no mind. We jus kinda gotta keep our eye on his mouth. You know these young'uns." His words sped up to keep track with his worry. "They need lickin more'n they need most anything else. I'ma make sure he gets his. He just tetched. Not disrespectful like it might seem at this moment. But not like that an excuse.

'Cause it ain't. No, sir. No ways." His words spilled out, trying to cover the moment with talk. The colored men and boys in the yard nodded and then *amen*ed. Like church and as if their agreement might help. "Yep. Yep indeed! That boy always been foolish like that." Folks were trying their best to help him.

"Sho nuff is."

"Peculiar since day one."

The truth was that Percy was already thinking of how Iredell and Lilah both had gotten their boy used to praise. How he recited his times tables at church when other youngsters said their Easter poems. How he helped Mrs. Bryant with the counting after Communion Sunday because he liked stacking the coins by denomination. How Iredell pushed him toward Reverend Wade on their way out the double doors so the preacher too could lay his hands on him and tell him he was smart. This was what Percy had come to expect. So he pulled at his daddy's hand and started up again trying to explain.

"Papa, that ain't right. You know I can do the numbers. He still got our money! It don't add up right." That was when one of the other colored men took another kind of action. He snapped the reins hitched to his mules, and the mules pulled his cart forward and to the side of Iredell's wagon like he was trying to pass him. But he deliberately pulled it so close his wheel spokes caught on Mosby's wagon and in the ensuing entanglement and the fuss, the colored men started up:

"Hey there!"

"Hold up, boy!"

"You cutting the line."

"That ain't right. It ain't your turn."

"Hey there!" Their voices blended like a bass choir one atop the other until the noise and some strategic pushes and dropped bushels allowed someone to snatch Percy off the platform, hold him by his shoulders, and speak clear and firmly: "You go home now." Percy shook his head yes. The chaotic scene scared him. "You tell your mama everything what went on here. Don't look back. Don't come back. Tell her without changing a single solitary word. Tell it straight on. You hear me?" Percy looked around at the dust flying, heard the donkeys braying and the men shouting. He couldn't see where his daddy had gone to. So he did as instructed and took off running for home.

4

From Peril to Promise

LILAH WRAPPED HER ARMS AROUND THE RUSH BASKET WHERE HER freshly dried clothes, just pulled from the line, spilled over its side. She liked the rough feel against her skin. She folded herself into the day's variegated textures—slick grasses and gritty soil from her kitchen garden, satin-ribbon streaks of sky, spiky pods bursting from crepe myrtles that shed their papery bark with even the gentlest swipe across their limbs and branches. She held the basket tightly round her middle, pushed the screen door open with her hip, and dropped it into the ladder-back chair at the kitchen table. She'd left a glass of purple ironweed blossoms on the table that morning. The water was still clear. And there were peaches in the blue tin colander waiting in the sink, ready for a warm rinse and peel for pie. Their deep fruity scent promised they would be ripe enough for her thumbs to pull apart from their stone, and she'd have to keep her men—well, Percy and Iredell—from eating them without waiting for the cobbler. So she put a few aside for them and pulled a fresh rag from the wash so they could wipe the juices that would fall as they devoured the sweet fruit. Lilah loved these summer rituals. She depended on their certainty—whether it was the fresh smell of line-dried sheets, a kitchen with a window and a door out to the back, the familiar creaks in their metal bed, the hooked rug that ran down the hallway, or the man who loved her so deep and dependably she'd melt just anticipating him. She pulled the basket close between her legs, enjoying the rub against her thighs, and started her folding. The overalls, sheets, and shirts, even the socks held on to the fresh air. She pressed the clothes close to her face to let their sunshine warmth fade into her cheeks and keep hold to their scent as long as she could.

Most things got folded with her practiced dexterity—first a vigorous shake, then turned sleeve to sleeve, seams lined up one side to the other, pants leg pulled out at the crotch, and each surface smoothed twice—front and back. For some she stopped to dip her hand into the tin basin filled with Argo, sprinkling the chalky mixture across the cloth. Those she kneaded and shaped into mounds that would hold the damp long enough for her to press.

She was well into the ritual of fold, smooth, sprinkle, and mound when Percy's little body exploded through the screen door with a slam. The door slapped twice against the casement before it stopped, and before it finished the second slap, he was breathlessly babbling about his time with his daddy down to the store. Lilah was so fixed on her ritual and the irritation of the door's slam that she was only halfway listening. Back then, Percy was such a fast and frequent talker that folks had taken to pulling her aside to ask if it was all right that the boy never hushed. But he was one of the kids who wanted to know why and how and be listened to and answered simply so he could have room to say something else. Sensitive to how he often "just talked," Gran'mam said, "to hear himself talking," every once in a while it didn't hurt to let him get it all out without being so attentive. So he babbled and she folded until he said, "And then the white man—Daddy say his name Mr. Bassett—the one who sets behind that big-ole desk. One day I want me a desk like that. But mines'll have some secret pulls. This white man, the one who got the same sorta desk I'ma have me one day, he say . . ." His mother stopped and cut her eyes over to her boy, slicing through what had been her afternoon reverie with a sharp fear. She stopped and listened in a way she wished she couldn't, didn't need to summon. At least that was how she chose to remember it. She clutched the shirt in her hands, making more wrinkles than freeing them, and her grip tightened as he slowed down and said it again. He told her with a precision well past his age exactly what had happened.

She listened to her son's story once more, and since nothing fundamental changed and there wasn't a single thing that might loosen the cold knot forming in her stomach or relax the tightening in her throat, she got busy. She lost some bit of time trying to process what she heard and maybe thinking about the right reaction; but she really couldn't remember much until her common sense took over, and she pushed the laundry basket away from between her knees, dried her hands on her apron, untied it, and draped it across the back of the chair. Lilah got to moving. At least her hands and feet still worked, even though it seemed like her heart had stopped. It didn't take her long at all.

Twelve short steps and she was down the hall and into the one bedroom and standing over by their bed, the one covered with the quilt she'd worked on all during the war. She reached up to the shelf above the metal rails for her mother's indigo blue carpetbag. M'dear had passed on before the war. *Good thing,* she thought. A small blessing given this thing here. She left the satchel open on the bed and rushed back through the kitchen and outside, letting the screen door slam and slap in its frame without even trying to ease it closed. Instead of plucking the clothes from the line and gathering the pins in her mouth and down the sides of her apron as she had just—had it been an hour or hours ago?—she snatched them, piled them into a bundle as large as her apron could hold, and let the clothespins go flying and land in the yard wherever they might. She paid them no mind at all. Back in the house, she dumped everything on the bed and began sorting what would go into the blue carpetbag and what could stay. No folding or mounding, no sprinkling, then pulling and matching up the seams. Her order and their lives had been upended. She jerked the jelly jar from the back of the kitchen cabinet, and when the top wouldn't easily twist open, Lilah smacked it on the table until it shattered. She gathered coins and bills without a thought to the cuts on her fingers, and when she finally noticed them, she shrugged and just wiped her bloody fingers down the front of her dress. She closed the family Bible on the table next to their bed and slipped the latch into the leather strap that bound its feather-light pages and wrapped some clothes around it before she slid it between some of the clothes she packed. It wasn't as if the Bible offered her any particular comfort. She liked the sound of the words, especially from the Old Testament, but too much of it ran against her common sense. But it did list the family record on the illustrated pages that divided the testaments, and somehow she knew the life they were leaving would need evidence to challenge the disarray that was quickly descending over this moment. She rolled Iredell's and Percy's overalls and shirts into thick tubes and stuffed them next to the book. She cradled the teacup—the one with the violets scattered across the rim that the white folks who held her family had passed down to her mama. For a brief moment she wondered at that story and thought maybe her mama just took it like they took their freedom when it came. But it was a stray thought, odd and inappropriate for the moment, so she brushed it away and spent a moment carefully wrapping the cup and its matching saucer in the cotton batting she'd bought from Bassett's to replace a seat cushion. She'd never linger there again, fingering bolts of material, choosing between one with more purplish blue than the other. Lilah shoved as much as she could select or snatch into satchels for the three of them to haul down to the station—the only thing she knew for sure that would happen next. She was just waiting for Iredell to bring the wagon round to the back of the house. Front or back would tell her whether her panic and plan were correct.

On any ordinary day, Iredell would stop in the front yard to unload the cart, leaving whatever supplies he'd picked up at Bassett's on their porch, placing things that were for the inside of the house as near to the door as he could, then he'd get back on the wagon and pull it round back to the shed, leaving the mule to wander the field. But what she knew for sure when she heard him come down the road at a clip rather than an easy roll, and when he pulled around back and come through the door after he replaced the mule's hitching for the field horse and when there wasn't any unloading to do; what she knew for sure was that everything she was thinking and doing and scared for them about, and everything Percy had said, was absolutely true. Their faded white clapboard farmhouse with the bluish blossoms now drooping over the lid of the glass jar and the dusty-rose peaches waiting in the colander were already slipping toward memory.

Bassett had never had any back talk from a colored man, much less one of their snot-nosed pickaninnies, but he was primed for exactly that kind of trouble. Ever since these colored boys got home, they had an attitude that needed correcting. They talked about it down to the lodge and fumed about it in their homes. There was already a war of words about how these newfangled niggers were overstepping. Stories floated in from other towns about how some had to be put in their place. Over in Greensboro, a noose corrected some right on the courthouse lawn, and a whole passel got toted out to the woods and left in some outcropping of trees back in Guilford County, or parts of them anyways. Folks took souvenirs. Truth be told, it was coming to a head in Sedalia long before little Percy Mosby giggled. Nobody needed much priming at all. Everybody agreed that it was the final disrespect, and nobody interrupted with "but it was a little boy what said it. He didn't know no better." It wouldn't have mattered. Percy Mosby was evidence that the boys who had got to be soldiers were teaching their swagger to their pickaninnies. It had to be stopped.

The news spread fast amongst colored and whites both, and it was as sure as the sun would set (and not long after that) when Bassett and his boys, along with any others they might find on their way, would find their way down the road, past the tracks, and to Sedalia's coloreds. Jugs of home brew got passed around the store where the men gathered to bolster and bluster their indignation. There was grunting and grumbling. Booze sloshed from one man to the next. Elvira Bassett made the mistake of coming in to ask when her mister would be able to unload some of the supplies so she could shelve them. She got backhand slapped and knocked to the ground for interfering. So she got mad at the colored folks too, and the women who iced her lip and brushed back her hair from her sweaty, puffy face joined her indignation and hurt, and lent her blame the company it had earned. The men were angry and drunk. The women were hurt and diminished. By sunset, things had gone way past ugly.

Nobody needed to let the Mosbys know. They were fully aware that they needed to be long gone by the time the white folks got riled enough to be on the move with their rage settled and focused. Households went quiet. Kids were called in and shushed. Shades were drawn and shutters fastened. Front doors were bolted, and nobody even thought twice about a lantern when the dark finally settled. Some folks took off to spend the night by the creek bed rather than in their own. Dusk-dark had barely settled into night when Lilah and Iredell took Percy in the wagon up the winding back roads out of Guilford, past Durham, and into Wake County, and pulled up behind the train station in Raleigh. The Mosby family huddled in a thicket of bushes to the side of the station, not daring to approach even the colored waiting room. They lay low, nestled into the dense roadside brush. At daybreak, just as the mourning doves' plaintive calls woke to dawn's haze, a train whistle sounded. The exhausted family crept toward the last car just at the edge beyond the station platform and scrambled furtively aboard, their belongings and their boy clasped tight into their bodies. Percy slumped asleep across his daddy's shoulders, fitting snug into the space he'd held since he was a baby. Being he was nearing seven, his long legs dangled under his father's firm cradling and his own arms reached fully around his daddy's neck. His head nestled into the curve of Iredell's shoulder and chest. Lilah and Iredell sat on the edge of the seats at the back of the colored car. For the two days and nights that it took (counting the platform change in Baltimore) to get up to New York City, his parents barely closed their eyes.

Mostly, June Bug slept. Sometimes he woke and looked out the windows, but he'd gone quiet. It was evident to him that something essential had gone missing. Even Gran'mam wasn't with them like she always was, and his pa said she wouldn't be coming. "It's just us, son. Just the three of us right here." Iredell didn't wait for his son's "Why?" and Percy didn't ask. He simply looked out the window and considered everything that had happened from his words in the store to the run directly home, to his words to his mother that fell out without stopping, to waiting for Pa to come, and how he came round back and how he just heard, over and over—*Shush! Shush now! Shush up!*—until he fell asleep. In his mind, his words were at the center of whatever this was and that called for some consideration. His mother and pa were obviously doing the same thing he was. Usually they would be talking and laughing and even singing some, and he would be at the happy center of their conversating, but none of his usual and ordinary was happening now. Even when the porter came back to the car to tell folks they had passed the Jim Crow line and people cheered and got up and moved around, the Mosbys stayed put, clutching each other like they had barely escaped the thing they barely had. They felt special and different, but the porter recognized folks like them and made sure somebody passed some of their carefully packed boxes back to them—a boiled egg, a chicken wing, some white bread, and even a freestone peach. Lilah nearly wept when she held it in her hands and dug her thumbs down its center, pulling it apart for her husband and son. That wasn't how it was supposed to be.

39

Percy was still. Except for his wide eyes that focused outside where the train's rhythms suspended the moment and followed the slow glide of landscapes that slipped in and out of view, and watching the way the dirt transitioned from red to black as if it were almost enough magic to displace the misery that brought them to the cramped quarters of the train car. When he wasn't looking out the window, Percy slept, slipped into the space between his daddy's shoulder and the glass. Iredell used the hours to remember what it was they had planned for and to focus on how it would have proceeded if this had been the leave-taking they had planned. He recited lines from the letters they had read, mumbling them in a subvocal hum that eventually blended into the train's low, rhythmic rumble. He focused on whatever he could recall about the new city that would shift the moment away from peril and closer to promise.

When they walked through the large glass doors of Penn Station and stood outdoors, the streets were so dense with color and full of movement and thick with smells that DeLilah could not separate one from the other. At first the Mosbys seemed not much different than any other southern coloreds seeing up north for the first time, families who struggled to define and then realign their dreams with what they actually saw. But her first remembered judgment, which turned out to be correct, was that this was a city that would take whatever she had to give. It was more, and louder, and brighter, and busier than she imagined. It unnerved her. Iredell grabbed her tightly around her waist—like she would be the one to go missing—and she shifted the long strap of the blue carpetbag, the one made from the rug that once lay in front of her mother's chifforobe, the one she used to sleep on, the one that got stitched into a carrying bag when she and Iredell married. She re-shouldered her bag and leaned into Iredell's embrace so heavily, he looked over at her and laughed. "Baby," he chuckled. "You looking at our future right here. This gonna be all right. We not only gonna manage this, we gon thrive." And then he asked her if she had the address they had copied from one of the church-basket letters about where to go when you were new to the city. She needed both hands to search her pockets and purse. She let go of Percy and slipped her hand out of Iredell's grasp.

She would come to blame herself for letting go. So you enter, is how you shall leave. And she stood there outside of Penn Station with all of New York close around her and dropped the clasp of the only two folks she had. *I let loose of them. Me. It was me who let them go. At the very moment I shoulda held on, I let go. So all this that done happened, this is on me.*

IT TURNED OUT THAT QUIET SUITED LILAH. STILLNESS TOO. SHE CRAVED it. The city's vigor unsettled her, and the nearness of their neighbors, especially in the earliest days in the city, felt odd rather than it being an ease. But she followed the plan for the sake of their son, and eventually for the child not quite here. She managed her way through Harlem, coming to know its stores and its streets, Chasen's Grocery and the Polish butcher, the barbershop where the men always made room for Iredell's boy, and sometimes even the church, where the music reminded her of Sundays back home, sweet voices muting the clamor bound by the church doors and people's spirits. But mostly, Harlem's streets were too loud for her liking. The voices felt flattened out of their warm southern fullness, and the smells that drifted out of windows and down narrow and dark hallways were greasy and sharp instead of green and lush. But because Iredell wanted her to and because his hope was so beautifully balanced with his caring for her and their boy, Lilah kept trying to find her place. She may have come closer to doing so if he had given her more time before his leave-taking. But barely a year had passed before Iredell died, leaving the two of them with his memory. It wasn't enough to keep them safe.

Like too many of the folks packed close in Harlem's tenements, Iredell got caught up in the last wave of the thing they feared the most and that made the burial business so profitable that Mr. Mason could open his Harlem Mortuary and Funeral establishment. Iredell died within a week of threatening to. The colored doctor made his rounds, toting a worn black bag that had nothing in it that could heal but only things that could measure—his fever, his breathing, his heartbeat. Lilah kept waiting for him to pull something out that would relieve her husband's suffering; but on the last visit she heard his bag close, its clasp a finished snap like it wasn't about to open up again. Iredell lay listless and desert-dry across the bed, making no noise except his cough and sometimes a rattled breath. Nothing stirred the night air, and the day's business outside their building kept its distance from the dying going on inside. There should have been more room if not time, Lilah thought. A place for the doctor's bag other than right there on the bed beside her husband. Somewhere for him to sit

41

and tell her what to do to make her beloved husband well. A place with a lamp beside it so he could read from his medical books instead of the lightbulb they moved from socket to socket that gave nothing more than a dim glimpse and bleak promise.

Iredell's dying began with a searing headache that kept him in his bed with the shades pulled—even in the day. A cough settled in after the headache. It was brittle and sharp—piercing through the fog of his sleep enough for him to moan, and then go silent again, his thin wheeze a worrisome accompaniment to each breath.

She kept a kettle on the burner, letting the warm steam mist through the air, hoping to loosen the cough that got tighter with each daybreak and break the fever that rolled in and rose with each sunset. The oils she rubbed into his skin seemed to do no more than fuel the fever. Phlegm blocked his lungs, and sometimes he was quieter than her whispered entreaties. She got so desperate for any sound from him, even the raspy sound from his tortured breathing gave her an assurance that he was still alive. Until he wasn't.

The night he died, the soul-withering pauses between each breath were more noticeable than the air he took in. She lay beside him worrying over the reach of the silences. She thought she should be saying something, sharing some words that might linger between them—making a memory that would arc out and carry her through. But no words came. She pulled his hands up to her face, letting his fever burn into her cheeks, longing for him to notice, and desperately needing him to say something that she could remember forever. But his flesh was already wasted, and although he trembled with his last breath and moved his lips some (or so it seemed), he said nothing to her that she could hear. His hands fell heavy and limp away from her grasp. Iredell Mosby was gone.

Percy stood at her side tugging at her dress, wanting her to hold him. But all she could do was hold on to herownself, wrap herself in her own arms, grasp her own elbows, press them into her sides, and then rock and wail until somebody called the undertaker because it was no use sending for the doctor by the sound of that cry. Until her beloved came back as a shadow crisscrossing the slender rays of the kitchenette's sunlight, her memory only held the weighty silences from that night. Iredell lay limp and lifeless between the sheets, his deep brown already gone ashy, his eyes already sunken back into his head rather than being the light on his face, all fleshy and full and searching for a smile from her.

They buried him without much ceremony. The undertakers were so busy that caskets came and went from the funeral home on weekdays and weekends both. Mourners stayed from one burial to the next—sometimes going out on the step for some air, but making their way back as the food and folks from one wake made their way to another's. No use in wasting a good section of pie. Or some fried chicken, even if it was mostly backs. Lilah was left with her son and a whisper of spirit that would soon be her daughter, Selma, still finding the form to join a life already tilted toward sorrow.

They didn't have much of a service to organize, nor a church ground to bury him in. There had been little time to pay up the insurance man who came by each month. It lapsed when you didn't keep up the payments, he explained to the distraught widow. And Iredell didn't belong to any of the societies that could help him out with a plot. The family was too new. They were not established. Lilah wondered how could anything or anybody establish in a town with no place to root, no soil to turn? Some of the men in the building arranged for him to be carried out to the city cemetery on Hart. Percy and Lilah stood hand in hand while the grave-diggers tossed dark loamy soil onto the pine box the city made available to the poor. Everything about it made her think that although he was gone, this was no home going. Not with this deep dark dirt, not with this semblance of a casket, not without the elders of their small frame church back in Sedalia preparing chicken and curing a ham and doing a requisite wailing when Reverend Wade spoke his obituary. This was quiet, foreign, and lonely. She stood at the grave for so long past the prayer and the first shovel of dirt that her neighbor Doris Gayles, who'd come along because it wasn't right the family didn't have nobody there for them, pulled her away from the edge. "Come on now, sweetheart. He's as safe as he will ever be." Lilah looked up, but there was nothing there that would make her believe in a heaven. "Come on now, Lilah. You got to think to the living. Your boy needs you to get him home, and you need your rest your-ownself, being you carrying company." Doris tugged at her sleeve. Lilah turned toward her, then looked back across the field of graves—mounds of dirt clumped together like there was some plan or purpose, except there was nothing other than bleak fields of wasted flesh that lay beneath. A dead cold light slipped across the sky and the small gathering followed it, first taking the ferry, then the streetcar back through the Bronx and into Harlem. Doris came to the flat with them and took their wraps and laid them across Lilah's bed. She reached under the sink for the sassafras root, stripped some bark, and poured hot water into the battered tin pan so the root could steep. Percy lay across the kitchen floor, lining up rows of dominoes like grave markers, as if the cemetery had stones. The tiles stretched from one end of the room to the other.

Iredell's dying faded almost as quickly as the illness that had taken him away. Lilah left something other than her heart at his grave after the minister said his prayer and they stood as if there was something that could happen besides him being dead and her being alone. The blue thread bracelet, tied and knotted from the remnants of the carpetbag her mother made for them, fell from her knotted fist down onto the loose soil at his burial site. She'd given Iredell the bracelet before he went over to France, and he wore it until she slid it off just before the mortician's boys lifted his body into the rush basket and carried him away. It belonged with him, she thought. Even there. Even if there was just a bit of color left to acknowledge there had been days different from the one they were struggling through. As they left the cemetery, a sliver of blue broke through the clouds as if something, or someone, acknowledged her gift—or accepted its purpose.

5

Selma Althea Mosby

SELMA CURLED DEEP INTO HER FRIGHT, HER FINGERS CLINGING TO THE intricately embroidered weave of twigs and branches twisted into the icy-blue pile of the carpet. She held on, as if she could slip between them and they might collapse into an impenetrable bush that would protect her from what was already finished. She was already finding refuge in shadows that would slowly, inevitably, crowd out the life that had been hers. He stood, buttoned and belted himself back into the "sir" that she'd learned to avert her eyes from, because ever since she started doing the third-floor cleaning for his mother, he made her feel uneasy. Never a courtesy, always a leer. Never a move away from her, but usually an aggressive grope or tug that, until this evening, she'd managed to dodge.

She came directly from school, just as her mother instructed, stacked her books on the ledge under the stairs, and changed into the gray uniform hanging inside the west door of the basement kitchen. DeLilah Mosby got her interview in the white folks' Upper East Side mansion through her church connections with the Women's Auxiliary in Harlem Heights. But it was her sewing skills that got her the position. She only had to show Mrs. Thayer her embroidered pillowcases and tatted collars with blossoms stitched in such elegant detail that she was almost afraid to touch them. She had practical skills too, she assured Mrs. Thayer. She could sew on buttons and fix a hem or turn a collar—whatever was needed. But it was her skilled needlework as well as her quiet, deferential presence that placed her in charge of the household linens. DeLilah Mosby was a success for the auxiliary's jobs program, and they pointed to her long-term employment in the real estate mogul's Manhattan mansion as an exemplary illustration of their project's impact. They didn't have that many to show off.

The Women's Auxiliary of the Negro Welfare League was a social club of upper-class colored women who lived up in Harlem's Sugar Hill. Other than tea parties and summer soirées and of course their signature event, the debutante ball, the women designed projects that would facilitate the uplift of some (carefully) selected Harlem women. Of course their plans did not include uplifting them to their own heights (only so much could be accomplished with women not born to their station), but they were fully interested, even invested in them being a credit to the race. Whites had a tendency to see all coloreds as being the same, so whatever they could do to polish the image of the race would assist their own social ambitions. Lilah was aware of the standard, grateful for her own opportunity, and already anticipating what her "connects" with these folks might one day mean for Selma. The auxiliary's uplift project gave her ways and potentially the means to be hopeful about her daughter.

Their most recently discussed project had an even greater potential than their usual offerings of etiquette lessons and household management workshops. This time the society ladies were considering how they could establish a college fund, perhaps even a scholarship for one of the daughters of the help. From what Sadie told her—and Sadie Mathis would know, being that she worked in the colored doctor's house— the plan still had to make it past a contentious review before it could become a formal project. But some of the ladies didn't like the idea at all. They'd worked very hard to make a practice of keeping their daughters away from and different than "regular" Harlem girls. Many of the ladies had horror stories of what the girls in Harlem were like, especially the younger generation—"nothing but a fast piece of furniture," Millicent Henderson huffed—but then one of the ladies, it was probably Mrs. Eula Ann Pettis, made a motion that not "just any" Harlem girl would be eligible, but only those who were daughters of the help and, by association, already tangentially exposed to the habits of the upper classes. These girls were more likely to have ambition to escape their circumstances. Lilah was determined that when Selma came of age, her daughter would be chosen.

DeLilah always kept Selma close. She might not have been a comforting presence, but she was constant. Selma's upbringing left little time for affection or indulgence. Lilah wasn't soft. She'd already practiced that with June Bug and look where it got them. So when Selma was too old to be looked after by neighbors and old enough to get into the kind of trouble that could not be spoken of in polite company, Lilah instructed her daughter to take the trolley down to where she worked for the white folks on the Upper East Side directly after school and wait quietly in the service stairwell until her mother finished her chores. Until the day Mrs. Thayer caught her there, no one but the rest of the kitchen help knew the girl came to the lower level of the grand Manhattan mansion after school. The discovery had its consequences.

It was early winter when Enid Thayer took the back stairwell that led to her house manager's small office. She was bringing her edits of a menu they had developed for the upcoming holiday season. Usually, she didn't go down at all—her help came up to her. She held on to the walls as she did, not wanting to share the banisters that the help used. Fourteen-year-old Selma was sitting on the window seat that stretched across the span of the landing. She'd positioned her slender body to catch the last of the day's sun even while she twisted just so, so some of the light could hit the page of the book she held in her hands. What made Mrs. Thayer's discovery of the girl worse was Selma's response to her churlish "Who are you and what are you doing here in my basement?" Without looking up to acknowledge the authority or away to indicate any interest, or startled to show a reasonable fear at having been discovered, Selma merely answered the two questions she'd been asked.

"Selma." Her eyes bent back to the book in her lap. "Reading." As put out as Enid Thayer was with the girl's insolence, and especially after learning that she was the daughter of her valued seamstress, she saw the opportunity the girl might bring—especially during this season when the family was required to entertain so frequently. So she put aside her considerable irritation and said it didn't do anybody any good to just be sitting around wasting time, because in her household, if she had to have any of them there at all, there would certainly be no shiftless coloreds. She told Lilah, "If you're going to bring your girl with you, I will indulge

47

you"—that's what she called Selma, an indulgence—"I will indulge her staying here as long as she makes herself useful." She didn't want to see her again with any books. A book was a waste, at least for her kind. So DeLilah's daughter was put to work scrubbing the bathrooms and polishing stairwell balustrades in the mansion's upper floors. Those were the house's least used areas, and Selma was often alone—a precariousness that the Thayer son used as invitation.

SELMA COULD STILL FEEL HIS STUMPY FINGERS GRABBING AT HER CHIN and squeezing. Later she recalled that she was thinking that the bones in it would break. She learned in science class that there were fourteen bones in her face. She had good reason to wonder how many of them would splinter. And there had been bruises too. These could not be documented, just remembered. She traced their blue-black outline on her thighs and arms as if they were a map of what had happened. Selma left some scratches in the baseboard as she tried to pull away from him, and worried that it would seem the room had not been properly done. Later, as she was putting herself back together, she attended to the woodwork by covering her marks as best she could with furniture polish. They left dark grooves and if you looked carefully, you could see how some went against the grain.

When her mother finally asked, "What were you thinking?" and not meaning it in the way she answered, she told Mama Lil that she wasn't thinking about anything but "connected to the chin bone." From the song. Because it felt like her chin bones were the ones being crushed. She said she couldn't say a thing with his hand squeezing her mouth. Not even to shake her head one way or the other, not yes and not no, either. But with all that was left of the habits she had—which was to savor quiet spaces and prefer silence over speech—she did promise him not to tell. It was the only vigorous move she could make, shaking her broken head and heart up and down, hoping it meant he was through with whatever it was he had done to her body—every part, front and back.

She kept her promise because the shame that might have lingered if she had stayed with the moment would be an open wound and more than she could bear. And because her mother had earned that job with the white folks, and they would let her go without a second thought if she dared to say anything at all about the behavior of their only son. And also because she still longed to be the girl she was before she sought refuge in a tangle of carpeted branches.

Given the surety of her losses, her silence made perfect sense. As did her twisting her panties into a ball and stuffing them in her pocket, because being ripped they wouldn't stay on. And taking the chance of using the upstairs bath for her own business. She stood there with the door safely closed and laid her head against wallpaper that felt like velvet. But this time she didn't stop to trace its patterned whorls, testing to see if her fingers knew where the ridges would rise and then fall again. With one quiet but vigorous and vicious act, she'd been shifted to the other side of proper, and now everything was filtered through an unspeakable horror.

Selma slowly went about what repair of her body she could and then to cleaning up. She was nervous and watchful because the help is not supposed to use their bath—just keep it clean and pristine. If she needed to relieve herself, the one for the colored help was in the basement, on the far side and behind the furnace. Knowing she had to find a way to make herself presentable in case she ran into anybody, she stayed long enough to be certain that there were no remains. She cleaned herself—washed and wiped her face, rinsed her mouth and spit and spit and spit, even though it wasn't enough. She was too afraid to use any of the products in their cabinets. She pulled her hair back into a braid and wrapped it with the headscarf, hoping that it looked the way it had when she put on her uniform and hoping that in case anyone, especially her mother, looked at her, they would see the same thing she did when she looked up and into the mirror above the porcelain sink. Selma glanced up, just to make certain. But when she saw her reflection, she sucked in so much air that she gagged, again. She held on to the cool whiteness of the sink until she recovered. Then she made her way carefully down the back steps, back to the kitchen, where her mother waited.

On the way back home, and for just a moment, she let herself remember. How she had heard the bedroom door close too quietly for it to be the wind from the window she'd opened so the room could be freshened. Selma liked cranking open the casement handles, watching the dark limbs of the trees slowly separate from the black ironwork on the window. She stayed at the window's edge just long enough to watch heavy wet snow threaten the few brittle leaves left with a coverlet that would eventually weigh them down. With one last deep breath, she savored midwinter's crisp clarity before she closed the casement, thinking how she had yet to dust and polish the stairway balustrades on her way down and how their dark heavily turned woodwork had once been like the trees that lined the pavement outside of the mansion's windows. There were few trees like this in Harlem. She was thinking about this shift in the circumstance and the nature of wood and its whorls when she felt his arrogant grab and brutal tug. She tumbled down into the carpeted pattern of leaves and branches that, being mere embroidery, could not save her from his assault.

Afterwards, she groped her way to the adjoining bath with a growing storm inside her that she would learn to accommodate as if it were ordinary. But there was nothing ordinary at all in the stain slipping across the floor's penny tiles and the pitiful thought that the grout would discolor if she didn't get to it quick. But every time she put her elbows into it—which is how work gets done right—a splash of blood would drip from between her legs and run down across another circling pattern of tiles, threatening to steep permanently into the pristine spaces that separated one from the other. Eventually she stuffed one of her cleaning rags between her legs to keep from having to clean herself as well as the floor.

She didn't say anything at all when she finally got back to the kitchen and changed back into her school clothes. Her mother's frown waited for her. For a moment something caught Selma's eye, and she looked briefly off to the side where she thought she saw something—a flimsy fluttering thing, just out of sight, like a feather or a snowflake drifting just outside of where she could have seen it more clearly. But her mother's voice snatched her away from the floating thing when she fussed about her taking too much time to do the little bit of cleaning that Mrs. Thayer gived to you and we done missed the streetcar. Selma heard herself say "have missed" but not out loud. There was more for her to remember than to say out loud. Like what Percy said to her before he left.

I gotta go, Baby Girl. I love you. Don't worry none. You can manage. Don't do me. Do better. Be loving. Take care of Mama Lil.

She tried. Selma was attentive and careful with her mother. She anticipated her moods and tried to stay out of her way unless she could be of some help. Despite her efforts to be dutiful and loving, she learned that her mother could only manage loss if it was unspoken and kept to its place. Recessed and removed. Keeping hurt at a distance was their well-practiced labor.

Lilah and Selma's walk to the streetcar and ride home was quiet. But there was nothing unusual about that. Her mother was often too tired from her duties at the Thayers' to "chitchat," as she called it, and certainly on that night, Selma was still trying not to remember, much less to say, what it was she had just endured. They waited at the corner, the freezing slush piling into icy mounds between the sidewalk and curb. And finally, when their streetcar came round the block, they climbed aboard and took their usual seats. She watched as her mother's eyes closed and then her head leaned back and settled into the corner between the seat and streetcar. She only coughed a little before she fell asleep against the cold glass window, with just her headscarf between it and her cheeks. Selma pulled her mittens from her fingers, reached over, and put them between her mother's scarf and the window, hoping to soften and warm the place where she laid her head. She stuffed her own cold hands into threadbare pockets. The kind of cold she was feeling would soon settle in and stay put.

Selma watched the flash of streetlamps as the streetcar jerked its way uptown. She felt the settling in of the frigid night air, leaving nothing of the dim warm twilight that grew shorter as winter claimed its days. In late fall, the twilight seemed to linger some, its dimming shadows holding just until the night's shade was thick enough to make its claim. But in midwinter, nothing lingered. Especially nothing warm.

When the two got home Selma moved the lightbulb from the bedroom to the socket that hung from the ceiling of the tiny kitchenette and sat at the table to study her assigned recitation. Whatever had happened was already ice inside her, growing layer upon layer, defying a clear memory of the deed. She whispered her words and the next day spoke them. No one noticed that her eyes watered, and no one asked why she kept brushing at her brow. A floating, icy thing seemed to graze her cheek before she brushed it away. She said her piece as she had practiced it the night before:

> In the fell clutch of circumstance
> I have not winced nor cried aloud
> Under the bludgeonings of chance . . .

She collapsed back into her seat determined not to give in to her grief. She remembered her brother's plea to "do better" and her mother's instruction to "be a credit to the race." In order to do or be either of those things, Selma needed the room in her head for recitation and geometry and civics, and not the twisted and frigid knot that felt like the branches from that carpet where he pushed down and into her. A clutch of spiked thorns threatened to keep her in that spoiled space, even though she had cleaned herself the best she could and even though the thing he did had already found the place to attach and grow.

When a brutal thing finds a child, even a girl child as smart and focused and ambitious as Selma Althea Mosby, it can lead to a vicious space.

PART II

A Great Depression

6

(No) Credit to the Race

IN EARLY MARCH THE CITY HAD NOT YET TAKEN IN A PROMISE OF
spring. In fact, the day was as grim and gritty as the news that blasted
from the headlines:

> Lindbergh Baby Kidnapped from Home of Parents
> on Farm Near Princeton;
> Taken from His Crib; Wide Search On

The large dark letters broke Selma's concentration. She reached the end
of the block where Chasen's Grocery wrapped itself around one street
corner to the other. She knew she was there before she looked up because
she'd been counting the sidewalk squares, letting her fingers slip through
and across the iron gates that held in a fenced row of brownstones. She
stopped seven squares from Chasen's because otherwise she would have
met the curb and cobblestone unless she turned and went into the corner
grocery or crossed the street. She didn't do either one. She simply stopped
when the newsboy's urgent, high-pitched call seemed to be directed at
her. It wasn't, the street was full of passersby, but she felt his call was waiting for her response.

That was how she remembered the moment. The day she heard about
the Lindbergh baby was the day she finally understood the full consequence of the terror that had forced her to the floor.

It was on the street in front of Chasen's Grocery, caught by the word "BABY" in a headline about a kidnapping and by the photograph of the women—the baby's mother and grandmothers, and the child itself—when Selma Mosby realized that the weariness, morning malaise, and a slight plump in her belly was evidence of her own impending motherhood. And she also knew, while attending to the photograph where the clasp of the Lindbergh's kinship was obvious, that there would be no circle of family for her. Despite her mother's efficient interest, Lilah's emotional energies were still directed toward mourning her loss of Iredell and June Bug's leave-taking. Back when it happened, the only thing her mother offered her was to say: "June Bug hadta leave. He can't come back. Less said the better. Now don't ask me nothing about that no more." Lilah shoved her hands deep into her apron pockets and her daughter hushed.

The efforts to find the sweet towheaded infant who just happened to be the child of the most famous person in America would consume the city, account for uniformed police being more attentive to things that seemed ordinary, make stories of Lucky Lindy seem brutal rather than simply pitiful, and would give the city a common conversation that distanced them, at least a bit, from the despair of soup lines, the disappeared surety of jobs, the very ones that brought them clear-eyed and hopeful to the city, and the pall of desolation that folded their days into depressions that were blamed on "stock" markets that—after serious and sustained discussions amongst whatever clusters of men gathered to pontificate on these matters—seemed to be not at all like the street-corner groceries they knew well, but a kind of market nobody could describe to anyone's satisfaction except it was clear to all that the disparities between the wealthy (those who survived, at least) and the serving classes of merchants, laborers, and immigrants became more pronounced and made their days even more precarious.

When Selma looked at the headline, she saw the story in the picture beneath—a mother and two older women, probably the baby's grandmothers, one who lovingly held the infant on her lap. The younger woman's arm stretched down and clasped her baby's hand. Lucky Lindy wasn't in the photo, but he was the reason for it. His heroic accomplishment elevated the event from the everyday to the nation's tragedy.

Although everyone else would be consumed by the story, Selma was disinterested. For her the word "BABY" in a screaming headline about a kidnapping and the photograph's pastoral domestic was a clarification that there would be no circle of women waiting for her. Her mother would have no room—not in her heart, not on her lap—for the kind of trouble a baby would bring.

IT WAS EARLY MAY WHEN THE LINDBERGH BABY WAS FOUND IN THE woods not far enough from the family's home to stem the fabrications that lay in wait for a thread to start weaving together a story. Not much was left of the body. The local papers reported that the child's skull seemed to have sustained a serious fracture and his little hands and part of his leg (his left leg) were missing from the ditch where the body lay, as if it had been dragged there, or perhaps dropped. There was speculation that animals may have attacked the body—which would not have been at all extraordinary for the forested area that surrounded the expanse of Lindbergh's property. It was absolutely reasonable to infer that there could have been vultures, raccoons, or maybe a fox had torn at the skin of the baby's body, and the gnawed marks on some bones and scattering of others in a way that would explain the missing limbs. To some of the forensic experts who surveyed the scene, it looked as if there had been some halfhearted attempt to bury the baby. That speculation was as horrific to contemplate as the one associated with a deterioration due to exposure. If there had been an attempt at a burial, why was there a kidnapping in the first place? What was the reason for the ransom demand if the baby was dead? Was the child's death accidental? Was it intentional? Women wept as they stood and read the news being shouted out by street-corner newsboys. White men strutted and fussed about the criminal element amongst the immigrant population. Because there had been official talk about a German accent in negotiations with the kidnappers, those families kept to themselves and stayed away from the press. The city that had been their promise became their prison. Their neighborhoods, so clearly marked with Old World words and New World dreams, may as well have had a target singling them out for suspicion and general ugly ways. Because Lindbergh was a national hero, and because being on his side was a consummate demonstration of American patriotism, the kidnapping and its aftermath was the nation's story. By the time more than one kidnapping demand circulated and after the dead baby was discovered in such disarray, President Hoover himself stepped in and ordered a search for the murderers to be organized by the Federal Bureau of Investigation and the National Guard. This was an important moment, and the city rallied to help it be exactly that. Blocks and boroughs cooperated whether it was by spreading the rumor and mistrust or organizing a fierce loyalty to the nation's hero and Lindbergh's dead baby boy. It led them, at least momentarily, away from the restless brooding that they brought to bread and soup lines and gathered them back into a manhood that was loud, aggressive, demanding, and more familiar.

In Harlem, self-appointed spokespersons took to street corners and soapboxes, loudly assuring anyone in their hearing that the Lindbergh outcome was a warning—a doomsday message about excess and ambition and the consequence of raising up anybody higher than the Lord, who watched and waited for His final judgment, and only the faithful could escape by paying attention to the signs. Some dressed for the occasion in elaborate and heavily draped fabrics, robes fringed with feathers and head wraps pinned with bejeweled brooches. These men, and some women too, claimed the tragedy was a lesson indicating it was past time for folks to turn around and return home to Africa where they would be queens and emperors and nobody's babies would be in danger. There was plenty of talk.

Mr. Chasen pulled the LINDBERGH BABY KIDNAPPED! poster from out his storefront window. The baby's body—what was left of it—was found the same day that Selma Mosby's mother took one long, quizzical, perhaps anguished look at her daughter and said, "It looks like spring ain't the only thing blossoming up in here." She'd been watching her daughter for some time knowing there was something she should know. It started out slight, then came to her thick and full.

There was certainly no necessary connection between the two babies, except the kidnapped baby made Selma realize her impending motherhood, and the dead baby news caught her mother's attention in a way that settled on her own child. By the time it had all taken the shape it would, Lilah's slap nearly knocked the wind out of her. Selma had been sitting in the corner of the worn sofa. She'd settled back into the tuck between the arm and the back almost as if she were making a space that she could wait for and contemplate the birth of her baby. It was the same sofa that was her bed at night and her mother's place to welcome company (who was usually and mostly just their neighbor Doris) when they didn't sit at the kitchen table. Selma's small body collapsed into the pillows, and her position accented the growing roundness of her tummy. She sank deeper, forced by the surprise and the intensity of Lilah's slap. She wasn't breathless. It didn't knock the air out of her. But her mother's slap did do damage. It loosened what seemed to be something like a snowflake (in the way it would accumulate and blanket), or an icy shard, a frozen splinter free to float free then down and burrow somewhere deep inside her, leaving a fissure that would not, could not be stitched closed. It made her take in a breath, and she couldn't tell whether it was hurt or cold that was so sharp she shuddered. She felt the trail of frost slice through whatever protective layers there had been. It crept into the place it would settle and stay. She tried to brush it away, and when she did, she felt the sting of her mother's slap linger like a mark or a brand from some other time or place. Lilah saw her child's gesture and took it for disrespect.

"You look at me when I speak to you. Don't you be swiping at my hand. You done had your chance to do that when you let somebody put his filthy hands all over you. In places supposed to be your privates. And do nasty things. Things ain't nobody can take back." Selma had no way of knowing that her mother's words were the very same ones she'd heard herself, those many years back when her own pregnancy with Selma's brother Percy became the talk of Sedalia. Caught between her memory of Sedalia's focused shaming turned Lilah against her lonely daughter. Selma felt the injury of her mother's words like a leave-taking. They stayed with DeLilah for all the years since her pregnancy, tucked in deep but not buried. She dragged them out from her memory and hurled them at her own child with an ease that only came from the weight of their burden. She didn't stop to think of what they had done to her. How they wounded and pierced. It was all about their release. She didn't stop to think that Selma might could hold on to them as she had. It was just that they were no longer hers to bear. The more she spoke, the more easily she remembered. She let loose a generation of accusations that rolled out like ritual. "Who the daddy? Who you been swishing around? When you start smelling yourownself? Who you let up in there? In the name of Jesus, girl, you gonna tell me!" In that moment, the difference between her slap and his slam was hard to distinguish. Selma stuffed herself into the corner as astonished at her mother's passion as with the ease of her diminishing. She felt herself grow smaller, shrinking away from her mother's words and up and then outside of her own body.

"I work night and day and weekends up in that house to make a way for you to have a better life than this one here!" Her hands came down in a fury, both of them, striking her child, the sofa, the pillows, the baby deep inside, still protected, but vulnerable. "And I even take you up there to keep you outta the streets and safe!" *Whap!* Deep sigh. "Have mercy!" *Slap!* Her arms got weak, but she struggled to keep up with what seemed the only recourse she had left. "You ruint my plans and your future because you couldn't keep your legs closed to some little no-good street trash. I had made it so you could get choosed to go the colored girls school back home and be a Bennett Belle with them e-light girls and get you a chance at something better than this . . ." Selma whimpered. "What people you a credit to now? What I'm gonna do now? You got an answer for that? Slut!"

Selma remembered that name past everything else because that was the name her mother pronounced on the street women, the ones they passed on Sundays who stumbled out of the alleys and lay across the brownstone steps still full of sleep and Saturday sin. Lilah sobbed with as much hurt as Selma felt. But her daughter had gone quiet.

Eventually, her mother's voice dissolved into a moaning despair. Finally, the mother and daughter fell together, pressed against each other with their hands cupped over their faces. Their shoulders heaved—up and down, in and out. Together. Kin-shared sorrow.

7

Tell Me

SO, YOU DONE IT AGAIN.

It wasn't a question. He didn't ask her. He said it plain. Like she was already supposed to know what he was talking about. Like there was no reason between her and kingdom come that she was supposed to knit her brows and wonder, then ask what it was he was doing here. Much less how. So DeLilah skipped the ambiguity and spoke to the air like it was a perfectly reasonable thing for her to be doing.

"You here today? I looked for you yesterday." It was bad enough him showing up in the sunlight, when a luminous dust drifted through the streams of light filtered through otherwise dirty windowpanes. Flecks of leftover soul-stuff from everybody who ever died (which was what Gran'mam had said this was and which made his being there make sense) that sparkled whenever the sun hit them just right. She wanted to dissolve into his light, fit into the spaces between the glimmering reflection that seemed to hold him so safely and with more assurance than she felt. But she held to her place outside. Her hands slipped into her pockets, and her fingers spread to hold on to her flesh beneath the apron. She needed some grounding before she responded. He sounded accusatory and she needed solace. Her response was careful and defensive. Still, she didn't want him to leave her. Again.

"What you mean again? I said I slapped her. This time. This one time. This one terrible moment. This one blinding . . ."

Just stop, sweetness. I ain't asked for no kind of sermon. Saying it don't make it so. Let loose of your words and look to what you tryin not to remember. I ain't tryin to make this thing be about you. It's our girl.

Her fingers began to press into her thighs. "I know that. You don't have to tell me. But it was me." She didn't want to escape blame; she just didn't want its condemnation. "It was me. I hurt our baby girl. I was afraid and I hurt her in order to . . ."

So we back at you again. In order to what? Words cain't do nothing after somebody takes you down. Or somebody knocks you out. Nobody listening after you make them too fearful to come close enough to hear. After that, it's way past too late for what you want.

She felt for a break in fabric, the frayed seams that would let her reach through to skin. Her hands fumbled beneath her apron, looking for a grip. "That's not what I meant. I meant . . ."

It's too late and it don't matter. It is what it seems like. And what it seems like is you got you a habit of some kind.

"No. Listen. Listen! You tryin not to hear what I'm saying. And . . . and too, you wasn't here to give me any kind of help. It was once. This one terrible time. I never hit her before. Never. Not once. It . . . it come out of nowhere and my hands, my hands . . ." She pressed down deep into tracks from an old scar. "It was like they was moving outside of me. I was out of my mind with grief. I ain't never felt that kinda way before."

The light or his shadow shifted with a trembling that made her hush. *'Ceptin that time you slapped Percy upside his head?*

Lilah's shock tried to speak over her memories. "Percy? My baby boy? No! Not at all! Not ever! I *never* touched June Bug. I loved . . ."

This ain't about love. It's about hurt. You can't twist one up inside the other. For a brief moment, Lilah wondered whether there was any talking going on at all. Maybe it was just whispers. A resolute sweep at that last, reluctant cluster of dust gathered deep and thick into the corners.

Whatever it or he was, she needed to hear what he was saying because it took her back to a moment when he was there with her. Not these lonely empty days when struggle and missing him went hand in hand. There was something precious and fine and necessary in his taking her back to a moment before, even if what he was saying was so horrid. Needing the solace from those days, she hushed and listened. As she did, her fingers tightened on a needle she'd already pushed through.

We talkin about hurt. His speaking was slow and solid, even though there wasn't nothing to him but light. *I need you to remember and here you is tellin me you forgot. I ain't here for no forgetting. This is all about remembering. You can't be forgetting how we left with him cryin so hard he fell asleep on my shoulder sobbing? How I had to pull him out from behind the stove where he run to, afraid of you being afraid? You forgot how we left our home with all of us sobbing? How we had to put our hands over his face to hush his left-over-from-crying-too-hard heaving when we was hidin in the bushes? You be the one so attached to remembering. How you done forgot all that?*

Lilah struggled to connect the memory he was urging when what she wanted was to stay in its space. Its expanse. Its capacity. Those times before he died. Before they came north. Before there was a cramped flat with neither sun nor son. "You talkin about that day we left? Is that what you mean? You sayin I hit him? That I hit our baby boy? He was our baby. He didn't know no better. I couldn't a . . . Not my baby boy . . ." Even as she said this, and despite the effort not to, she was remembering. First, the heat of her rage and how it melted into her insides and like to have pulled her down. How she wanted to fall still but how she couldn't. She remembered how her hands got to be almost too heavy for her body. How they acted out what she could not.

You did.

"None of what happened was his fault. He wasn't nothing but our baby. It was them white folks. Harassing us, coming after us and what was ours . . . Ripping apart what we had planned . . . They was planning on taking him." She said that aloud. To herself she said, So we had to go. And time came I had to send him away. And now Selma. Who be good as gone herownself.

No doubt. He shifted into a side shadow. *But like I said. Again?* A still, small quiet settled in the room, reached into its crevices, draped across, and bound the two souls until it was the only thing left.

LILAH KNEW HOW FOLKS WOULD LOOK ON SELMA'S PREGNANCY. ANTICI-pating their judgments, their *tsk-tsk*s and side-eyed *I told you so*'s took her straight back to Sedalia, and how her being pregnant without Iredell being there was an opportunity for gossip and self-righteousness. She remembered the patterns of hurt; the way that what was said and who said it lingered long past the moment. The rehearsal of words and the way they sliced, burrowing in and making borders, etching her shame into a landscape. She could have stayed in that space of her own memories, but by that time Selma was talking. Once she started, it spilled out like a torrent mixing her memory and the violent and sordid circumstance into a thicket of vines that coiled around the moment and trapped her. Some of it was nonsense talk. All about trees and branches and spitting and shoving. She didn't so much as let go of the story as she let it shed. But some stayed with her like crepe myrtle bark back home or the city's birches. Even when you peeled it back, beneath it lay fresh skin, ready for wounding. Unlike her mother, Selma had no loving moment to return to when the meanness shadowed her. No memories of a soon-to-be soldier boy whose hands were gentle and tentative. No shivering from desire. No words that mattered, soft and whispered, curious and caring. Words that took DeLilah through her pregnancy and Percy's birth and those months before Iredell came back from France scattering folks' ugly ways and making room for the protections of kin. Selma had no sheltering memories, and DeLilah, consumed with her own grief, overwhelmed by loneliness and the fears of her failures and losses, let that gather until it governed. She acted as much as from what had happened to her precious girl as from what she did to her. Anguish emptied her out. Contrition left her remote. But the echo of her slaps lingered. As if that made a difference.

The truth was, ever since Iredell died and then later, after Percy left, she figured out that she had finally learned something. Instead of soldiering on (which would have been her mother's advice), she spent her days waiting for the next loss, for the absence that would crush and how whichever would be the one to come, it would be the one to extinguish. It was certainly a contradiction. Nurturing and caring for and embracing her precious daughter could have helped her slip past that result. But she couldn't see past the grief she'd had and the grief she anticipated. When she was confronted with her inability to keep her daughter safe, or her failures to have done so, what seemed possible—or at least familiar—was adding one more assault to the mix. Lilah knew how to act, that was how she spent her days. Acting like somebody's mother. Acting like the help. Acting like church was salvific rather than ceremony. She practiced how to act instead of how to be.

She knew that working for white folks came with a certain kind of nearly unspeakable danger, but she never warned her daughter. Sure she told her things. Telling was always easier than listening. She could direct her in where to sit. When to leave or enter a room. How to polish silver without leaving a print. How to be quiet when they in the room. How to make it easy for them to go on ahead with their chatter, even when it was about one of them or their people, with her standing right there holding a tray. Outside of her instructions on the proper ways to do and be, she left Selma mostly to her own devices. But and in fact, her daughter had none. And certainly no way to develop any. The company of her classmates could have made the difference of girls together, but her mother's rigid schedule made certain that friendships couldn't carry over or come with her. There were no slow walks home for her, no stops at Chasen's for Mary Janes or a nickel bag of peppermint pillows, no giggling with girlfriends. After school she went straight to the trolley and took it downtown to the Thayer mansion, quietly descended the side steps, then through the kitchen and halfway up to the landing, where she found a seat and some sun. The only thing that came with her were her schoolbooks. They suited her because she was bookish. It was a perfectly natural development since she had no time to practice the careless and carefree talk of girlhood. No stolen moments to share secrets or intuition with her age-mates. And as far as her mother was concerned, being bookish wasn't demanding in ways that would make it necessary for her to give more than she was able. If her Selma grew to prefer them to her—to want words on a page rather than words from her mother—then there was less for Lilah to worry over. Her precious girl, which should have meant exactly what it said, wasn't treasured, was innocent until she wasn't, and was alone until something cold and somebody foreign took up residence inside her. Lilah's failures dead-weighted her days and diminished her daughter's.

So when Iredell came back, more shadow than substance, it was like forgiveness. And when he said, *Tell me*, it seemed like invitation rather than admonition.

"We came on home that day. I remember it because I left Selma's gloves on the streetcar. She gived them to me to slip between me and the window, seeing I was tired and was going to nod off and she wanted me to have some kind of comfort for my head."

She that kind of caring? She didn't get that kind of spirit without some kind of love. She had to at least know what it was she wasn't getting. That says something. Don't know whether it's about you. Maybe not. But maybe.

Lilah looked away from the doorway because she could not bear to notice whether there was a glistening or fading. "You got to understand," she pleaded.

Got to? He said it as both statement and query. Here he was offering either/or, and she was focused.

"What I'm saying is you got to understand it was like my slap on her was the onliest way I could touch her. I didn't hold her none. She wasn't used to that from me. And even when she needed it the most, I didn't. I didn't grab my baby girl and cry with her. I didn't wrap and fold her into my arms. What I did was to whup her up and down her little body. Probably hurt the baby, too, for all I know."

He shook his head. Spirals of dust swirled around him—more shadow than light. But there was no telling if it was to shame her or to let her know he understood. Lilah turned away. "I know the whole building got to be talking about how I laid into her and be wondering what Selma had gone and did to make me lose myself like that. But that's what I felt. Like I had lost something. Again." Then she did look. She looked over and waited for him to say something, to nod, at least. But he didn't, so she went on with the story, feeling the weight of it slip away as she told it all to the one person who mattered. Her words flowed out and away. Like river water. Or tears.

It ain't meant to be easy. He said it as if an answer to the question that lay between them. She slid her hands under the table and into her over-large apron pockets that she used to pick up buttons or coins or whatever else she found lying around and without a good place to go. Mostly she used her pockets to hold her hankies. The ones she used these days were the ones her mother had stitched, and they had her initials in one of the corners. She slipped her hands into her apron pocket, found the sewing needles she kept there—the ones with just a piece of thread left attached that otherwise could be stepped on or lost. She pressed the needle through the apron, through her dark broadcloth skirt, letting it pierce the layers of cloth. Lilah slit a fresh space on her scarred skin. She pushed into, down, and across her thighs until she felt it.

"You right about that." She sighed into her cup of sassafras, blowing her words across the surface as if it were hot, even though the cup had cooled during her telling. "These days, I don't even look to imagine what easy means anymore. When we come up here, we didn't intend on easy. All we needed was safe. Then when we got to feeling safe, we wanted better. Then you left me and . . ."

Awww, baby, don't be saying it like that. You know it wasn't like that. It wasn't that kind of leaving.

"Felt like it." She heard the raspy edge in her voice and couldn't smooth it away. "We needed you with us sure and certain. But here you is this shadow."

Ain't nothing ever sure, sweetheart. Sure means still. Life be quick. A moving thing. Shifting. His angle of light moved just slightly.

"No. Not that kinda still. Not fixed. I mean it more like looking for something to depend on. Like you were to us. Depending on you being here . . ." Lilah looked over to his shadow, which had lengthened as the day crossed the room. "But not like this. Not like you is here now." She let go of the needle and pulled a hanky from her pocket to wipe her eyes. "I wanted to do the kind of things that would give me some say, you know? That could be like, since you done this, this is what good can come from it. Didn't seem like too much to be asking. Do right and right come back at you."

Yeah, but this here ain't no kinda right. It looked like his shadow shifted when she heard him say that. He didn't usually take to complaining. Most often it was her. Maybe what she'd done to Selma got to him. She didn't know whether "ain't right" was about what had happened to him, or what she'd told. Lilah leaned toward the window. It looked like he leaned against the door. Their shadows touched.

"Well, then, maybe you do understand. Enough hurt without me helping it happen." She pushed up the hair from the back of her neck that had come loose. Her small tortoiseshell comb tucked some wispy curls back into place, but sometime during the passing of years, her aging touched them as well. No longer spongy, now they were instead silky fine strands that did little more than make her feel even less like the self she remembered. The one whose dark tight curls could hold a blossom on its own now was mixed with fine strands of silvery gray. Would've been a time she cared. Or let the lady who pressed it add a bit of tint. But now . . . Then he said what she needed to know.

What you did come from you being fearful and letting that lead. Fear empties you out, sweetness. Makes ways and means for wrong. Lilah could feel the tears that had welled in the corners of her eyes spill out and down her cheeks. She left her hanky in her hand but pulled the needle back from out the layers of cloth and wove it through the inside seams of the pocket. *We got a grandbaby coming and with that got no choice but to move away from hurt.* Lilah shook her head.

"We? It's just me left up in here."

Uh-huh. What's the plan?

He'd always said that. From the days they started thinking about coming north. Even on the night they had to leave—which was not in the plan—he was talking about what they planned to do when they made it up north. Way before either one of them was sure they would make it out of the county. *You the one planned with me back then. You the one left here now. What's your plan?*

Crying made her cough. She tried to muffle it in her hanky. She looked up, her hand over her mouth. When she did, he shimmered, grew brighter, and then—just as quickly—dimmed. Or was it the other way round? She heard him like an echo—*What's your plan?* Lilah wasn't through. Somewhere in the pale light lay a promise of clarity. Something in his telling made way. If only she waited, there would surely be a response to his call. Some grace if not devotion.

What's your plan?

"I knew their boy was trouble. Always lurking. Shifty-eyed."

What's the plan?

"I taught Selma how to act instead of how to be."

The plan?

"Those people always getting that boy out of some kinda problem or another with their money. They that kinda rich. The kind that fixes things with they money."

Make a plan.

Again and again until there was nothing left but her tears and his words, and not until then was it clear that there was no instruction in her tears, but there was something to do between her words and his whisper.

Lilah stayed at the window most of the day. At least until the sun reached the other side of the house and his shadow was too dim to make out. It was quiet between them. But there was a comfort there too. And by evening, when Selma was back from school saying she couldn't go back because people were beginning to notice and she'd have to stay home and wait for the baby to come, her mother was the one saying, "That's not the plan. Oh no, sweet girl. It's not gonna be like this."

"Mama, there ain't nothing to do. I'm spoilt."

"Spoilt? Spoilt?" Lilah held her daughter's head between her hands. She cupped her cheeks and looked straight at her until Selma looked back. Her eyes were full and watery. "You listen to what I'm telling you. You ain't no kinda fruit. You about to be somebody's mother. And one many times better than the one you got here. But until then, you got me to stand with while you get to growing that baby."

Selma tried to twist away from her mother's hands. Something was shifting and she couldn't bear the difference it introduced. "But I'm your baby girl."

"Not no more you isn't. You carrying somebody that's gonna need tending to. First part of tending is planning. Right now, that's for me to do. I done practiced planning before. Now it's a baby to plan on. Same process." Later she thought if she had pulled Selma into the planning, given her something to do other than wait, she might not have slipped away. Selma settled into tears.

"But I'm Baby Girl. Me. Me. June Bug gived me that name." She remembered his urgent whisper, his instructions, his soft gravelly voice, the love in it, the safety. The belonging.

Lilah looked over at her daughter, worried over the tiny voice that warned her then, that if she was going to be able to keep these two, she had to choose from the same kind of strength she used that night they had to leave home. Strength motivated by love, not fear. She had it in her. She brought it out.

First, she would go to the Thayers. She would stand up for her child in the Thayer household and name their son. Then she would stand with Selma while ugly comments slid past her in church, or when the kitchenette door was opened to let in the breeze and they could hear folks in the stairwell. She would stand still and keep the hot comb steady when dirty whispers drifted up to their flat. She needed something that would make the gossip not matter as much as the plan. She'd seen the Thayers use their means time and time again for their boy, and she would make sure she had something to speak up for her girl. Even if it did have to come from them. Even if it was ill-gotten, it would be gain. They had lost too much. There would be nothing else gone on her watch. She chose necessary. No different from when she was carrying Percy and folks waited for her to show she was fallen. Or when Iredell died and she had to stand up when all she wanted was to lay down with him. This time the plan was to hold her daughter close and herself up.

Tell me.

8

Kin

OF COURSE LILAH WAS DISMISSED FROM HER POSITION WITH THE WHITE folks. She came up there knowing the consequence, even while sitting upright and proper, her feet crossed at the ankle, in the Thayers' upstairs parlor. She laid her small cloth handbag across her lap, smoothed the creases in the dress she'd chosen for the encounter, plain—but with a large deeply embellished lace collar smocking that showed off the skills the family would lose. DeLilah spoke forthrightly and without drama first to Mrs. and then to Mr. and Mrs. Thayer. Her courage came from her having made and now her carrying out a plan. She was able, and her composure and certainty carried the moment.

Both Thayers were eventually there, even though she had just started out the talk with her missus, feeling it was most appropriate to speak to the boy's mother. What rankled Enid Thayer was DeLilah's presumption that their both being mothers gave them some shared sensibility. The conversation started poorly when DeLilah asked to speak to her, "mother to mother." Enid was already disoriented by the house girl's direct ask to speak with her, and "in confidence" too, even indicating the place. "Perhaps your upstairs parlor, ma'am? It be away from ..." Lilah glanced around where the help made their ways past the two of them standing face-to-face in the narrow hallway, already unable to look away from the oddity of the colored maid speaking directly to the lady of the house. "It'd

71

be away from those not concerned with a matter that be personal to us both." She noticed her employer's confusion and hesitancy, and had prepared for it. "It be something you want to know, ma'am." In Lilah's mind, this boy's mother looked as unmoored as she had felt once she learned what had happened to her daughter. The white woman's irritation noticeably bordered on fear. Enid only indulged her because it would have been awkward to remind her to speak with the house manager, especially when she was told it was "woman's business."

When the focus of her meeting became clear, Mrs. Thayer pulled a delicate lace handkerchief out from her sleeve and held it to her mouth, as if what Lilah was saying needed some filter, as if her words and their focus were so foul that it spoiled the very air between them. Her other hand grasped at her pearls. But as much pity as Lilah might have felt for Enid Thayer, her being the mother of such a monstrous son, the woman's ugly demeanor closed any portal that might have been forged between them.

At some point, much more quickly than either had anticipated, it was all said and the two women sat with the Thayer boy's deed, its consequence, and Lilah's demands laid out between them. Nothing bridged their gulf. The bitterness in the room expanded with each breath.

Lilah wanted accountability and stiffened against the other mother's shrill but scarcely credible denial. Her eyes had already betrayed her belief. Nevertheless, she attempted an ugly rebuttal. "I will not be spoken to this way in our own home. Mr. Edward Jr. would have nothing to do with your little slut. How dare you even bring her into our home?" Lilah blinked back her rage. Hearing Mrs. Thayer say the very word she'd hurled at her daughter was punishing. But the woman's haughty shock and vehement repudiation reinforced her resolve.

DeLilah spoke the whole story, exactly as she'd heard it from Selma and without shielding the sordid, hurtful details. Her voice got fuller with each detail of the accusation, as if saying them there, in the very house where her daughter was attacked, was testimony. She managed her final words just as she had practiced them. "What Mr. Edward Jr. did was plain evil. Wicked." She shook her head back and forth. The telling was visceral and she hurt for her daughter, perhaps for the first time. But she couldn't stay paralyzed in that place. Instead, and as instructed, she'd made a plan. "And too, Mrs. Thayer, ma'am, you and me both knows it was not lawful. There be rules even for you folks. We up in the North now. This New

York City." Enid's eyes darkened as she focused on her maid's audacity and the danger in her words. "My girl Selma is not of age. So however you people will want to think about it, y'all keep this in mind. My girl is just a baby herownself. So any ways y'all try to add this up, my Selma just a girl child. That's the law. And because now there's a sweet and innocent baby to come out of this, that mean you and your family here have some accounting to do."

"How dare you!" Enid Thayer gripped the upholstered arms of the chair to steady herself. She knew it would be impossible to recover even the veneer of her authority, but she rose with whatever poise she could command and walked over to the fireplace to ring the service bell. She'd never felt more vulnerable, even though she'd become unhappily familiar with handling difficulties that came from their son's conduct. But this time there was an implicit threat that ran deeper, and this time, perhaps for the first time, she was afraid in a way that felt unrecoverable. The butler came to the door, took in the odd scene, and made it plain, as gruffly as he could, that he was more than ready to escort "the lady" out. Mrs. Thayer's face blanched and her voice trembled, but she explained that that wasn't necessary "at this time." She glowered over at DeLilah, as if there was some possibility the situation could be handled in a way that would maintain her authority. She directed the butler to summon Mr. Thayer. With dispatch.

When Enid sank back into the chair to await her husband, she was already receding into the truth of the matter. Enough had already gone awry with Edward Jr. to forecast the boy's dangerous potential. She was quite well practiced in managing it. While she waited, there was enough time to recall the acts that she'd excused or denied or negotiated around. The memories left the air around her thick and cloying. She moved the hanky to her forehead as if to press the pain back inside. She used it to fan the air to try to make it thin and clear enough for a breath. But the space of terrible outcomes already filled each corner of her every thought about the son she loved deeply but who also taught her how love and terror could occupy the same space. Lilah was still talking, still explaining, and still filling in details. She wanted the woman to be quiet. She wanted her gone. She wanted to disappear herself. But none of this mattered. Her fears took a shape and had a presence she would not have predicted—at least in this horrific detail and intimate specificity. Her son's potential for harm was always more dramatically possible in her imagination for him than his potential for anything else—a family, a future, or even a position in the society she and her husband had so carefully cultivated. Despite her desperate attempt to bury the raging thing inside him, she'd failed. It grew as he did. And it was loose.

Her husband's brash confidence accompanied him when he pushed the door open and demanded to know why he had been interrupted to come to some meeting between his wife and the help. He glared at Enid but didn't even acknowledge DeLilah. He listened without comment and then managed the asked-for solution as if it was not at all personal. Mrs. Thayer was grateful for the shift that her husband's presence brought to the room. She moved to stand beside his desk, hoping to benefit from the haughty expression of his authority. He angrily pushed aside the paperwork detailing plans of the new hotel and the city blocks that would soon carry the family's name. He pulled out a ledger and wielded his fountain pen as if this event were ordinary. She needed distance from DeLilah and proximity to her husband, even though somewhere inside she knew she shared more with the colored woman than the man whose efficiency was thankfully managing the situation. But now, with the boundaries between them leaking, she needed her husband's presence to reinforce their distinction.

He said the girl was whorish.

Lilah said my baby girl is just fourteen, and she got this baby because your boy is a monster.

He said there was no way to prove their son had been involved.

She said that she'd been in service with them for enough years to have heard a whole host of stories about their boy. And too, she knew some of the folks that had come to their door before she did. Folks downstairs talked about what young Mr. Edward been doing for all the years she worked there. Loose talk don't always stay to where you want it to. My folks got connects down to the *Amsterdam News* and the *Negro World*. Stories about babies get news these days. People all riled up after what happened to Mr. Lucky Lindbergh and now with all the news reporters . . . Lilah could see Mr. Thayer stiffen. Well, she was sure her baby would get some kind of attention too. Or at least she was sure enough to try.

Thayer's remonstrance stumbled. Still, without proof . . .

Lilah said there was blood on the upstairs carpet—her girl didn't know not to put hot water on stains. And the baseboard was scratched where her daughter had tried to claw her way away from their boy. Would he care to see?

He said that wouldn't prove a thing.

DeLilah said there are colored policemen now. Things are changing.

He said she and her girl were no more than trash.

She said trash will cost you and that was no way to talk. ". . . considering this baby that my Selma is carrying is your kin too."

He said, "You go too far."

Without breaking her rhythm, she said, "A check will do, sir, or cash. And if you would be so kind as to include my wages—seeing as I won't be back . . ." And she let that trail off, so it could be either a fact or a promise.

Later Edward Thayer was left only with his wife, Enid, as a reasonable target. His accusations were bruising. He violently grabbed her shoulders and shouted that she had mismanaged the only real job she had by letting Lilah bring her slut of a daughter along with her to work. He blamed her. If only she had been a better mother to their son, all of this could have been avoided. He pressed Enid against his desk, his thumbs digging so deep into her breastbone that she could barely breathe. She tried to break his grasp. Even in the midst of their battle, Enid wondered if he knew their son at all, or whether she had spared both of them while she consumed the day-to-day, month-to-month, year-by-year terror of rumor, gossip, and innuendo about their son. But perhaps it didn't matter what he knew.

When Lilah left, Edward Thayer was still seated at his desk, turned away from his wife. "It's done?" She needed to finish this interlude and then get back to a space where she could build the energy to manage the weighty sense of inevitability she always carried, whether it was fear about the next telephone call or hand-delivered message or—God forbid—aggrieved visitor at the doorbell. Another lawyer. Or the police. Her husband always completed these frightful events the same way. He wrote a check. But she was the one left to do the comforting and assuaging of headmasters and coaches, teachers and camp counselors, and friends' parents. Complaint, resolution, silence. As much as she dreaded the aftermath, she needed this one to follow that pattern. "Is it done?" she asked again. Thayer wondered whether Enid was becoming as much of a problem as their son. He turned toward her.

"There is nothing more to speak of." He locked the drawer of his desk and laid his hands flat on the surface, as if to prevent any leak. He pulled the architectural renderings that had been on the desktop back into sight as if they were the only business that was of interest. "There will not be another word in my household about any of it." Enid sighed. It was the assurance she needed. But, in fact, her husband's officious pronouncement came from his own insecurity about the boy. He had to assign blame. That was the difference between them. He managed the event while she handled the residue. He had to distance himself from the unpleasantness despite the fact that his wife would bear the brunt of his privileged distancing. "You must find a way to assure our family is never put into such a compromising position again." It was not a question.

"Yes. I will make certain of that. I . . . I'm sorry . . . I . . ." She stopped midsentence, not only because he wasn't listening but because she'd glimpsed out the window. Just past the curtain she could see Lilah closing the gate that led to the downstairs. The corner of the envelope Edward had given her had caught in the clasp of her handbag, but that wasn't what drew her attention. It was that no one could have guessed from her bearing any of the trauma that had just played out in the Thayers' front parlor. She was walking straight shouldered and upright, as if she hadn't been shamed by Edward's tirade about her loose morals and the way her daughter had picked up the worst habits of her people. As if she hadn't been humiliated after making her demands known—which was what to call them—that she and her girl and the baby be compensated for the costs they would "incur." That was the word she used. She'd never heard the help speak with such authority or self-assurance. DeLilah Mosby sat in the Thayer front parlor as if she were fully entitled to be there. She didn't waver from her text: "A check will do, or cash," until her husband finally went to his desk, withdrew the leather ledger from a locked drawer, and wrote a check. She didn't even examine it. Instead—almost casually, DeLilah unsnapped her worn cloth handbag, placed it inside, and clasped it back. She could see from the window that the edge of the envelope peeked out. Given the circumstance, it was more self-possession than Lilah had a right to exhibit. "Did you write it for what she asked?"

"In its entirety. Her wages included. This sordid matter is over. But you will need to take your role more seriously. Your son has always been a challenge, but this kind of expense has become problematic."

She didn't say, *But he is our son . . . ours.* Instead she struggled to explain: "I know. I mean, I won't, it's just that, well, yes. Of course I'll make certain of that. I'm sorry, Edward. I . . ." and that was when Enid glanced out the window again and saw Lilah Mosby walking down the street as if the entire scene that had played out in the upstairs parlor hadn't been a shared mortification. As if she were immune to the insult and the accusation. She should have moved more slowly. Her head should have been bowed. Enid Thayer wanted some visible indication that her family had prevailed. Instead the linens girl walked away from their home as if she had just completed a business transaction that did not diminish her at all. Especially in the way it left Enid Thayer reduced. The woman's dignity made no sense. Given the circumstance, how could she manage to carry herself away from their household with a calm that seemed prideful?

In fact, Lilah's relief came from the certainty that she had at least trimmed some of the troubles that had twisted their way between mother and daughter by going to her white folks and making the demand she'd carefully rehearsed. She knew that Mrs. Thayer believed her as soon as she saw the color drain from the woman's face. It was absolutely evident that this was a troubled woman just waiting for the next version of whatever it would be that would threaten them. "Here," Lilah offered, as if she were the one directing their meeting. "You set down and I'll get you a glass of water." She walked over to the bar, reached into one of the overhead cabinets for a glass, and filled it with tonic water as if she did the same thing every day of her life. Then she took a seat in one of the upholstered chairs and explained the business she had come to discuss.

Enid Thayer listened to Lilah Mosby as long as she could, managing some facet of a cut-crystal reserve before she rang for Mr. Thayer.

At that moment Lilah knew she had won. But she had no idea of the danger she ripped open when she told the Thayers that her daughter and the baby would need the finances so that they could go on and get a life somewhere else now that it is ruined for them here. It was when she said that they should remember "this baby is your kin too" that she made the irreversible error.

9

The Words to Say It

THE TWO CIRCLED AROUND EACH OTHER AS BEST THEY COULD IN THE small flat. The daughter was not speaking at all, and her mother's remembered grief and regret grew large enough to fill the void. Lilah struggled with her new understanding of how easy it was for her to shift from fear to fight. How it was she could hurt her child—no, how she could hurt her children—and how it now felt more familiar, even more ordinary than she could bear. She ached every time she saw her daughter look away or watched her shrink back from her touch. Regret as thick and viscous and unyielding as pinesap settled over the tiny household.

She knew now that when she slapped—no, when she beat Selma—it came from the same kind of helpless fear she'd felt back when her own pregnancy with Percy was questioned and side-eyed. When love felt like hurt. Discovering what *her* white folks' boy had done to her own baby girl left her with a sharp and unforgiving grief. She could not neglect the pain. Her apron pockets leaked with threads, sun-soaked yellow like summer sun, green like after a rain back home, red like sunset, or bloody—like soil after a slaughter, or rain-soaked clay. They were the only reliable reminder of her days.

The family that disembarked from the Southern Sky might have thrived in this place where folks and their buildings and their necessities covered everything, taking up space like a dense country landscape.

But cityscape was different, and the ways and means of living here either folded you in or left you out. In fact, Lilah's familiarity with fear was already too brittle for Harlem. When Percy took to the streets and she let go of asking questions about what he was doing and with whom, it was in part because she was already afraid of what his answers might be. Harlem didn't settle on in-between when it came to living right or not. And when the thing happened that made it necessary for her to send him back home, she grieved his absence like a dying. Then, after she discovered Selma's pregnancy and learned the event of it as well as the circumstance, it moved her fear so close that nothing else seemed possible. She mapped the route onto her thighs.

Lilah tried to explain some of this to the only real friend she had in the building. Doris lived alone, up the hall at the front of the building in rooms with two real bedrooms and windows that looked out on the street. She did what she could to shush folks when they got to talking about Lilah and her daughter, especially their thoughtless giggling over how the mama "laid into that girl" when she found out. Doris was the one waiting for them when they came back from Harlem Hospital with the baby, and perhaps because Lilah was so successful in shutting other people out, but also because her neighbors gave up on her too easily, Doris was the only one to help get them settled in. This morning the two women were alone with the baby. Selma went out, Lilah explained when she answered the quiet tap at her door and shrugged away the other woman's "Where to?" They sat together, folding diapers and delicately embroidered baby gowns and caps, and talking in a way that left Lilah so grateful for compassionate company that she confided in her the real story about what had happened to Selma.

"I knowed about this kinda thing happening and didn't save my own child from it. And then, I went an—" She stopped and sobbed, but Doris helped her find the words to say it.

"Girl, don't I know. I useta work for some folks, and the daddy came after me the same way this boy come after your Selma." Lilah nodded. "Sweetheart. For womens like us that a story's old as our days. We don't never get no kind of say when that happens. We just got to deal with the grief we get . . . if we can." She reached over and tugged Lilah's hand from her apron pocket and held it tight. "Not everybody has what they need to make it past that kinda hurt." Doris held on to the hand that slapped Percy and walloped Selma and that now wanted desperately to reach down for a needle embedded in her pocket seams. Lilah's sigh was deep and long. Like a cutting.

"I know. I know you right. But what breaks me is how I already sent one child away from me. And Selma? She good as gone herownself. You seen her. She don't never say nothing. We been back from the hospital going on a month now, and she not at all interested in this sweet baby like she ought to be." The two women looked over to the baby swaddled and sleeping on the sofa. "So what is it I got in store for my grandbaby over there? I can stitch her these kinda things . . ." She pressed the growing pile of baby linens down, then separated them into two stacks. "The Thayers made it so I am fixed to buy her what she needs from now well into her growing up. But knowing what I done to my own, seems reasonable that I ought to worry. What I done with my own hands . . ." Doris wouldn't let her finish it and took hold of her other hand, moving it from the way she clutched it to her chest.

"It ain't about our hands, Miss Lilah. It's about our hearts. We stay scared for the children. If you gotta hold on to something, hold on to your heart."

"I think I lost that a long time ago." Tears streamed down her cheeks.

"That ain't true. Your love for Percy right here." She touched Lilah's chest. "You love Selma, else you wouldn't be so worried about her. And that gived you the strength to force that family to step up for your grandbaby and not give in. But it's just that, with what all you been through, you got the kind of love that's pressed up close to worry. It's nothing wrong in that. We do what we know. And what we know and what we been through means sometimes we just got to be hard. The kind of ease you missing don't always come when we need it to. Sometimes love means firm and certain." Lilah looked toward the door, as if Selma might come in to take in some of this wisdom. "And sometimes, sometimes it comes out in a kind of touch that hurts rather than holds. That don't make it right, but that's what it is."

Lilah spoke to no one in particular: "It feels like I'm always just a step away from pieces. And with Iredell not here to hold me together . . ."

Doris took her friend's hands into her lap and held them there. "I know that's how you think it was. But you done some of that stitching yourownself. You done held together when others pulled at your seams."

Lilah looked back at Doris, grateful for the company and her words.

"It's likely gonna get harder now. Even with what that family turned over to you. You still got to figure out your ways."

THE FACT WAS THAT IN SOME WAYS, IN IMPORTANT WAYS, THE MOSBYS were no better off than the days they first arrived and tried to understand that if they wanted flour there was a store down a corner rather than the next town over, and there was no need to wait for a weekend to hitch up the wagon and go into town for supplies. They felt the city's large offerings, and Iredell made plans for them to grow along with it. They had every intention of moving someplace where at least there was more than the one bedroom. But sooner than they could follow through with that wish, Iredell lay dying in the very rooms they found when they first spilled out of the train with all those other colored folks searching for the freedoms or security or a star. And after he passed on, they were mostly lost in a city that held out a promise like it was something that might be found but made it difficult to discover. The idea of moving now, even if she had the money to do it, felt overwhelming.

Their tiny kitchenette was at least familiar, and it kept her company with his spirit and her memories. There was a stubborn window—more likely to be stuck than glide like the rope and pulley inside was made for it to do. It was over the sink and actually useful because she could wash right there and string and pin the clothes out and run them right down the line without changing her place. It did require her to step up on the stool and reach across the drain. At first, she'd been excited at its ease. There'd be no more need to dash out the back door, hearing it slap against the jamb, and rush to gather up her wash from the lines before the rain. But she came to miss the run and the rain, the stiff sunshine smells left in clothes off the line, and the way a porch could hold a whole company of women rocking in bentwood chairs, sitting across a railing and leaning back against the steps. The scent of summer-splashed washes was nearly, but not quite, faded from her memory. In fact, they seemed to glisten.

The one other window was in the back-room bedroom. It didn't open and was grimy from the city's dust and progress; but it did show some sunset if it was winter and if you were standing in the kitchen or seated at the one table at just the right time to catch fall colors. Otherwise it flung late-afternoon shadows out across her worn counterpane and into the other room. It was a mere and slightest blessing of light. There was a table and three chairs, one that wobbled. She thought at one time they would need another chair, but then Iredell died and what they had was enough.

Homework, eating, sitting, reading, braiding hair or pressing it, talking to a neighbor with tea, waiting for coffee to percolate on the stovetop, all happened there. There was barely room enough for the faded sofa that Selma slept on at night and was saved for company during the day. It lay like a way station between the two rooms where the family did its living and Iredell had done his dying.

On the night Iredell passed, the walls seemed closer. His dying filled every crevice. These many years later, it still lurked in darkened corners. Or he did.

She remembered the only space that mattered. And mourned its loss. The one where he held her sweet and close. Like they knew how deeply they needed something familiar and were sure about. Even when they had lived in Harlem long enough to know it—the rhythms of shopkeepers and dray horses clopping down the street, the trolleys with sharp new colors and their clanging announcement that they were there for the time being and the times coming, the slow summer and dreary winter afternoons, even after they were no longer surprised by any of it, it was only with him, nestled in the hollow of his arms, whispered to and touched as intimately as she could be touched, that Lilah felt safe. When she said she was afraid, he pulled her into his lap and held her there and said *unless you afraid of this*—and he'd touch her in all the places, and have her touch him. In those moments, the crevice in his shoulders, the smell inside his elbow, the feel of his fingers tracing down her body until they stopped and pushed, fear was the last thing she felt—*you ain't got nothing but me to worry about.* He told her again, *I got you, girl. I do.* He did until he died. His safety and promise was buried along with him and the blue thread bracelet she'd tucked into the burial ground.

NOW HERE SHE SAT WITH DORIS GAYLES—WHO, FOR REASONS OF HER own, was not frightened away by their loss, their sorrow, her failures, or what was now the relentless wailing of a newborn. Doris would listen to her trying to explain why her fear was far more reliable than her hope, and even though she tried not to, she wished for the thick quiet of Carolina's summer nights. Outside, while Harlem's gas lamps flickered, Lilah remembered fireflies playing in the dark, and she wished for home and the clutch of longleaf pine and drone of Ju-ly flies. Doris set her teacup down on the table. Lilah pushed aside the basket that held a stack of papers and manuals that the ladies who worked for the colored betterment folks were passing out amongst the women who worked in proper homes—because they were the ones most exposed to what they all aspired to. The ones promising a scholarship for one of their girls to go down south to one of the colored colleges. DeLilah told Selma about the girls who went to the Palmer Institute, back home in Sedalia, then on to the college for colored girls at Bennett. Instead of bedtime stories, she'd preached to Selma about the attributes of the Bennett Belles and how at the train station all the students would arrive in bright white dresses, and then the wagons and even a few automobiles would come for them to sweep them away to elegant lives behind the walls of the college. She lectured on how to keep to her lesson, and the ways she could to prepare herself for something more than what they had. As far as her mother was concerned, Selma had been right on the path to be a Bennett Belle until she wasn't. Until she stitched herself into that shroud of white.

After Doris left, Lilah held the baby in the crook of her arm and reached into her sleeve for a hanky to catch her cough. Ever since she left the Thayers, her cough had become more pronounced and now, having to move around toting Selma's baby, it seemed every time she bent over, she'd cough again. She had no idea how long she could carry on, caring for a newborn that her daughter did not even notice because her mind had loosened. She shifted little Chloe onto her hip while she warmed the formula. If she had been born up in the Heights, the baby's caramel curls and rosy complexion would have made her ideal for exactly the life she had imagined for her Selma.

Chloe's rosebud lips grasped the bottle's nipple. Lilah closed her eyes and remembered crepe myrtle. Their delicate blossoms, feather light and crinkled, would just now be tightening into bright green knobs, readying for the winter. If she were in Sedalia, the red dirt roads would already be grooved with the trails of late summer rains, and the porch swings and rockers would creak back and forth, appreciating the generous touch from Indian summer when snap beans weighted aproned laps and punctuated stair-step gossip. Pots too large for the burners would bubble mason jars and their lids, the clink of bottles, one against the other, as reliable as stovetop steam. Lilah stuffed the hanky into her apron pocket, and her fingers brushed against the letter that she'd shoved down her right-side pocket without reading it when she came home yesterday. Given what she found upon opening the door, it was not surprising she'd forgotten it. She rocked more vigorously, as if the energy would shift the image. Lilah fed little Chloe with one hand and read what Percy had to say in the other, her fingers shaking as they moved slowly across the page—then back again, as if to affirm she'd read it correctly. She looked up at the calendar over the kitchen table to check the date and be sure. By the time she finished, the baby was asleep, and she was near to drifting herownself. June Bug's letter was still clasped in her hand waiting for her to figure it out. Sleeping is best for making up your mind, her mother always told her. That's when the ancestors will come and tell you what you need to do.

10

Just Prudent

LABOR DAY WEEKEND THE THAYER CLAN GATHERED IN THE HAMPTONS to conduct the annual meeting of the board. Edward Thayer Sr., the current chair of the corporation, repeated the phrase "your kin" in his report. He offered it as explanation when his brother Alden asked about a line item from the report of a rather hefty expenditure with no explanation other than "personal privilege." Edward was not at all hesitant to fully explain that he had used that account to pay off the Mosby women, a decision absolutely within his purview as chair. Because the board had full review of all expenditures, Alden's inquiry was appropriate. "It's insurance," Edward clarified when he noticed the anxious glances being exchanged by some board members. "And it's not as if these funds haven't been used for various personal matters in the past. I need not remind you that many of us here this afternoon have made use of this kind of opportunity our operations make possible . . ." He put on his reading glasses for effect and pointed to the page in the notebooks that had been prepared for each member. Clearing his throat for effect, he noted aloud: "The line under question is appropriately debited from the Chairman's Reserve." He took off his glasses, laid them carefully over the page, and folded his hands on the table. "And of course we know that many of us have had the advantage of these funds as your own family's needs have come into play." With this reminder, several seated around the large table indicated they were ready to move the pace along rather than linger on an item that might cause more detailed discussion than they'd want. They pushed their chairs back or noisily turned their pages. Everyone understood the necessities that came with managing a family corporation—keeping the family name pristine, protecting its interests from those who made malicious claims (not, of course, depending on the truth of the matter but its potential for harm), and keeping their philanthropy the focus of public scrutiny. The era's economic challenge pushed the lives of those whose wealth was as reliable and flush (or even more so) as it had been before the crash to the forefront. Intense scrutiny of families who managed to escape the nation's economic horrors became a habit of those who had lost everything as well as of those who had nothing to lose and were living even more precariously than they had before. Those whose wealth survived became a spectacle that was greedily consumed with a mix of hope and jealousy. So the family's investments in the city were at least some balance to the gossip about their outrageous parties, excessive expenditures, and their ostentatious consumption, as well as the questionable conduct of its younger generation. Luxurious hotels, parks, and whole neighborhoods would soon bear their names, and the Thayers, whom some took to calling the "landlords of New York," appreciated that their credibility and stature came with a certain precarity that could not endure a scandal. They also appreciated (and some even came to depend on) the private perks that made monies available when special needs arose. The younger generation of cousins, those who would soon be appointed to positions on the board, was in the room as observers, learning the ways and means of the family business. They took up seats on the sofas and chairs that lined the library walls and included Thayer's son, Edward Jr., who shifted uncomfortably while his father repeated the story of his folly. His father told the story of the colored girl's seduction, as he called it, in hopes that it might serve as a cautionary note. He looked directly at those seated along the bookshelves. Edward Jr.'s cousins nudged him, and during the break for private discussion, the young men crowed about their successes in keeping their own dalliances with their household help out of this particular realm of trouble. As far as business matters went, the financial report was accepted as offered.

Just before the dinner bell, Edward's younger cousin Cole—Alden's eldest son—repeated the gist of the meeting to his wife, Adelaide, who had the unbecoming habit of overstepping her boundaries in her inquiries regarding the family's business matters. Since her puzzlement underscored Cole's own worry about this most recent matter, he tolerated her interference.

Adelaide's planning for their ascension amongst the family's elite had been well rehearsed, even to the point of selecting Cole as her target (rather than the elder cousin Edward) well before he became predictably besotted with what seemed her charming playfulness and just-naughty-enough habits to string him along. They were married not a full year after her debutante season, and she was still beaming from her family's approval of her keen and strategic placement in New York's best social circles. She took on her new duties with a relish that was sometimes overly interested (at least that was the comment of some of the elder women in the family). But she was strategic in using the time to urge her husband's leadership potential as a viable option to his cousin. And since Edward Jr. was as yet unmarried, she had some time to indicate her husband's reliability and maturity, especially in contrast to his cousin. She used every opportunity to do so.

The Thayers were real estate magnates, and what were lean financial years for their peers had seen extraordinary growth for the corporation. Cole was the second eldest heir in the Thayer family, following his cousin Edward. Adelaide's mother had heard enough about Edward Jr.'s weaknesses to suggest that her daughter consider a match with the cousin. Adelaide was given careful instruction on how to nurture her future husband's potential as chairman of the corporation at the same time she cultivated the potential that there could be a break from the tradition of simply choosing the eldest because he was "presumptive" heir. The decision would be determined by a vote rather than by seniority. "Presumed is not the final word," her mother insisted. "You make your own destiny. If you don't claim the opportunity that this marriage gives you, you have no one to blame but yourself. You must plan for what you want." Fortunately there had already been enough whispered gossip about Edward Jr.'s propensity for embarrassing conflicts that led to questions about his potential for stable leadership. And this event, which took up a bit more time on the family's agenda than had been allotted in their meticulously planned schedule, may have given the final proof to that potential. It would be a matter of time and circumstance.

Adelaide turned away from her dressing table, unable to contain her amazement: "The colored girl called the baby 'kin'?" Cole's silence was answer enough. "*Our* kin?" Adelaide pressed the point with her emphasis. "And you said what?"

"Nothing. Nothing at all." His temper flared slightly, in part due to his own unease with the situation. "You have to understand the protocol. It wasn't my place. We're sidelined," he said. "Quite literally." Cole was thinking of the arrangement of the room, where he and his cousins were seated along the wall. "I've explained this to you before. I don't see why we are discussing it now. It's not your place." He directed his irritation to his man, demanding that Hobart adjust his collar again. "It's just not sitting right," he complained. "Can't they do better downstairs? It's a damn collar for chrissakes."

"Yes sir. My apologies." The manservant removed the collar and replaced it with a fresh one. He fumbled for a bit in the drawer of his linens box. "This one should fit quite well." He fastened an identical collar onto the shirt.

His wife knew she had to negotiate this terrain carefully, but she wasn't ready to relinquish the opening it gave her. "Oh, darling, I do apologize. Of course it's not my place. I'm just concerned about you—about our little family. This girl's mother called that baby 'kin.' That just makes me ill. And what if . . ." She shuddered at voicing the thought. "What if that child were to orchestrate some future claim?"

Cole obviously had already thought of that potential but dismissed it, assured by the discussion and action of the board. "I understand your interest. But it is nonetheless misplaced. There's an order to respect," Cole replied. "And Uncle Edward handled this to everyone's satisfaction."

"But that's just it, my darling," she explained, as if she were agreeing with a perspective he, rather than she, had offered. But the fact was this moment helped to clarify his own discomfort. Adelaide noticed his puzzlement and took advantage of the opening. "You and I both know that that colored tart and her bastard baby could eventually be quite disruptive. Your uncles and aunt will all have retired from the leadership, and you'll be at the table if and when Edward's little colored bastard shows up. And it could happen at a most importune moment. We'd spend our days guessing when there might be a knock on the door, or a letter from a solicitor . . ."

Adelaide knew her argument had had the desired effect from the hesitant tone of his response. "No, she won't. Or she might not. Or shouldn't. There were papers. Legal papers were drawn up. The family knows how to protect itself in these situations—"

Adelaide carefully cut him off, knowing she was as close as she was going to get with the argument. "Well, of course, he would have, darling. But as you well know, that baby didn't sign a blessed thing. When it comes of age and shows up knocking on the family's front door . . ."

"Please, sweetheart, please let it rest. Or at least trust me to handle the matter." Adelaide gave him a frustrated look, which he didn't see. He was finished with the conversation. She had done all she could, and she knew by his discomfort that she had planted enough of a seed for him to think about it later. "We should go down. The dinner bell has already sounded." He took her gloved hand and tucked it firmly against his own tuxedoed arm. Outside of their suite, they joined the rest of the family in an orderly descent down the grand staircase. After everyone was gathered and the requisite exchanges of pleasantries about the day—tennis, boating, weather, and other seasonal talk—waned, his Uncle Edward and Aunt Enid and Great-Aunt Ophelia led the family into dinner. Falling appropriately into the generational custom of hierarchy, Cole and Adelaide followed his parents, who followed his cousin Edward Jr. The rest of the clan followed them. Cole couldn't help but notice his cousin's obvious sulking. It seemed as if the residue of the meeting's personal agenda was visibly attached to his mood.

The long mahogany dining table was elegantly set with the blue-and-white summer Wedgwood and freshly cut flowers. Candlelight enhanced the brilliant crystal, and the silver service sparkled in its glow. The staff quietly served dinner, their presence never acknowledged by the family and yet the protocols of service rigidly observed. Their scripted but seemingly casual conversations were correctly paced and chosen for banality. But during it all, from the first service to the dessert, Cole was preoccupied enough with Adelaide's remonstrance for it to show. At one point, he caught her eye as she gestured rather emphatically toward his Aunt Ophelia—they called her "Aunt Phee"—to remind him to direct his conversation and attentions toward her. She held, after all, the most important vote. He momentarily buried the thought of his cousin and turned to cultivate the affection and interest of his aunt, the only surviving member of the first generation of Thayers. It wouldn't be long before she not-so-subtly reminded her kin that, as the eldest, her preferences should be the family's guide. The fact was that she could effectively hand Cole the chairmanship if he was seen to be her preference. The will she often talked about as still being in draft form was a considerable weapon—so deference to Aunt Phee was a substantial investment.

By the end of the evening, Cole was convinced that his wife had a point and that the family was not sufficiently alarmed at the breach his cousin's carelessness might constitute. A claim against them would be, at the least, an unfortunate distraction. He made himself a promise to attend to the matter. After all, there was the Rhinelander affair some years back that taught them all how even the potential of an illegal or unwanted heir could disrupt the legacy they so carefully guarded. Or, and at the least, bring unwanted public attention to a family who cultivated their privacies and exercised extraordinary control over their public images. Who amongst his kin would want their name to be headlined the way the Rhinelander family suffered? Especially since managing that public image had become so much more critical during this unfortunate time of public scrutiny of the very few families who seemed to prosper despite the depression that gripped America. So, although there was no one who thought that the amount tendered was at all consequential (if not a bit high, for a colored family), the meeting concluded as if the item, and the baby, were disposed of in a manner appropriate to the occasion. His uncle had assured them that the woman was no longer employed by them and added that Enid had been appropriately reprimanded for allowing the help the latitude that led to this unfortunate event.

Following dinner and after the women excused themselves, the men gathered in the smoking parlor, and after more liquor, some high-stakes poker, and accompanying braggadocio, the evening came to an end. Cole noticed how easily Edward's genial ways made him a favorite amongst his cousins as if none of the embarrassment of the board meeting adhered to him at all. He could shrug it off with his appealing personality and ingratiating friendliness. It was the way he'd managed throughout his school years and now into his young adulthood. Nothing ever stuck. His cousin's naive and easily earned embrace were enough to encourage Cole's thinking that Edward's social acumen (not to mention that he was the son of the current chair) might overshadow his own potential. It could be necessary to take a more pronounced step—at least one, and possibly two—to guarantee that his and his family's situation were not endangered.

He wasn't being selfish, just prudent. Somebody should have the health and welfare of the family at the forefront of their thinking. Everything couldn't be cured with a cigar and another brandy. At minimum, he might find a way to exercise some leadership that may eventually return to his favor. Then find a way to discreetly share how his brilliant leadership better, and more responsibly, positioned the family's future.

Back in Manhattan, Cole Thayer made certain to find someone who could take care of the matter he'd become convinced was a liability. By week's end, a man who was known for his experience and his discretion in matters relating to the family was ushered into his library. His nervousness showed in the way his hands kept circling the rim of his dark brown fedora and fingered the chain of his pocket watch. Thayer was efficient and unambiguous. "The child could become a problem and we can't afford one now, nor will I tolerate any surprises in the future," he said to the man facing his desk. "Do I make myself clear?"

"Yes sir. Absolutely."

"Fine. I will anticipate hearing from you again only when the matter is—shall we say—disposed of. Needless to say I will not anticipate your even approaching the messiness and certainly not the publicity of the Lindbergh affair, but, nevertheless, be aware that its most unfortunate outcome should be your guide. Do we understand each other?"

"Yes sir. Fully."

"This should do for now." He slid an envelope across the desk, then signaled the man's dismissal by turning to the papers from a file that he'd opened earlier. When the door closed, Cole Thayer poured himself a glass of whiskey to calm his nerves. What he had done felt like a solution—and one that ought to be celebrated. He decided he would surprise Adelaide by taking lunch with her. He found her at her writing desk in the morning room.

"Lunch now?" she asked quizzically. "But it's not yet noon. The staff . . ."

"Follows *our* instructions, my dear. And at any rate, an early lunch should suit your growing appetite." Cole stood behind her and wrapped his arms around her, carefully patting her belly. Adelaide hadn't seen him this interested in her since she told him about the baby. She rarely had a chance to enjoy her husband's company. She rang the staff bell and informed the housekeeper that she and her husband would take an early lunch together in the sunroom.

11

Far to Go

IN AUTUMN, THE SIDEWALK'S THICK BLANKET OF LEAVES ALMOST HID the thin stretches of pavement that lay between the cobblestone street and the dense walls of the academy. When the children of South Buffalo ran or biked or skated down these walkways, they scattered a leafy congregation that swirled into the streets or clustered against the rugged walls of Mount St. Joseph's Academy. Rumor had it that there was lush and plentiful acreage inside—manicured gardens and hedged mazes. Except for the small chapel for Mass, Communion, confession, and other Catholic sacraments, the only things visible from the street were the upper floors of buildings on the other side of the wall. Outside, the wall's massive rocky fortification nearly met the sidewalks where a narrow patch of dirt that lay between them and the dense stone foundation burrowed deep and unyielding into the earth. The wall was more a part of the neighborhood than what lay beyond. The only hints of life from the interior were the sightings of the Sisters of Mercy. Always in clustered company, their hands tucked behind dark scapulars, beaded rosaries taking up a rhythmic swing with each step, the sisters would quietly emerge from behind the iron gate next to the huge wooden doors that opened for deliveries. Even when the gates opened, hedges blocked a clear view and left in place the neighborhood's imagination of what lay inside—which was nearly always something grander than what was actually there.

In fact, Mount St. Joe's was partly orphanage as well as a home for girls described as "wayward" in polite society. Its shrouded mystery was so fully woven into the neighborhood lore that occasionally a father threatened to hoist a poorly behaved daughter over the wall and leave her to the whims of the strong-willed nuns inside. Because no one knew differently, and the nuns never spoke (except to shush a noisy parishioner during Mass), the threat was usually enough to correct the conduct before it became a habit. The academy was the locus of the community's imaginative life. Its lore, shaped by the formidable wall, grew in proportion to what they did not know. Generations of South Buffalo neighbors passed the stonework. Children brushed their fingers against the rugged rock, adults lowered their voices—respecting and adding to the imagined mysteries that lay behind the nearly seven-foot-high rocky barrier that either protected the residents or imprisoned them.

The only public entrance anyone knew of was the chapel that buttressed the east wall. There was a stained-glass window in the apse, and families stopped to admire the rose window above the entry door because it was their grandfathers who had been brought in from Italy to do the leading and bevel the glass pieces. Beneath the window, seven stone steps led to the city's sidewalks and marked the boundary between the diocese's propertied wealth and the city's south-side immigrant poverty. The steps were worn smooth with the comings and goings of neighbors who entered for Mass but rarely ventured past the Communion tables or beyond the confessionals. The chapel gave frame and function to their lives, within and outside of its walls. Its rituals bound their days and circled their traditions. From Communion to burial, despite the fact that what they knew about it was less than what they imagined, St. Joseph's was their foundation.

Inside the chapel and on either side of the massive arched doors that met the steps to the sidewalk was a small niche neatly carved into the stone. A gleaming white marble baptismal font was stored in one. The other held a small rush basket that was used yearly to hold the baby Jesus in the children's Christmas pageants and then returned to that dark corner for a need the community understood but rarely spoke of. When a need arose to leave a baby born under questionable circumstances and better left to the cloistered care the sisters were dedicated to provide, the basket was there to take in an abandoned infant. Every once in a while, and only at night, the tinkle of the small bell hanging from the archway signaled that a newborn had arrived. After enough time to allow the person leaving the child to disappear into the night, her secret intact and her reputation left to her own repair, a nun assigned to the watch would appear and gather the baby into the world behind the walls. The only evidence of these children would be school day recitations from the orphans, chanted from opened windows floating down to the streets from one of the buildings within the walls. The academy's children—nearly all of whom were girls—were schooled, churched, and trained there until they were adopted out or entered the novitiate. It was true that a very few neighborhood girls, lured by the mystery of the place, entered the cloister. Every spring there would be guesses as to whether or which one amongst a circle of girl friends would disappear after eighth-grade graduation, leaving parents to whisper how their daughter had taken the veil and playmates to decide exactly what that meant. Certainly their imagined destiny was richer and more complicated than the simple rituals and unpretentious patterns of claustration.

There were a few boys amongst the orphans. If a boy baby was left in the basket, the most ordinary move was to immediately place him out to an adoptive or foster family. However, a very few were kept and trained to perform more tasking labor on the grounds. While they were infants, they gave the older girls experience in caring for boy babies. As they grew older, the boys were trained in various jobs around the convent that would help in its daily operations. They never knew whether their staying was fortunate or not—they had no means of comparison. But each of them knew that on their thirteenth birthday, they would meet with the priest, be outfitted in new clothes, and handed a suitcase packed with their clothing, some toiletries—nothing much more than just the basics—and a train ticket on the Empire State Express. They carried a letter with directions on how to find a YMCA in New York City and that testified to their good character and readiness to join the labor force.

Ned Raddice was one of those boys. On his thirteenth birthday he was given new suspenders, pants below his knees, a suitcase, and a taxi ride to Buffalo's train station, where he presented his one-way ticket to New York City. He was excited and frightened, but fully ready for a life beyond St. Joe's cloistered walls. Ned had a tenacious willingness to do whatever was necessary to earn the very best position he could manage. He was motivated. Before ten years passed in the city, he'd worked his way out of a factory shift (because he was literate and well-spoken, having been schooled by nuns to be more presentable than a run-of-the-mill street urchin). He worked with numbers runners for a short time, collecting debts and managing block assignments. And although he didn't like to think of it, he did what was necessary to keep his business profitable, including the one time he killed the man who couldn't come up with the cash. The ease with which he drew his pistol and shot the man, even with his own "accountant" in the back of the room, bothered him, and he knew then he had to refine his line of work. The messiness of that job and the way he managed to handle it without anything more than a passing concern for the boy who watched him shoot the man and walk past the corpse nagged at him. So when the opportunity to take on security work for the Thayer Corporation came, along with the ability to use his own judgment on how to accomplish his assigned tasks, he preferred the independence, the pay, and even the formality that working for the Thayers afforded him. He was now "Mr. Raddice" instead of "Boss" and wore a classier suit and tie. His carefully blocked brown fedora came to be his trademark. Raddice willingly took on the duties of discreet professional services for his employers over the flash and perils of working the streets. The skills he'd developed from those days in the streets did come in handy for some of his assigned tasks. That plus his Mount St. Joseph learned habit of discretion led him to occasional, and then more frequent, contracts with executives like those who worked in the upper echelons of the corporation. His maturity and experience meant that despite his bosses' ideas about solving a problem—like the ugly direction to go ahead and dispose of the baby as if it was mere trash—he had ways that were as cautious about his own complicity as theirs.

After hearing Mr. Cole Thayer's directions, Raddice did indeed know how to disappear the baby in a way that it was never heard from again. He was just more compassionate than the Thayers; or more cautious; or he had had enough of the kinds of bloody and permanent solutions like the ones he once managed when he collected monies for the Mob. These days he prided himself on being able to meet his employer's needs without endangering his own potential. Except for the episode some years back of that messy shooting in Harlem, his hands were clean.

Since a baby was involved and because he didn't want to draw any unwanted attention, he used his wife, Juanita, as his assistant. They could take the train together, appearing to anyone interested enough to notice them that they were just an ordinary family with a newborn tucked into a bassinet. The train they chose would arrive after dark. Juanita would wait at Buffalo's Central Terminal while he caught a taxi to a street near enough to walk the short distance to the chapel, enter the building, leave his bundle, and ring the bell. The baby would then disappear into the rituals and routines of St. Joe's, and he could tell Mr. Thayer the plan had been executed. Thayer executives never wanted to know details anyway, and with this plan, the baby would be as good as gone. He and Juanita would board the train back east, and he would collect the remainder of his salary. Done. And frankly, he didn't mind the task at all, being of the opinion (had he been asked) that the orphanage would surely be better than being raised by coloreds or especially being done away with by the Thayers.

AFTER SURVEYING THE JOB, RADDICE DECIDED IT WOULD BE AN EASY snatch. He watched Selma Mosby long enough to know the girl had a problem with attention at the very least; but it was probably more than this. She was a curious study, and he spent more time than usual trying to understand her routine. She would take the baby out, put her down on a blanket in the churchyard, and leave her there on her own, while she went off to pick wildflowers or walk the rows of gravestones, leaving pebbles on some and fading blossoms at others. He knew he could snatch the kid and be gone before she turned around or came back from the fence where she spent most of her time picking the violets that grew there. More often than not she had strung some of them around her head like some kind of wreath. Sometimes she dug around the fresh graves trying to plant the blossoms she'd pulled from elsewhere in the graveyard. They'd never grow, being without roots. Sometimes the holes she dug were much too deep and wide for the blossoms she'd brought along to replant. But it was like the girl didn't even notice. The task seemed more important than the result. Raddice saw his way clear.

On his first attempt, he got to her as easily as he had planned. He just walked the path until the girl went off behind a tree, reached down, and grabbed the baby. Just outside of the churchyard, the kid started fussing.

He looked down in the bunting for a pacifier, mad that he hadn't discussed with his wife how to quiet a fussing baby. But when he looked directly at the baby, he immediately realized he had picked up the wrong kid. Raddice was flummoxed and angry. He prided himself on doing his homework and knowing everything he had to about a job. He had no idea this girl was a nursemaid for some white family—but it was clear to him that the baby he had was nobody's colored kid. The hair was white people's hair—golden and wavy. Her skin was fair, even her lips were rosebud pink. This wasn't no colored kid. For a few seconds, he didn't know what to do. But he stepped back inside the churchyard and saw that Selma was still nowhere in sight. So he took the baby back, laid her on the blanket, and walked away. The city didn't need another white kidnapped baby and, even more than that, by what had happened to those even suspected of involvement in the Lindbergh baby's killing, he didn't want to have any connection to a kidnap like Lucky Lindy's. By the time he got back onto the sidewalk, Selma emerged from the copse of trees holding a bunch of violets and dandelions. Girl doesn't even know the difference between a weed and a flower, he thought. He waited until she gathered the baby's things, then he followed her, so he could see whose baby she was keeping. He needed to fix the lapse in his own research. To his surprise and puzzlement, the girl went straight back to her mother's apartment building. "What the hell!?" Raddice exclaimed. He told Juanita what had happened.

"Ned, sweet pea." His wife shook her head and sucked her teeth. "Sugar, that wasn't nobody's white baby. That was hers. That was the one you was supposed to take. Don't you know nothing about how the coloreds get their color?"

"Huh?" he asked, still huffy with the inconvenience and ineptitude of it all.

"Me, I saw some of their babies when I worked the colored ward at the hospital. They can be born to look as white as you and me. They don't come with their color when they first born. Some of the mothers showed me how you can tell—it's something about behind their ears or at the edges of their fingernails. But other than that, some of these babies come out looking like white babies—no different from what one of ours would look like if, well . . ." Her thoughts wandered off, having gotten too close to the sadness of her own failed childbearing. Raddice's mouth gaped and he tried not to choke on the coffee she'd poured into the mugs for them. "Sure seems like God's plan to make a fool outta all of us, I guess."

"Well, I'll be," he sputtered. "I'll be damned."

Juanita let go of her reverie and returned to the situation before them. "Well, at least now you know more than the average white man. But remember, this baby's daddy is a white boy. There's bound to be some lightness in her somewhere. Think about it. You seen some coloreds with all kinda shades to them. Dark brown like the boys that worked for you back in the day. And lighter brown like some of them be that chauffeur for the Thayers. No telling how it's going to show up or what they grow up to be like. But the basic fact is you had the right baby and you gived it back."

"It won't happen again."

"It *can't* happen again. With everybody talking about the Lindy baby, this kidnapping business is too much in the news for us to take too many risks."

"It's not a kidnapping. We're transferring care. Like they do in the system." He was remembering his own youth. "And anyways, nobody notices coloreds that go missing. Light or not, ain't nobody who's going to care if there's one less of them. In fact, some folks will say good riddance. It will be a flash in the pan, and then Harlem will go on and do something else to get folks riled up. Something always going on uptown."

"Maybe so, but I'll still be glad when we're finished with this business. It don't feel right to be messing with a kid," Juanita said. "Something wrong with somebody who'll hurt a baby."

"Who said anything about hurt? What I'ma do . . . No. What *we* going to do is give this baby a better chance than what she got now. That mother she got ain't right in the head. Something off about her. We doing this baby a favor, for sure." He stopped pacing back and forth and said more quietly, "It's a real favor, 'specially considering what Mr. Cole instructed me to do—not in so many words, but I took his meaning."

"I guess . . ."

"No guessing. When we get that baby to Buffalo and away from this girl I seen her with, she already better off than how she started." He slid his thumb against his fingers and rested them in a fist that pointed to Juanita. "And you and me, babe, we will be set with a payday that will take us a long ways from where we sitting right now." He thought further. "Maybe even Connecticut." Juanita looked up at him in grateful anticipation.

"Okay, sweet pea. I'll exchange the train tickets. You go get the kid."

"Good as done. The Mosby gal walks every weekday. Tomorrow is Thursday. Good a day as any." Juanita remembered a verse from her youth. *Thursday's child has far to go.*

"Indeed," she said. "As good a day as any, and better than some."

12

Marks Like a Map

THE CHATTERING WAS LOUD, STRIDENT, SHARP. THEIR WORDS WOUNDED.

She left the baby all by itself out here?

She ain't nothin but a baby herownself.

Who the daddy is what I want to know?

They shoulda took the pram, left the baby. Coulda got some bills for that fancy contraption.

It was a pretty baby. Light-skinded. Good hair.

Oh.

Empathy, accusation, speculation, and judgment mixed one into the other until there was no difference that mattered. It was all piercing. Bystanders exercised brash authorities and pronounced their own nearness to the danger that had attached itself to the girl in order to establish their bona fides:

I was in the store this morning getting me some Argo and some of that new "It's Lysol Time" disinfectant.

That stuff work?

Don't know yet. Didn't get a chance to try it when this here happened. Where was you?

Me? I was just down the street. Come soon as I heard. Maybe first one of all y'all.

Wasn't five minutes passed since I myself walked out of there, but I had two sacks and couldn't hardly see my way over them.

I heard that screaming and came straightaway . . . Soon as I could get a babushka since my hair ain't been pressed this week.

Me and my cousin know her from when she still went to school . . . know the family . . .

My brother played with June Bug 'fore he ran off.

What kind of name is June Bug?

Kidnapped too?

With a name like that, it makes you wonder.

Lotsa folks named June Bug when they young.

Humph. Common.

Folks don't kidnap Common.

Well, there is that.

The loud and competing familiarities shattered what had been early autumn's serenity. Now a motley crowd pushed against and soiled what had been freshly wiped storefront windows. The *Amsterdam News'* reporters were already scattered through the crowd shouting questions to any who would answer. Plenty of folks had answers. But none that mattered. Photographers jostled to get a good picture of the baby's perambulator— which still had the bag of apples inside. Once the door was locked and monitored, they pressed their lens up against Chasen's windows trying to get a glimpse of the mother. Their bulbs popped with each click of the shutter, hitting the glass as they ejected. Selma shuddered alongside the sharp explosions.

With enough regularity for rhythm, women with just a sweater thrown on over a muslin dress or no covering at all came looking for the children who had lingered at Chasen's. They sought them out in the crowd, grabbed hold of tiny brown arms, clasped, cuddled, and snatched with the kind of brusque motherly insistence that fell somewhere between anger, fright, and relief. Canopies of sun-speckled color in the street's sparse scattering of trees, which just hours ago had been a welcome advent of the season, dimmed as the morning moved into day and the day clouded over. The laughter that had accompanied children's joy as they burst into the store for a before-school candy faded—replaced by the crowd of broken-voiced neighbors. Women wept over the baby's likely danger, especially the way it followed the notoriety of the Lindbergh kidnapping. Men and women both fussed loudly at what they already knew would be a stark disparity, trying to find a residence for their anger and frustration, as much of it predictable as it was already present.

101

Y'all brought out the National Guard when it was Lindbergh's baby. Weapons and everything at the ready. Like the WW all over again. And all you got up in the store is two police with billy clubs? That ain't right.

Who gonna call Hoover and tell him to bring his Federal Bureau up here to Harlem?

Where's all them what was up in New Jersey for his baby?

Shoot! There so many come to Jersey, they spilled over here to New York. Jersey couldn't hold all of 'em come out to find Lindbergh's sonny boy.

You think somebody left over from that investigation could manage their way up here to Harlem. We ain't hiding where we are.

Ain't none of them G-men could find Harlem on a map.

Don't need no map. Just keep going north till there's more colored than not. That'd make anybody backtrack.

Need to make you some tracks 'fore you can take them back!

Inside the store, a clutch of women gathered. Selma had been guided to a bent cane rocker and sat there trembling without leaning back into its willing shape. She was cold and frightened, or both. And then there was a part of her that was feeling more than she had felt in too long. It noticed the attentiveness directed toward her. Full-bodied and not at all stingy or cautionary. It began to feel welcome, if late.

Two policemen, well—one cadet and one officer—worked their way through the outside crowd, inside the grocery, and back to where Selma sat and women rocked the chair for her. It didn't take long for Officer Weldon Thomas to make his way down to the grocery as soon as the call came into the precinct. He'd already clocked in at the station even though it was early. He had full access to the same locker rooms as his fellow officers but never found it an easy space to share. There was locker-room ribaldry amongst police and, too often for his temperament, the comments were racial and disparaging. Like: *Man, I had to rescue a colored boy what fell in the East River yesterday.* And the retort: *Why'd you bother? Coulda been one fewer delinquent to process next week.* And the too-raucous laughter at the pitiful humor. And the looks at Weldon daring him to join in, daring him not to. Weldon either had to retort, take it, or seethe. Coming in early prevented him from having to make the choice. So he was ready for duty when it called, except he did not anticipate this kind of trauma. He called for his cadet LT Mitchell to come along with him, and it didn't take long at all for them to get to Chasen's. They were the first cops on the scene. Which was a good thing, because these were their people, and a not-so-good thing, because it showed the city was not taking this seriously enough to send in the white folks, which would have indicated they meant business.

It could have been worthy of comment that Thomas—who was Harlem's first colored policeman—now had a cadet taking orders from him. But things were too chaotic and troublesome for that kind of comparison. It was no day to report firsts. Mitchell stood respectfully to the side, up against the shelves lined with boxes of Fels-Naptha, Chipso, and Oxydol. He held his tiny pencil stiff and spiral notebook flipped open and at the ready as if an attentive posture might compensate for the confusion. Thomas looked around to see that this was a waste of time, since nobody from the detective agency had showed up at the scene, so he sent the cadet—who was also his protégé—outdoors to guard the baby's pram until the investigative unit arrived. Things were quickly devolving into a generalized panic that was going to do nobody any good. Too much chatter, too many people with nothing to do but make loud protestations, commentary, or declarations, and too many others willing to respond. So with as full-on a projection as he could manage without hollering, Officer Thomas inquired of no one in particular whether anyone had sent for the girl's family, and if the day nurse was still at the church clinic down the block, and maybe somebody could ask if she might could come over to the store to give them a hand. Also if there was a pastor around, how he could be helpful to our situation while we police do our work. Maybe folks who had seen something could line up on this side. The disorder was already settling into something more manageable. As folks took up his tasks and followed orders, it released a good portion of the tension.

Selma rocked and tugged at a loose thread.

Mrs. Chasen came from the back room with a coal-stove-warmed blanket that she wrapped over Selma's shoulders because she was shivering, and Selma relinquished herself to the women who brought out large lace hankies to wipe her brow and then to the one who pressed her hands to close around a hot cup of sweet-milk tea. She was settling into their care. It had been so long since she had received this kind of tender regard. Noticing her relax, they brought their fingers to their lips and encouraged an enveloping shush. Some took up sentry-like postures at the front door instructing that the officers had asked that nobody but family and police officials be allowed to enter. Others, who had been there from the beginning of whatever this was, lined the aisles. An elderly woman, with silvery-blue hair and a stalwart posture that would make anyone's slouch shameful, stood behind the girl and let her arms slip down across Selma's shoulders until her hands met in a tight clasp across and against the girl's chest as if to shield her from further assault.

And then somebody's hands, someone's sweet loving hands, took a brush to her head. Just pulled it out of her bag like she carried it around for occasions like this one, pulled the loose hairs from between the bristles until it was as clean as it would be, and started at the girl's temples. Selma leaned into the bristly tug and tingling strokes and the palm of somebody's hand.

She talking yet?

She got anything to say?

Tears or no?

Umm-hmmm.

Who she say done it?

She asked for anybody? Say the baby's name?

What she say it is?

Chloe who?

Chloe Mosby. Lives over in Mrs. Griffin's building.

Oh. Then we should just go on and ask her. Nothing gets past a busybody.

Isn't Mosby her mama's name too? Why she got the same name as her mama's mama? That tells you something right there.

No it don't. Be still. Keep a civil tongue. This girl done lost her baby.

She the one leave it outside while she went in for some candy.

Who said it was candy? Coulda been something for the baby.

What do any of that matter?

Selma could hear their quiet questions, and despite the implicit criticisms they conveyed, there was still something soothing in their hum and whisper, at being at the center of somebody's words. Nevertheless, there was a competing mix of voices in her head. Nobody could hear them but her. And they were moving from whisper to words. The ones she heard come in from outside were simply querulous. Yes, judgmental, but curious. Wondering after her. The murmuring from inside once had been no more than an icy feather's fierce flutter as if something brushed up beside her. But now it seemed to have sliced its way inside and done damage.

Now that these women's voices had company, it became very confusing. Which does she listen to? Who's asking for her response? Who's that who said *You better tell*? Before there had only been a soft, flittery *shwoo-shwoo* in her head, but it had morphed into a conversation that was leaving her out. And too much of it was sharp rather than soothing. So she just listened, frightened by how many there could be inside of her head and distracted because she had nothing to say that anybody would stop and listen to. Shushed. Again.

The investigators, which meant the white detectives from the precinct, finally arrived, walked through the crowd outside, pushing folks aside like they weren't there for compassion and care and even information, looking for somebody in charge. They began with the Chasens, who directed them to the girl. Mrs. Chasen pointed to Selma and insisted on respectful treatment. Things seemed to be standard in their inquiry, and polite until it was apparent they weren't going to get anything from her. They tried abrupt and brittle, but their tone made no difference. Selma wasn't speaking, and it was soon apparent that nobody near had any usable information. Neither of the Chasens had seen anything except the empty perambulator. Officer Weldon Thomas's questions were official too, but unlike his colleagues', his gentle inquiries were a surround of solace.

Your mother be here soon. Anybody else you want us to call for you? You want something to drink—maybe something hot with a taste of sweetness to it? You have a picture of your baby girl?

He hoped his tone would open her to his inquiries.

Anybody stop to peek inside the carriage when you went walking? You push her very far this morning, or did you come out just to go to the store? I'd be out, too, on a day like this one. All the leaves turning. Where did you and Baby Chloe go? You been at the churchyard yet? Trees are real pretty in there. Did you meet up with anybody? See anybody?

But Weldon's gently nudging questions and compassionately expressed concerns or knowledgeable commentary didn't matter. Selma had slipped into silence, lulled by the gentle strokes, the soft caresses, kindnesses, and the women's warm embrace. Their presence was almost enough. It had been so long since she had earned this kind notice and this caring attention. The voices around her were settling into a deep-toned hum, thick and dense. Even if she had been able to speak or tell or answer or explain, or had she been able to lift her own voice over the babble in her head, she couldn't have found a ways or means to do so. There was too much in between. So instead she settled into the silence. She was marked anyway. Anyone could read the damage in her eyes as easily as they might have seen it up under her mother's skirts.

For Lilah, it was her dress, then her dark slip (to hide the rusty stains) that masked the terrains of her hurt. An etched landscape of healed and healing routes and ridges navigated cross-stitched patches on her thighs. Marks like a map. As if you could follow one and find a way out until it merged into another and then another. For Selma, it was her quiet. At least on the outside. Inside, a brittle chill of voices battled for her attention. Most of her quiet was spent trying to listen to them. In some way, both mother and daughter held on to their wounds. Wounds like words like ripples on a pond.

13

Where You Been?

LILAH MOSBY'S FEARFUL ENTRANCE BROKE THROUGH THE STORE AND disrupted the jittery calm that had settled over and shrouded the scene behind the counter. She'd heard the news in the worse possible way to hear anything terrifying. She was making her way down the long block toward her building when the curtains from Leona Griffin's open window billowed out. As soon as Leona saw her coming, she left her apartment window and hurried down the stairs to the sidewalk in order to meet her neighbor. She needn't have hurried. Lilah's walk was slow and measured.

Leona's rooms were much more accommodating than the Mosbys' kitchenette. She had a first-floor flat proper. There were windows in the front that looked out onto the street, and another one facing the well between buildings where women hung their laundry. Leona had already started her day's work. She'd perched herself at her window closest to the front stoop. From that vantage point, she watched the comings and goings, noted the times folks left, when they were supposed to return and when they did, who was talking to whom, who had dropped a friend and who picked one up, and whose man stopped off a couple of buildings down before he headed to his own home. Her lacy curtains parted just enough to look as if they shielded her vigil—but everybody recognized her as the busybody at the window who knew everything, and if she didn't would make out like she did, which was its own kind of dangerous. Every once in a while, somebody asked after what she had seen, or heard, or sur-mised—a mother or a wife would knock at her door and get invited in for tea and talk. Even in winter her window was cracked just enough to let in some voices. She told folks that the radiator heat needed the fresh air to break it up some, but everybody knew she needed to listen as much or more than she needed air. On this Thursday her window was pushed up as far as the sash would allow and she was sitting inside, watching. Usually, she didn't move from the spot; but this morning was different. As soon as she heard the news, she went up and knocked at Mrs. Mosby's door. No one answered. She didn't think either one or even both of them could've come back without her noticing; but she needed to check because she'd seen both women leave the building, one early, the other later. And she'd been waiting for their return. Just in case she missed it when she went to use the toilet and turn off the teakettle, she went upstairs and knocked. She was known for being gossipy but reliable. After hearing about what had happened down to Chasen's, she sat waiting for Lilah to return, fairly certain that Selma would not be home anytime soon given whatever was happening. Her mother should have been the first one there with the girl. And no matter how wayward she'd become, there wasn't much that Leona could imagine as being a good-enough reason to keep her away in the midst of such a crisis. She was somewhat relieved when finally she saw DeLilah making her way slowly down the block, but irritated as well. Leona thought that she should have been rushing given the seriousness of the situation.

But Mrs. Mosby was walking slow as molasses, and it wasn't that she was overloaded with packages or anything. There was nothing in her hands except her cloth purse that she held tight against her chest with both hands, like she was holding something in, or expecting somebody to snatch it from her. She should know better than that, Leona thought. Ain't no pickpockets out this early. She was moving like she had time to take. Or like she was holding on to some unwanted company. It was obvious to her neighbor that she would be in need of somebody to alert her as to what had happened. So Leona left her perch in the window in time to meet Lilah on the sidewalk in front of the stairs. Lilah had just about reached the ornately carved balustrade that indicated the building had once been a single-family home before it was broken into apartments and flats. Her neighbor stopped her cold.

She had planned to stop at the steps anyway, even if Leona hadn't come down and blocked her way. Her pause would be respite, because everything, every little thing, took more effort these days. When the children were little, they used a shared rhythmic stair-step mount, their mother in the lead and their tiny determined voices matching the rhythmic chant: *Keep step. Keep step. You've got it, don't lose it now, keep it, gosh darnit! Keep step!* Nowadays her most constant accompaniment was her cough, so persistent that she kept a hanky up her sleeve to hold over her mouth so as to be polite when she had company.

These days no children's voices joined hers, and what once seemed to be an endless store of raising-these-babies energy had dissipated. There were no moments left or available to savor the feel of sweet sweaty baby hands clasped in hers. No endless toddler's asking "Why?" Just memories that haunted each stair rise and that waited with her at the short landing inside where she could lean in against the railing, catch her breath, and still maintain her dignity around those who'd pass her by—climbing up with enviable ease, with or without grocery bags or babies—politely excusing themselves around the woman who felt her days folded around her like a winding sheet. She hadn't even turned toward the steps when Leona stepped out in front of her and transformed the rest of her days.

The unspoken code of how many words were proper for passersby to exchange got left behind as soon as Leona met her at the sidewalk and remarked: "Girl, you sure out early this morning! Where you been? I went up the stairs to your door, but you didn't answer." Before DeLilah could nod or note her neighbor's presence with an *And good morning to you too, Leona,* her neighbor had moved past her perfunctory greeting and on to the business at hand.

"Oh sweet Jesus, to have let this happen to all y'all with everything He already gived to you to carry. He might not give us more, but this seems even to a good Christian woman like me more than you deserve no matter what the girl did in getting herself pregnant. I was going to knock again soon as you got back from wherever it was you went so early . . . where you said you been?" Leona didn't break for a reply. Even if she had, none would have been forthcoming. "But given what happened up at Chasen's, I just had to be down here to meet you to see how you must be beside yourself?" Her words were a rush, and she really wasn't looking for an answer or a conversation, she merely wanted to let Lilah know she knew something her neighbor would want to know. And then to be there to see how she took the news so that she might properly share the story later.

Sometimes a neighbor's sorrow was the only way to be sure their own had been forestalled, and at least for the moment, instead of being the one soothed, they could be the one who knowingly spoke of the tragedy and who would be eagerly available to share with others how well (or how poorly) the prayed-over were managing. Leona Griffin's quizzical solicitude reached inside and left Lilah motionless, frozen in a viselike grip of icy potential. She listened without trying to understand. She listened, trying to take in the words and put them in an order that she could manage. She listened. Then, without even looking directly at Leona, she gathered herself up and straightened her shoulders and, as best she could she set her face like a mask so that whatever Leona would say (as she surely would) about how she received the news, it wouldn't be from any disarray she displayed there on the streets. Lilah pushed her weight up from against the railing and made her way down the sidewalk continuing down the block until she turned the corner toward Chasen's.

She heard the crowd before she saw them good. She noticed the grocer with his frail wife weeping into his shoulder. She saw the police and she even saw the white man across the street, his arms folded across his chest and a brown fedora pulled low over his brow. The rest of the crowd was made up of neighbors, street folks, ordinary residents of the corner and the block. But that man made her shudder. She recognized him from before, from those years around the time Percy left. Back then, he took up residence on her corner and block for too many weeks after Percy was safely away from the city. It made her grateful that she sent her son away, and it made her distraught that she had been right to do so. This wasn't the first time during the month she saw him taking up his vigil outside her building. And here he was again, still on the lookout. The crowd noticed her arrival. "It's the mother."

The girl's mother?

Her grandmother.

No, fool. The baby's grandmother, the girl's mother.

Which she got? Grandmother or mother? Me, I got both.

Fool, this ain't about what you got.

Y'all move!

Make some room for the lady, she got enough to bear without all of us stan-din in her way.

Let her in to reach her baby.

Her baby's gone missing, fool!

No, let her in to her own baby girl.

Who? The mother?

Grandmother.

On whose side?

There ain't but one side. Baby don't have a daddy.

Every baby got a daddy. What you mean is, there's no daddy that's stepped up to the plate.

This ain't no picnic. This people's lives.

Then let her pass on by!

When Lilah finally pushed through the crowd and entered the store, her pitiful cry *"Baby Girl?"* broke through the gathering. Selma recognized her mother's voice and in that brief moment engaged the wanting in her words long enough to wonder which baby girl it was that had earned her mother's attention. And more because she wasn't sure whether it was her or her Chloe, a great heave, a full ballast, gathered up her insides and held them tight. Which would have been normal except that just as suddenly as her breath came up, it stopped—gripped by the pain of it all. She closed her eyes waiting for its release, but it took longer than she expected and the pause, as well as her need to exhale, startled Selma into a loose, deep, guttural sob that sounded enough like the kind of cry the women had been waiting for. It was as painful to hear as to witness. But it also gave them a way to focus.

That's right, sweetheart, just let it out.

Let go and let God.

She's giving in to it.

Just go 'head and cry, child. We'll hold on.

Seems like she can't get her breath. Give her some air.

Some space.

Some room. She 'bout to grieve this thing.

Have mercy!

Let the girl catch her own breath.

By the time her mother got to her and pulled her into her arms and Selma almost gave in and settled into longed-for gathering up that finally felt familiar, she hovered somewhere between a breath, a sigh, and the women who thought she was finally ready to cry deep and good let it go. Weeping was something they could recognize.

Just go 'head and set them flowin, sweetheart. Tears got to find their out.

Lilah moved out of duty and practice, but the truth was, this particular horror, public and perilous as it was, felt like the last time. As Selma stiffened in her arms, it reminded her of that day when she came home to what seemed like a blizzard. Lilah closed her eyes, trying to focus on this particular moment with her daughter. She was determined to push aside the intrusive worry that other day had produced. But try as she might, it lay too near to the feeling she'd had when she grabbed Selma into her arms, and her daughter's stiff silence remained unyielding despite the mounting desperation around them. This time she could feel the difference. That time had been private. Nobody's curious stares. No one's unpronounced judgment. Nobody watched and listened so they could tell the neighbor or kin who had not had the fortune to be "right up in there, when it happened, when her mother showed up at the store" exactly what was said, and by whom.

The way she had to carry the memory of that terrible day when she came back home and was nearly blinded by the white made this desperation even more worrisome. Back then, when Lilah had walked into their kitchenette, it was the brightness of it all that stopped her. She stood still and quiet just long enough to survey the scene and understand it wasn't a covering of snow that had somehow found its way inside and nearly blanketed the room. Which, given what it turned out to be, would have been more manageable. The glaring patches of white were as pathetic as it was pitiful—especially once she realized what it was. It wasn't too long (although it felt like a lifetime) before she let loose with a series of questions she already knew were all too late to ask and so, not expecting answers, she did not get any. DeLilah Harrison Mosby reached out for her child with no words to say how fully her Selma had come undone. She only knew she had to make a plan.

14

A Wild Tangle

IN THE DAYS BEFORE SHE STITCHED TOGETHER HER WHITE DRESS, Selma pushed her daughter's pram down the street. She walked the three blocks past her elementary school, PS 119, beyond the pawnshop, and toward the corner where the church stretched across one side of the block and then down the other. It was a long walk, but she had a particular destination. The first week she'd gone to the park with Chloe. But then she found a more secluded spot in the churchyard that felt safer. When she got to the corner church, she walked past its massive stone steps, turned the corner, and pushed the pram past the row of arched windows to where a small iron gate opened onto the side yard. Down that stone path lay the gardens and burial grounds. She reached inside the gate (she knew it latched from behind), lifted the lever, and maneuvered the shaded pathway toward the back.

The grounds were small, but there were enough headstones to show the church had some history—folks to bury as well as folks to baptize. If the groundsmen left a pile of newly turned earth pushed up against the far wall, it meant that somewhere would be a cleared space waiting for a Saturday service. There would likely be a tent lying folded nearby, ready to erect to shelter the family. Early on the day of the burial, the undertaker's maintenance men would drop off some wooden chairs, just enough for immediate kin and not too many to fit under the tent, along with a lectern where the Right Reverend would speak whatever final words there would be. Folks buried in this churchyard had means. Episcopals were select like that. Even though they were colored, the seriousness of their rituals matched any of the white congregation down in Manhattan. They were the only Harlem church with a burial grounds, and even though a lot of the tombstones there did not belong to black folks, and had been established before Harlem took on its newest group of immigrants, the colored congregation took pride in having one—especially if they could afford to occupy one of the few plots left for members only. The congregation spent a good deal of its annual budget on keeping the grounds pristine. Selma took notice of the preparations, and whether the clearing was small and made to fit a child's casket rather than an adult's. This Saturday's body was almost certainly a child's. The small grave waiting to receive the casket and the tiny pile of dirt beside it seemed a mere mound barely rising past the earth it would need to fill.

Selma learned how the day's patterns practiced a churchyard routine. She knew when the sunlight would hit the bench under the chestnut tree, which patch of violets were ready to open and spill over and cover the in-ground markers, what shadows would hit the stained-glass windows and hide the figures so it seemed as if someone were missing from the biblical text she'd memorized as a child. Her days there were dependable in a necessary kind of way. She brought little in the way of ritual other than being there in the morning and leaving before noon. She did understand how the churchyard was better than the park. Here no one asked to peep at the baby, no one clucked over her "misfortune"—hers, or her daughter's—no one reminded her of the future that she had thrown away and what a shame it was. Here her only company was blades of grass that held the sunlight in shifting shades of green and soft loamy soil waiting for either a body or a blossom. Of course Chloe was there too. But being so tiny and so new, she mostly slept, or took a bottle, and then slept again. It never occurred to her that the baby would one day need more than this. It was easier than folks had warned her it would be and not at all difficult to ignore her baby. She pushed the pram toward the shade on the other side of the yard where the ground had not yet been turned up and over for burials. The prime spaces were still those just under the stained-glass windows. But nearer the center, the grounds were not yet claimed. Here ferns still hugged the trees and some grasses were left long enough to ripple when the wind came through. It was so closeted that the air seemed to lose the smells of the city. Instead it was heavy with dense pine and weighted with the late summer's leafy green of chestnut pods. The congregation's garden club had taken on the project of planting the grounds with trees and evergreen bushes thick and lush enough so that when a burial was needed, these folks could feel it was in as good a place as possible to leave their grief. A wild tangle of ivy pushed out from the shadows and cascaded through the grounds, making it enough of a sanctuary to offer the mother and her baby girl respite. Some weekdays the groundsmen tilled the soil for planting, and the gravediggers moved it to other side of the hedges so the burial could take place and the mounded soil would remain out of sight of the congregated mourners. But even as they worked, they faded into a background that allowed them to leave Selma and Chloe alone to their quiet. No one troubles folks sitting in a churchyard. There, silences were dependable and even expected. Chloe usually slept through the morning. Selma may as well have been there all by herself. Today, just before she left, she had an autumnal memory of fried pies and her mother's ritual of making the dough, boiling down the apples into a sugary cinnamon and nutmeg syrup, and then pulling circles of dough over the steaming filling and closing them tightly with forked folds. She thought that maybe that would bring them back to days they once had, when June Bug was home, when she was the "Baby Girl," and when her mother was still trying to make their family full despite the absence of their daddy. His name was Iredell, her mother said, but never much more than that. Although his absence was a constant, there had been enough happiness, enough effort, enough of them to make some things worthy of today's memories. Certainly enough for her to want them back. She made the dress because then she could help her mother consider her future. And when that didn't work, she looked for apples in order to help her remember days passed.

LILAH HEARD THE BABY SCREAMING ALL THE WAY DOWNSTAIRS. Despite her being winded and needing the stop at the landing, she stuffed the mail she'd been thumbing through down into her right-side pocket and managed her way up the staircase without stopping to see why Selma couldn't quiet the child. As soon as she crossed the threshold, she came to a full-on stop. It was all too much to take in while moving.

Selma was sitting on the ladder-back chair by the table, her white-gloved hands calmly clasped together on her lap, her wan smile garishly obscured by a brilliant red lipstick that bled outside of her lips, which were parted as if she were about to say something. But she didn't. She was as quiet as a specter. Even if she had spoken or tried to, the slash of color streaked across her mouth seemed like a muzzle or a mask and, anyway, the baby was alternately shrieking and then gulping in heaves and deep sobs, as if it had been going on for some time. Selma's cheeks were rubbed full of the same color that was smeared across her lips. It was hard to look at her straight on. But what sent her mother nearly to the floor was her dress. She reached out to the wall to steady herself and looked around.

"Sweet Jesus."

Abandoned pieces of cloth scattered across the tiny room like a flight of spring-white butterflies had landed and stayed put; or a flock of feathers burst out of their casing, or maybe it was like a cotton field—pods snapped open and ready to tear. But mostly it was like snow. Icy and pristine in its ambiguity. A dishcloth, the hem from her late mother's Sunday slip, and even the baby's sheets and a blanket, the lace-trimmed pillow she'd sewn just for the pram, her used-to-be-edged-with-lace Sunday hanky, the baby's only bonnet, whatever was white or near-white and could have been cut, shredded, hacked at, or trimmed lay wherever her daughter had left them when she brought her scissors to the fabric and went to cutting. And now she was sitting at the table, wearing whatever pieces of white there were that had been sewn into the garment that she smoothed down across her thighs, as if the pitifully stitched together shreds, pieces, remnants of fabric might be tamed into the shape of a dress.

It looked as if she'd thought of a collar, but only one side of the neckline was stitched with the small ribbon of lace that a few hours ago had edged her mother's hanky. The sleeves were obviously from the bedsheet—there was only one (nearly) white one in their flat. But Selma had cut it so poorly there wasn't enough left to fashion a whole skirt and a bodice. So she used the sheet for two pitifully disproportioned tubes that she'd stitched into the shape of sleeves. Some had made it onto the bodice, but so did little Chloe's bath towel, the one Lilah bought after the Thayer settlement—its dense and fuzzy fabric a stark contrast to the threadbare and dingy sheet. And the way she had stitched the eyelet from Chloe's bonnet into the middle front of the dress left it looking like a stain—or some other kind of mark.

At the back, instead of buttons and buttonholes, a series of ragged slits held a long shoelace that tied at the waistline. Lilah didn't even need to search for her white work shoes; she easily recognized that it was their shoelaces pulling the fabric together. She could have spent the next hour tracing the origin of each piece of cloth, following the progress of Selma's madness across the open cabinets, toppled dresser drawers and shelves that gathered up unwound spools of thread—a rainbow array of tangled webbing that stretched from her bedroom to the kitchenette—stray buttons and the miscellany of needles and pins from the sewing kit that was usually in the chifforobe but was now on the floor, its contents splayed out over the worn wood planks. A map of her daughter's madness, strewn from one wall of the room to the next, spilled out and cobbled together showed DeLilah how it was much too late and too thick for her to think at all about stepping back, or away, or starting over as a family of three—a grandmother, her daughter, and her daughter's baby, who was still bawling from inside the drawer they used as her crib. Thank goodness the cotton batting that lined the sides was blush colored, and the little yellow blanket that had swaddled the babe did not find its way into her mother's creation.

If Chloe's pitiful wail hadn't called her back from her shock, she may have stayed put or else lit into Selma. But her grandbaby's shrill cry refocused her, and she bent over and scooped the child into her arms. That was when she saw the bright glisten of shears lying underneath her, their ends splayed open, where it would have taken only the baby's slightest shift to slice through a cheek or a finger. That potential brought Lilah all the way to her knees, cuddling her granddaughter in her arms as she sank down—"*Hush now, hush, sweet child*"—desperately, gently, carefully running her fingers across the baby's body. She pushed back her soft-as-velvet new-baby skin, uncreasing her folds, running her fingers behind her little ears and through her silky hair, stretching out her arms and pudgy legs to make sure she was not crying from something that her grandmother could not even speak. She did not exhale until she finished, instead she looked back over at her daughter—who was as oblivious to her mother's panic as she had been to her baby's cry. Selma had moved from the kitchen table and now sat with her back against the sofa that had once held her lace antimacassars—they had been her mother's and before that belonged to the wife of the man who owned Gran'mam. Now they lay in threaded disarray, fallen across the sofa's patchwork cushions, having failed, likely because their intricate network of knots was too challenging to become a part of the garment. Selma smiled, or it seemed she did. With the smeared lipstick, it was hard to tell whether it was a smile or a smirk. She stood up and twirled slowly around.

"Look, Mama! It's for school! You told me how all the Bennett Belles wear white dresses on the first day. I'm your college girl! Me! I'm so pretty! A pretty Bennett Belle. 'Hail the light that I doth bring!' Sing it! And tell me I'm pretty, Mama. Tell me!"

Lilah could indeed see how the pockets from her white folks' apron had made it onto each side of the dress—one lower than the other—and how the apron's bow was tied in front and circled her daughter's waistline. The difficulty she'd had in finding enough fabric was also painfully apparent when her daughter's slim caramel-colored legs slipped into sight from a gap at the waistline that seemed to repeat the break in the girl's sensibilities. She even noticed Selma's white anklet socks with the little ruffles that she'd worn as a girl and the thick smears of Vaseline from an obviously impaired attempt to polish her patent-leather Mary Janes. For just a brief moment, she found herself thinking how the socks could have been fashioned into dress cuffs, but the idea left as quickly as it tried to insert some sense into the nonsense spread out around her. Chloe squirmed and began whimpering, so she pushed herself up from the floor, shifted the baby over to her hip, and walked slowly into the kitchen. Selma's slow twirling stopped only when she noticed a thread that had come loose from the used-to-be-apron-pocket, and she knelt in place to knot it. *"Mama, you seen my shears? They were right here last I remember. But now I can't recall where I laid them down."*

Lilah held her granddaughter tight against her chest and walked past her without comment, filled the buckled tin pot halfway with water, placed it on the stove—the baby's bottle inside—and turned the flame on low. When she bent over to check the bottle's temperature, the almost-boiling water left a steamy glisten on her cheeks, offering cover for the stream of tears that would not stop, despite her focused industry. It did not matter. No one but her daughter and grandbaby were there to notice the unraveling. She turned to look back at Selma, who was now using her teeth to tug at the knots of the—were there dozens? scores?—of bright blue threads that she'd used to stitch together her first-day-of-college dress that hung loosely, untethered and frayed. Without comment, Lilah carried the baby and warmed milk bottle and pulled a kitchen chair over by the bedroom door so she could have a view into both rooms. She sank into its thin wooden seat and looked past the bed frame and outside. She could not bear to focus on the kitchenette or the girl behind her. Low streaks of clouds caught the last reddened lights of the evening sun and etched the late-day sky in dusky shades of rose, amber, and finally a deepening cerulean that would soon drift into night. Watery shadows slipped like tears across the counterpane. The baby snuggled, and they both closed their eyes.

15

The Web She Offered

DORIS GAYLES AND CADET MITCHELL GOT LILAH AND SELMA BACK TO their flat. They left the perambulator in the front hallway niche near Leona Griffin's windowed door, where nobody would dare tamper with it. Mrs. Griffin watched the pitiful parade up the back stairs, but LT put his hand up when she tried to follow. Once they got into their rooms, the girl dropped wearily onto the tattered sofa and Mrs. Mosby took one of the chairs at the table. Selma was already feeling the absence of the women from the store who had clustered around her and folded her into a circle where she felt safe and embraced. As much as she wanted it to be otherwise, Mama Lil's motions weren't as gentle as theirs had been. Her mother's touches were heavy, weary, and heartbroken. Which should have been expected. She was, after all, maneuvering through a wicked sense of dread. Lilah was remembering a flash of her daughter in white and the room that seemed an abundant flowering of misshapen white petals or snow. For a moment she looked around frantically, hoping that she hadn't missed a petal or piece of frayed fabric in cleaning up. There was no way she wanted to or could explain that to the police. Doris saw her desperate glance and, because she had been there to help the day after, when Selma left for the park as if nothing at all had happened and their flat was still scattered with fabric and threads, shook her head no, indicating that things were all right. There was no evidence of her daughter's fragility— well, none except for her missing grandbaby.

Cadet Mitchell was saying some things, asking others. "Can I get you something to drink? Maybe a cup of tea? Did you see anything strange? Any honey up in your cabinets? Who tried to talk to you today you didn't know? Some sassafras up under your sink? You want help to tell the baby's daddy? And his name would be?" He had his notebook at the ready because Selma looked as if she was trying to speak.

"Hush," her mother said. *"Just hush."* She took her daughter's hand in her own, longing for the grasp to slip into a clasp, where her daughter's fingers felt her mother's and reached toward what she offered.

It may have been the fullness of the moment, the crush of events, the peering, interested inquiries (official and not; thoughtful and not) that eventually urged her to keep to her quiet. It may have been she was simply being obedient and doing as her mother instructed; or that she was already "taken up residence amongst the addled," given that less and less of what she did say made any kind of sense. Selma's silence began quietly enough. And it was occasional, not full-time. But then it blossomed. As if the icy fluttering that had followed her from that Manhattan winter's day at the Thayers' to this one finally caught up and descended, covering her . . . folding sense and sorrow, hurt and helplessness, stitching them one to the other. And her mother, traumatized by the series of days that had tugged at her sanity and sense, couldn't even answer questions that may have helped by recalling what she did see, what seemed out of sync, what or whom she might have remembered, or could have said if she hadn't been so occupied with her own fear.

After the investigative officers arrived at the store and the detectives questioned Selma and her mother, Officer Thomas noticed that the Mosby women—well, one woman and a girl—were looking more and more fragile the larger the crowd became, so he sent them home. He was increasingly worried about the folks keening at the window, lingering across the street, finding occupation in the event, and sorting out their roles. And those who had nothing to do and no one in particular to look at were getting antsy.

A newsboy picked up a pile of papers from the knotted stack where the delivery truck had dropped them. Before he could start shouting the day's news, his mother came and grabbed him home, saying no nickel's worth of newsprint was worth losing her boy over. As usual, the paper carried a story about the Lindbergh kidnapping. And this just encouraged the comparisons. An elderly man with white hair haloed around his nut-brown features, deep creases in his cheeks, and years of thought lining his brow brimmed full of indignant outrage and was shoving the newspaper at one of the *Negro Daily's* reporters, stamping the ground with his cane and pointing to the report—this one an editorial about alternative Lindbergh scenarios and a rush to judgment.

Who gonna write up an editorial about our baby? Any of them city reporters coming down here to Harlem?

You right. Where they at?

Fool, we up in Harlem not down there in New York. City reporters not into what happens to our chirren.

Harlem be more New York than downtown.

Tell that to some of them folks live down there.

They looked everywhere but here for the ones took that Lucky baby and killed it.

Yeah, we shoulda been up under their suspicions too. They down here fast enough when somebody done stole something.

And now we the ones with the trouble.

Preach! Them kidnaps that they didn't catch prolly hid up here in Harlem all this time just waiting for the chance till they could snatch one of our babies.

Who gonna pay a ransom for a Harlem baby?

Who gonna want a colored baby for money?

You all outta your damn minds. They can skip the trial on those fools. Got 'em dead-on. Fingerprints an all.

Fingerprints?

Fingerprints is everywhere, fool. Course there are fingerprints. Trouble is a kidnapper's fingerprints don't say "I be the kidnapper y'all is looking for." It's just circles. Everybody has 'em.

A few in the crowd could be seen examining their own fingers while a rather heady discussion of scientific methodology, led by the old man who had the advantage of his cane to punctuate his remarks, engaged others, each with a more current and vociferous perspective than the next.

Somebody stood on a box and read the editorial. It called for continued vigilance. Which this crowd thought was an appropriate strategy for this occasion.

Look out now! They can't be the only ones got them some vigilance. We can get us some too.

You ain't lyin!

If I'm lyin, I'm flyin!

There were chuckles and a few outright guffaws until the women nudged the men to remember why they were there and it may be there was another baby dead somewhere.

Weldon heard the speculation and worried over it. When lay folks got into police business, no good comes out of their engagement.

Chasen, he a German, just like the Lucky baby kidnappers.

No he ain't. He a Jew.

No difference in my book.

Sure they is. One got a country named after them. Germany. Our folks went there in the WW and not all of 'em came back. The Jew ain't got no country. So it's a difference.

Not around here!

Their logic was loose, tortured, and dangerous. Weldon could sense the deterioration. And even though he needed some time to consider and organize the events, to gather his impressions, the situation was messy and confusing, and this talk about the Lindbergh baby, Germans, and Jews was not helping. This one was going nowhere fast. Plus it didn't feel right.

By this time Reverend Charleston had come from someone's bedside at Harlem Hospital and made it to the street corner. He saw the disarray as well and recognized the opportunity to get folks into church. Weldon could already hear the sermonizing rhythm creeping into his appeal to organize a community meeting "over the tragedy that has occurred in our very midst. The lamb that has gone missing from our flock. The babe that . . ." His voice was beginning to develop a tempo, and Weldon knew he better step in quickly. "As if the devil himself reached down here to Harlem. To our own star, our North Star, and troubled these waters . . ." And then there was more than one "Amen," and Weldon knew he'd better step in before hell on earth was described as having descended onto the streets of Harlem and folks got it in their minds to compete.

"Reverend Charleston, might I ask . . ." Weldon interrupted. "Reverend Charleston, might I ask you to share your very generous offer with everyone here?" Orage Charleston wasn't used to being interrupted, but the ask did allow him to take the crowd's focus with the official Harlem policeman having just endorsed his authority. "Reverend Charleston has some words about a community meeting. Y'all need to hear this because the police will be closing down this store for the moment for investigative

123

purposes. But we want you all to stay involved, and Reverend Charleston has some good advice for us."

It worked. Folks were directed to share the news with neighbors, to reconvene tonight, to pay attention to everybody around them now, to think over and compare notes about who was seen where and when, and who had been there at the beginning. The policeman promised that he would see everyone tonight at the church hall. It was a specific-enough request to redirect the energies. "Go home. We gonna meet again early evening down to the church. Go on home now. We'll see you then." Officer Thomas and the police and detectives had blocked off the door to the grocery and were beginning to create a perimeter around the building itself. The mother and the grandmother had already left, so that focus was missing. People dispersed, trying to look around and notice the neighbors they knew and the folks they didn't. A little boy in a green shirt looked around for the man who stopped him from running across the street against the light. He wanted to say thank you. It was a white man, he told his mother. A white man with a face like moon craters. She was one of the ones who had hurried down to the store to retrieve their children, knowing which ones were likely to stop there before heading down to the school yard. She was right. Her boy Sam was milling about the crowd, hanging around the bigger boys, trying to learn something he had no business knowing. He kept trying to tell her his story about the white man in the brown fedora who helped him. She snatched his arm until he said *Ouch* and reprimanded him for stopping on the way to school. It was against their rules and he knew it. But she did listen, and later that night at the community meeting, he'd shared enough about the stranger's presence for LT to put it in his notes, and also to recall that just before the meeting started, there was a man who looked similar enough to that description standing over by the detectives who showed up for the occasion. *Probably one of the plainclothes investigative fellows I don't know yet,* he thought. But he wrote that down too, having been schooled by Officer Thomas that his personal notes, the ones he did not have to turn over with his reports, were where he could write down things to think over later and make associations that might not have seemed related on the first go-round.

Weldon sent LT home with the Mosbys and used the other recruit who'd arrived to escort the stragglers away from the storefront. He needed help creating a space between the act and the evolving aftermath. The day passed without anyone's notice of anything in particular other than the collection of evidence, names, the removal of the pram, the return of the women to their home, the crowds to theirs. What began early morning passed into late afternoon. The day's light deepened into an autumn twilight. Sharp city noises would soon take on darker and longer night tones, and forlorn wailings looped into the chill night air.

16

Home Training

"MRS. EARLENE KINSDALE'S RESIDENCE. HOW MAY I HELP YOU?" LAVERNE Caver spoke into the receiver with the precision and cadence that she'd been instructed to use on the telephone.

"LaVerne! It's me. Sadie. I'm over here at the Scotts'. First off, I'm calling because my Mrs. Vera wants to talk with your lady about tonight's cotillion ball. And too, given how upset she got once she heard the story from me, she likely gonna share what I just told her. You hear tell about what's going on down in Harlem?"

"Girl . . . I been up in this house since dawn trying to get this lady ready for tonight. She barely let me out of her sight. 'Find me this.' 'Get me that.' When I work up here, nothin to know about except what she says is important. So nope. Not a thing. What's going on down from here?"

"Too much! And I was there. Right there at Chasen's where it happened!" Sadie's story was whispered and urgent. She was eager to tell her about the kidnapping, but she had to get it out fast. Neither of them could afford to let their employers hear that they were using the household telephones for personal business. Sadie Mathis shared what she knew as quickly as she could; but since the story was confusing, she had to frequently correct her friend.

"No. No. Not the baby's mother. Her *grand*mother. There's two Mosby

126

women, well, two women and the baby girl what's gone missing. It's DeLilah the grandmother, then Selma the daughter—the one folks be sayin is not quite right about the head, and then the girl baby named Chloe. I was headed to Chasen's Grocery to get some caramels for the Scott girls. She don't never let these sweeties have something special. But there was too much going on for me to get anywheres near inside. People crowded all around outside the store. Lotsa police. Even Officer Weldon . . ."

"Officer T. there too? So colored and white police both?"

"That's what I'm telling you. Him and his deputy—LT look like such a fine young man since they gived him the uniform—well, both of them trying to get some order to the whole mess. Folks hollering and talking all over each other. Womens crying. Whilst I was tryin to make sense of what had happened, Officer T. and Reverend Charleston announced a community meeting for tonight. You and me, we got to be there. So hurry up and get your missus ready for the cotillion. I'ma do the same with my Mrs. Vera."

"She know you on this telephone?"

"It was her that asked me to call for your lady."

"I know she heard it ring, she gonna be ringing on that little bell she keeps on her dresser table for me any second now to ask if didn't the telephone sound. She real particular about this. Always thinking somebody listening on the line."

"Well, we get every opportunity on the party lines. How many on your line? Neverminds. I heard that it was her ring they use—two short bells. Right? But you can't never be sure. But still, before you put her to the line, promise you'll meet me at the church. We can get all the information there from the po-lice and Reverend Charleston."

"If Reverend get to talking, any information gonna have to take a seat." Sure enough, a bell tinkled down the hallway followed by Earlene Kinsdale's aggravated query.

"LaVerne? Didn't I hear the household telephone? LaVerne!" Earlene Kinsdale had gone past curious to irritated.

"Girl, I gots to go. I'll do what I can." She shifted back to her formal telephone voice. Her children called it her church talk. "Just one moment, please, I'll see if Mrs. Kinsdale is available for a call from Mrs. Vera Scott." LaVerne placed the heavy receiver onto the hall console, straightened her starchy white collar, and ran her fingers around the uniform's scratchy lace cuffs. She walked the length of the hall to Earlene Kinsdale's dressing room with a brisk purposefulness, paused, then knocked softly and opened the door. Earlene Kinsdale was seated at her vanity, pulling her cheeks back toward her ears and peering deeply into her mirror to see what (if any) difference that made. "Ma'am, if you available, Mrs. Vera Scott is holding the line."

"I knew I heard the telephone! Whatever took you so long?" she complained while clearing a space on her dresser for the extension. "Of course I'm available. Plug it in and hand it to me. We've already been kept waiting by your dawdling."

"Yes, ma'am. My apologies." She placed the extension onto the space Mrs. Kinsdale had cleared on her dresser and spoke into the receiver. "Mrs. Kinsdale is on the line." Earlene irritably grabbed at the receiver.

"Hello? Vera? Hello?"

These exchanges, first between the Hamilton Heights maids, and then between two of the most prominent members of the Negro Welfare League, helped spread the news of the kidnapping from down in Harlem up to the Heights. For the ladies in the Heights, the timing was an uncomfortable inconvenience.

"Surely not one of ours?" Earlene Kinsdale tucked the telephone's receiver down between her shoulder and her ear while she pulled the left hand of the glove past her plump fingers, gradually working it up her forearm. Beads of sweat broke over her forehead, and she directed LaVerne to powder her face again.

The pitch of Vera's voice on the other end of the line edged upwards.

"Earleeeeeeene!" Her friend's unusually shrill tone redirected Earlene's attention back to the telephone. "Did you hear at all what I just said? A Harlem infant has gone missing. A baby girl. Taken straight from her perambulator. Whatever shall we do?"

"We?" Earlene was taken aback. "Sweetheart, please. You can't be serious." She straightened the glove's seam. "*We* can't have the auxiliary get involved in something just because somebody's baby has wandered off. And too, you might want to consider that a mother who loses her child—and who probably has too many anyway—is *not* our kind of people." She paused to let Vera appreciate the distinction. LaVerne pulled the hairbrush through Mrs. Kinsdale's auburn hair with a decided tug. "Ouch! Whatever has gotten into you, LaVerne? This is my hair you are doing.

Not one of your people's nappy heads. You know better. This carelessness is exactly what happens when you bring the street up in here!"

"Yes, ma'am. I do apologize." She took up the brush again, and this time started from the end of her hair shaft. Mrs. Kinsdale's hair was as taken to kinks as her own. Nevertheless, she didn't interrupt her employer's pretense that living up in the Heights was enough to give you good hair. Earlene returned her attention to the call.

"Vera my dear, I was about to say, how can you be certain that this lost child is a tragedy?"

"Now that's simply cruel!" Vera snapped back. LaVerne responded as well. She slapped the brush back down on the bureau and turned away so that her annoyance would not show. "And I didn't say she was lost. She's . . . she's . . . kidnapped!" Vera expected more empathy. "Somebody took poor little Chloe!"

"Chloe?" Given the occasion, Earlene's amused chuckle edged toward being mean-spirited. "What kind of name is that to give a little baby? It sounds like . . . like an old lady. Gray-haired. Large. Stern." She shifted the telephone into her left hand and let out an exasperated sigh. "Gracious, Vera! This whole conversation is a nuisance! Whatever goes on with Harlem's mothers, these matters are agenda items for the meeting, and I'm not even on that committee. You know I've done the arts facet since . . . well, since forever! For heaven's sake! Why are we wasting time talking about them now?"

"You can't be that critical, Earlene. By your logic, you'd blame the Lindbergh baby's kidnapping on some failure in that child's family too?"

"I do, indeed." Vera Scott let out a small, but noticeable gasp on the other end of the line. If Mrs. Kinsdale had been listening at all, she would have heard LaVerne suck in her teeth.

"*Sth.*"

But she wasn't. "If you remember, Vera, one of the Lindbergh maids took her own life when the police started investigating her. Just goes to show somebody wasn't properly vetting that household staff. Clearly the maid was unstable. Likely foreign born." She sniffed her disapproval. LaVerne stuffed Earlene's pinkie into the other glove with a jerk. "Good gracious!" she snapped. "Is it too much to ask for just a smidgen of gentility?"

"Lene, you're too harsh! And, if I might say it . . ." She gulped but then delivered the critique. "It's unbecoming. Especially as it seems we've now got one of our own gone missing and likely kidnapped."

"There you go with that 'we' again. I simply refuse the community it implies! That baby belonged to the help. Not to *us*." She slipped a bejeweled cocktail ring over the gloved finger that still smarted from LaVerne's shove and rooted around the drawer until she found another to put on her index finger. She held her hand up to the lamp until the ring's glass facets caught the light and glimmered. She was accustomed to brilliance.

Earlene Kinsdale's judgments about the difference between the problems in Harlem's households and those that might be encountered in Hamilton Heights were attached to the assumed obligations of their social set. "You know how careless these Harlem women can be. The last thing we need is their tendencies toward negligence associated with those of us who live up here." Vera had gone quiet on the other end of the line. "From what you've said, it seems apparent that the mother did not raise the girl to place a value on her innocence. For example, you say there's no father. And so what does that tell you about her home training?" She took her stridency down to a whisper, as if her judgment could not be properly voiced in genteel company. She didn't wait for an answer. "I'll tell you." She gestured LaVerne toward her perfumes while answering her own question. "None at all. At least nothing that would exemplify moral clarity. They spend entirely too much time outside of their own homes. This unfortunate result speaks for itself." LaVerne liberally sprayed Mrs. Kinsdale's neck and shoulders with her new bottle of Arpège. Despite the seductive advertisement for Lanvin's new scent: *Promise her anything, but give her Arpège!* Earlene had to buy it for herself. Being widowed was such an inconvenience. She took her irritation out on LaVerne. Again.

"That's enough! Enough! Good Lord, you'll have me smelling like a Harlem brothel!" She sniffed the room. "Well, at least a heavily scented one. I must admit that his new fragrance is quite lovely." She looked around at her room's clutter, anxious to exert some control. Her hands fluttered anxiously outwards. The closets were still open. The gowns she'd considered, but then discarded, were draped one atop the other across the velvet divan, and her drawers spilled out their contents. "LaVerne! Now, don't you even think of leaving here without returning things to good order. I don't care one whit about whatever dramas beckon from Harlem's streets. It has no place here. Remember, orderliness . . ."

"Yes, ma'am. 'Orderliness is the outward manifestation of character.'" She began gathering the clothing that would hang back in the closets and the gloves and jewelry that would be returned to her drawers. Once Earlene felt satisfied that the maid was appropriately focused on the room's clutter, she seemed to remember her telephone conversation. "Vera? Vera!" she shouted into the receiver. "Are you still there?"

"I'm here, Earlene; but I insist that we have a role to play. It's an innocent child, and this is *our* community. We must consider that we have an obligation!"

Vera's protestations were beginning to be an annoyance. "I'm not asking you to ignore the infant. And it would do you well to remember that *we* live in what's quite appropriately named Harlem *Heights*. We're situated above those neighborhoods for good reason."

Vera tried again. "But a baby was kidnapped!" Earlene didn't let her get further than that.

"Sweetheart—please don't interrupt. You called me, remember? I haven't finished my point." She heard Vera's frustrated sigh on the other end of the line. "You know how they are always saying, 'My Lord, have mercy'—like the Lord belongs to them alone? 'My' Lord. Gracious! The ego that takes! But *my* point is, they are always complaining even as they spend their days looking after everything but what should matter." She called over to LaVerne, reminding her to wrap her evening slippers—the ones they had not selected—in fresh tissues, and not to reuse any of the wrapping they had pulled away from the boxes.

Vera tried again. "Earlene, that's not quite fair, they . . ."

"Vera, please! Our auxiliary simply can't abandon our social calendar for every Harlem mishap."

"But I . . ."

"Now, then. As I was saying, they think everything belongs to them 'my polishing, my wash, my floors . . .'" She paused, correctly sensing that Vera was still distraught. "All right, then. Perhaps your instincts are somewhat reasonable. Let's see . . ." She heard the intake of air. Vera was about to continue her protest, but Earlene persisted. "No. Wait. Here's a suggestion. You know we have to come up with a neighborhood project on our agenda for the next meeting. It sounds, from what you've been saying, that this grandmother—what's her name?"

"Ummm . . . DeLilah?" She looked over to Sadie, who nodded and whispered the last name. "Yes . . . it's DeLilah. DeLilah Mosby."

"All right. Mrs. Mosby. And I suspect she's unemployed?"

"Well, what I heard is that she had a job in Manhattan's East Side as a seamstress and head of the linens wardrobe before she had to take care of her daughter and the new baby."

"Well, let me just say that 'taking care' seems to be up for debate." Vera started to interrupt. "But . . . just wait." She took in a breath, almost making up the proposal as she spoke. "If she has the kind of skills that would get her hired in Manhattan, it's entirely plausible that we can use her as a viable candidate for our jobs initiative. If she's had experience in Manhattan (hopefully it was Upper East), she might well be a reasonable candidate, even—" she paused before her suggestion, understanding the potential for gossip, "well, even in one of our own homes. I've heard the Middletons are looking for some household help. At least we can bring this forward for discussion. As unpleasant as it may be, given these events, her responsibilities might have become somewhat less consuming."

"So what are you suggesting?"

"If you allow the two of us to go ahead with our preparations for this evening's cotillion, I'll do this . . . I'll promise to put her name up at our next meeting. And, truth to tell, perhaps quite fortuitously, it has all the markings of a splendid service initiative!" Not hearing the eager affirmation she hoped for, Earlene Kinsdale went further and extended what she'd describe later as an overly generous offer. "How about this? You and I will be co-chairs. We'll share the project. It will be our baby. Agreed?" Earlene didn't even wince with her unfortunately selected phrasing, but Mrs. Scott did, even while understanding the suggestion had some appeal.

"Well, it does seem responsive." Vera sighed. "It's all so sad."

Earlene sighed loudly, relieved that she wouldn't have to argue the point again.

"Fabulous! Then we've agreed! I'll see you at the ballroom. Make sure to get there before the circle. I hear they've come up with a new promenade. Eula Pettis saw it in Europe. If she got it right. Which, we will only be able to discern after the girls execute the final rosette and curtsy. We just can't miss that. It's the highlight. So . . . do I have your promise?"

"Yes. All right. If we agree to engage the matter at our next meeting, I'll see you shortly."

Earlene Kinsdale finished her preparations and walked slowly enough down the brownstone's front steps toward her waiting car and driver so that watchful neighbors might have the opportunity to notice her fine attire. Her day maid hurriedly stuffed her employer's remaining gowns back into the wardrobe with little attention as to whether or not they might wrinkle. She came up the steps from the brownstone's lower door and rushed down St. Nicholas Avenue past the park to the trolley stop. LaVerne Caver, and eventually Sadie Mathis, joined the flow of folks who solemnly headed down to the Baptist church basement for an official update on the kidnapping in Harlem.

17

Women's Work

FARTHER UP IN HARLEM WERE THE HAMILTON HEIGHTS FAMILIES. THE ones that lived up in Sugar Hill had a sweet life that followed what it could discern of the habits adopted by Manhattan's wealthy. They focused on a program of similar rituals to bypass the Harlem life that was less becoming to their goals of racial uplift. Their Sag Harbor summers were near enough to the Vineyard and East Hampton; debutante balls and cotillions were modeled as closely as they could be on the ones written up with detailed flourishes in the society magazines. Their membership-exclusive societies designed increasingly elaborate rules of induction and secrecy in order to establish their selectivity.

Even though Mrs. Earlene Kinsdale (widowed) and others of her society set were merely a few blocks removed from Harlem's working class, they used that distance to maintain a social line as fierce as the color line. They called what women who lived "down in Harlem" did "make work," like it wasn't real. The constant busyness of the "girls" who worked for them discomfited their own elite ease.

However, and as quiet as it's kept, a goodly number of Harlem's women did indeed manifest a nearly obsessive and intensely personal focus on cleanliness—as long as it was the next-to-godliness kind. Things they could control received devoted attention. Everything else in their challenged days was a matter for prayer. Whether it involved their children and families or the things in their households, everything under their control was relentlessly attended to. Sunday socks were carefully folded over so lace edges circled their daughters' ankles without a break. Sunday shoes would get biscuit shined—girls and boys both—and, if necessary, a bit of Cleopatra hair grease got rubbed into the surfaces to get the intended glisten. Sons and daughters both were subject to a daily monitoring of knees and elbows for any sign of ash, and a tin of petroleum jelly was ready just in case. They rubbed their children's cheeks with it when winter's bitter cold hit and used it on their shoes for first Sundays. Those who could afford it used Vaseline for shoes and cheeks and Vicks for chest rubs when cold season hit. Others used Vaseline for both. They were careful about their families in every way their precarious living allowed. Coat linings and hems were inspected for loose threads and expertly stitched up before a seam unraveled. Tender headed or not, your hair was brushed and braided and brushed again right at the scalp and with extra effort at the kitchen. On special occasions, the hot comb came out, and if you could sit still, girl children got to listen to the women's talk where seemingly casually told stories or reporting or assessments were shared with full awareness that the attentiveness of their captive audiences was a constant. You might could get a jam sandwich while common sense got braided tight inside each cornrow and a freshly ironed plaid ribbon got wound through the braid, and only a tap on the bottom would dislodge the girl from the sanctuary between her mother's thighs.

When the women gathered, for hair or cooking or instructing, they took on whatever task there was to be managed and practiced it with deliberate intention as to how they handled self-respect. To the extent they could, their homes took up this same focus, where—even if they were knocked about outside, they straightened right back up when they came back in. Sometimes this meant facing trauma by a vigorously determined attack on wood or linoleum floors; tabletops, legs of any furniture, and wooden bases of lamps would earn extra thick dollops and vigorous rubs of Lightning Furniture Polish. In fact, floors were polished twice because, with Lightning's new product, you could clean your floors and get rid of insects at the same time. (It must be noted, however, that a good many women were beginning to sing the praises of the newest disinfectant, Lysol.) Their homes were witness and citadel . . . places for painfully learned (and taught) lessons, but also sites of sanctuary and solace. They didn't save you from tragedy, but you could sure clean up afterwards. Home held on to their shadows. Ancestors lingered there. And memory, that most precious and precarious space, had a room when it seemed there was no heart space left. Harlem's black folks were migrants from red dirt roads and clapboard houses with some land between them and sweet gum trees in summer and enough wood to be gathered that could fuel a winter stove and leave wisps of piney-scented smoke behind. Home was witness and memory.

So, in deference to the heft of responsibility held between paper-thin walls and noisy stairwells and windows with a mind of their own, Harlem's women were persistent in inspecting underneath and up above for cobwebs. Whatever windows could be opened, even if only to be held up with the temporary prop of a stick of wood or a hardback book (never the Bible—the Lord's word is not your prop, it is your purpose), until dusty counterpanes and throw rugs and anything else that needed a shake and a time-out in the fresh air could get some. Outside ledge hooks suspended laundry with a system of ropes and pulleys that made neighbors out of folks who might otherwise just share the same floor in the building. Along with a general interest in the welfare of the building, neighborliness included keeping the lines running. If you needed to holler out your window for somebody to check the line, you'd better be in good standing with the person on the other end. Shared work was ethic and purpose, and orderliness was either invented or rigorously maintained. No telling who might come up those steps or knock on the doors or come looking in on their insides. So they lined up shoes outside the chifforobe, stacked cans and packages by shape and size, savory and sweet inside cabinets and across whatever surfaces might hold the excess, if there was any to be had. They folded sheets and shirts, the extra set of towels, ironed and starched Sunday dresses (and sometimes the underwear) and weekday aprons, and kept empty coffee cans or mason jars to save whatever was left over, be it bacon or sausage grease or coins. Mirrors got wiped with old newspapers and then with a damp rag. Carpets were swept until dust rose in insistent clouds settling on baseboards and inside door frames, which was why the first thing a child learned was the order to cleaning a house. "Sweep, then dust." And that meant every single picture frame and each saved memento and holiday card and candlestick and china figurine that shared a space on a mantle. A side table got wiped down with a wet rag, with special attention to family photographs—the ones of Aunt Sis down home standing in front of tasseled corn and Uncle Son on that bright day when he pulled the mule cart in the watch-night day parade, cousins and kin hanging out the windows and off the edges of a clapboard porch—the ones they left back home, the ones who wrote letters that got filed between the pages of the family Bible. Harlem's women cared for what they had with measured and full devotion. Home was a sacred text.

Weekends were for catching up with mending. Shirts without buttons, straps detached from slips, lace fallen away from the edges of a hanky or Sunday socks—all found their way into the sewing basket. Everyone knew where it was and how to bring it and put it by her chair so she could reach inside and find just the right slot for the color of thread she needed. A luxurious sateen-tufted inside cover held needles and pins, and the wonders of the inside tray, with slots of different shapes and widths, held a tightly wound circle of measuring tape, odd lengths of ribbons, small buttons, larger ones, thimbles, and needle threaders. Underneath the tray were the crochet hooks, yarn, and pieces of cloth that could be a quilt when (and if) she ever got to it. Those baskets were cared for as lovingly as some of the most precious of women's possessions, and guarded with the same fierce authority. Rainbow-like spools of thread were tended to like jewelry. Sewing kits kept buttons and stray ribbons, snaps and buckles, and bits of fabric that just might come in handy one day. You never know.

Despite the loyalties imagined by white women down in Manhattan or the aspiring race-women up in Sugar Hill, Harlem's women worked with far more energy and passion than they ever brought to their white folks, or even to colored households up in the Heights. It wasn't always kind or considered or empathetic. Necessity was their prompt. And, of course, hope. And love, tough as it could feel. But they proved it with the stringent scent of Breath O'Pine, and their preparedness for illness or soothing came from gnarled roots of sassafras kept beneath the kitchen sink, and when it got past a vigorous chest rub with Vicks or swallowing it with sugar sprinkled on the teaspoon, they kept up with the lady down the block who kept roots and recipes most folks left back home. Harlem's mothers took comfort stretching out the lace antimacassar across a sofa back, in fluffing tired and well-shaped cushions, in having a rag rug beneath their feet at the sink, in making certain that their homes held to whatever was in them—children, husbands, lovers, brothers, kin kept as safe and protected as they could manage. The jobs their men and boys could depend on were scarce and precious. And the ones that took on skilled labor were constantly in danger. Girders that stretched their way across the skyline for new bridges and future trains killed as easily as the gritty labor in the tunnels that snaked below the city's streets, where being buried in a dynamite blast or a tumble from a loose cropping of rock happened so frequently that the whistle announcing a work stoppage because of accident became as much a dependable annoyance as it was a fright. The somebodies who got themselves this kind of work were just as likely to be a body that would need burying. Insurance collectors, the ones met with "Mommy told me to tell you we not home," and undertakers, the ones who vied for your body when all was said and you were done with, gained the most regular work. And because what was left for them to count on was stressful and precarious, Harlem's women worked for their own with twice the vigor they used up elsewhere. Women knew and girls were taught that anything inside was better than the streets. So they practiced the task of home with fierce love and willful intent and an exquisitely practiced ritual of loss.

Harlem's women worked to keep things safe and solid. They made city rules to take the place of country freedoms, like when the streetlamps came on, you best be in this house; and if you can't hear when I call, you too far away; and don't let your daddy get here to the table before you in here to clean up and get ready to sit down together to have supper like a family should. They practiced being prepared because the cold and drafts and troubles that ran through Harlem flats carried all kinds of treachery and some sickness too till it seemed sometimes like the funeral directors and ministers (who were usually the same person) were the only ones destined to prosper.

Women and their girls worked to keep their men and boys sane and wanting home, folding them so securely into family rituals that when they had to release them to the streets to do whatever it was they could to make it work, up there would be something good and wanted and especially something familiar and safe to return to. These were folks once bound to the South in ways that were as treacherous and cruel as the commerce that would have kept them there. But families who worked their ways north found an underground so deep it could bury a dream, and skies too cluttered with a weblike tracery of wires and cables, and concrete that stretched across the streets and over the river to ever remember they had come north because of a song and a star.

18

Quem Quaeritis?

NEITHER THE BABY'S MOTHER, SELMA, NOR MAMA LIL WENT TO THE community meeting. *Still in shock,* it was whispered. Folks nodded their compassionate understanding. The size of the gathering illustrated its seriousness as much as its novelty. The Masons and Knights of Pythias were there because attending functions was a part of their mission. Some even wore full dress including the fez, like they were at a call meeting. A small scattering of representatives from the NWA—the Negro Women's Auxiliary—did attend, mostly a disgruntled contingent of those who had declined to purchase cotillion pageant billets because of the increasingly steep financial commitment or the sheer boredom of the evening unless you were a parent and you bought a membership because the fate of your children's schooling and marriage and your whole family standing depended on your finding a way to manage the cost. A group of Harlem's ministers clustered with the morticians. Unless they wore their collars, it was difficult to tell one from the other, except the morticians were inclined to have lighter complexions and their slick hair suggested they had been indulging in some of their chemicals for personal use. They were the only ones certain that, in one way or another, their services were likely to be called on before this whole affair was over. Schoolteachers and day workers stood in small clutches. For the few children who were there, nobody let go of their hands, no matter how much they twisted and complained. Older kids actually sought out the clasp of a parent's grip, unsettled by the sense that something had happened and nobody knew what to do. Men who'd just left shifts above- and belowground both stood wide-legged, arms folded and angry at the vulnerability this loss represented. And there were the old folks who scattered through the crowd, punctuating everything with a *Do Jesus* or an *Amen to that*. Mostly, they were grateful for a night out, for the change in their routine, being away, even for a brief moment, from their ordinary evenings, but nonetheless shaken and unprepared with the words they usually offered when things went awry.

Everybody there knew that this kidnapped Harlem baby would never have received any kind of collective attention if it hadn't been for the precedent of the nation's baby—the Lindbergh infant. And given that, everything took on an unusual veneer of importance and performance. The organizers of the community meeting stood around the room like sentries. It was expected of church deacons and members of the usher board. That's what they did Sunday after Sunday. That and offering a shush when there was too much whispering during the minister's sermon. But the police were out of their element. Weldon's young cadet Mitchell surveyed the gathering from the back of the room and looked to Weldon for direction. He stood with his gloved hands behind him (just like one of the deacons, somebody said before they were corrected to understand that was his regulated stand-at-attention position, and then they remarked how much they appreciated him giving his own people that formal respect). There had to be something complimentary to say about the handsome young man. His freshly uniformed figure easily drew the attention of the younger women in the crowd, who made sure to speak to him and compliment him on his graduation from the academy. LT's success had been big news in Harlem, and there was a write-up about it in nearly all the church bulletins as well as in the *Amsterdam News* and the *Negro Daily*. Weldon anticipated the kind of attention and even adulation that would come to his young protégé and helped to prepare him to handle it modestly. Years back, he had been Harlem's first colored policeman, and he knew the challenges that accompanied the notice of his appointment. The expectations could get to be more demanding than the requisites of the position. It could be daunting for anybody to handle the sudden wave of attention and public interest, but it was something

Weldon had already experienced and he'd managed it nicely. Folks were ready to give LT respect because they acknowledged what a fine example Weldon had set and how if he had not been a credit to the race, LT wouldn't have had the chance he now held. They wanted them both to be a success rather than an experiment, so the community's support for colored policing began with a willingness to give the colored cops their propers.

Officer Thomas had known LT almost from the first days he and his family moved up from Stump Sound, North Carolina, to Harlem. When the captain assigned him to Weldon to complete his cadet training, it elevated the elder cop to senior officer status, and LT Mitchell got the continued mentorship of the man who saved him from ruining his life in the streets (which had been his mother's abiding concern).

When Officer Thomas started to make his way to the front of the auditorium, he nodded to LT and motioned that he should keep to the back of the room. Later, he explained it was as good a place as any, and better than most, to do some observation. Keeping watch was always a part of his job, no matter the situation. They had gotten to the place where they understood each other almost without having to speak. Weldon walked up the stairs to the raised platform. With so many people there, he would need to be seen as well as easily heard, even though his ordinary advice was that if you needed to stand on something to get somebody's attention, you're likely doing something wrong. This was different. But he didn't start speaking right away. He just put one hand in the other, behind his back like LT had done, and looked around until folks stopped talking. He hoped LT noticed. He didn't ever want to hear the boy shouting like he heard white cops, "Hey, youse, listen up! I says, listen up!" louder and louder until folks just gave in and got quiet. His way was to wait until folks noticed he wasn't going to start until they were quiet, and then when he got their attention, that's when he'd start speaking. When there were more folks noticing his exercise in patience than there were talking amongst themselves, he used his regular voice to politely ask folks to kindly take their seats.

Weldon had his work cut out for him in separating this baby's disappearance from the one that almost everyone was already trying to make it be "just like."

Mostly it was his people who crowded into the church hall. He knew most all of them. Even some of the white folks. The pawnbroker and

Mr. Chasen (who came alone because his wife was still too distraught), some cops from the precinct, and some detectives in plainclothes to blend in, which was hard considering this was a Harlem community meeting. In a corner near the back stood the same white man who was outside the store early, when Selma tried to get the carriage through the door and settled instead for lining it up outside by the vegetable and fruit bins. He was huddled up alongside the detectives. He didn't seem much different from the police. Pipe in his mouth, fedora still on his head, even though he was in a church. Even though it was the church basement . . . but still—no respect. The only difference was that his hands were stuffed in his pockets instead of scribbling on a notepad like the police or the newspaper reporters. Weldon noticed every idiosyncrasy he could about the crowd. He knew the likelihood of discovering something that might help solve the case, even something about who did it, diminished with each hour passed. He hoped LT was taking the kind of notes that he wasn't able to given his role in bringing the crowd to order and general supervision of the way the evening would proceed.

Folks soon quieted, and nervous coughing and grating of chairs took over the room as if to say, *We're giving you our attention now, so it's time for you to tell us what we need to know.*

"I'm going to do two things tonight, folks." Officer Thomas's deep baritone soothed the rustling and focused their attention. "First off, I'm going to tell you what we know up to this particular moment. I'm going to need you to put aside any comparisons you have in mind. We got to come to this one for what it is, not what it looks like." A few *Amens* confirmed he had advocates with this perspective, but there were some grunts as well. He ignored those. "Second, if you've got ideas to share or witness-type things to say, standing there in the back there is Cadet LT Mitchell, who will direct you to the proper official who can take your statements." LT nodded briefly, to acknowledge the notice. "Those men over there, the ones that got suits on, that's some detectives from the precinct, and they stand ready to do the same thing. Now, some of us might have questions for you. I'm going to ask you to answer straight and narrow, as best you can. No speechifying, if you know what I mean." Some in the crowd chuckled. "This not the time or the place."

Amen to that right there.

Aww, hush. Let the officer speak.

Ain't nobody stopping him.

143

You is. Hush!

"And while I'm on that note, there is a third thing. I'm going to task everybody here to do some thinking, give some consideration—especially if you were in the vicinity—and if there's something that strikes you as having been off, no matter when you were there, I want you to say it tonight, or if it comes to you later, to get in touch with us. Cadet Mitchell has contact information. And anyways, y'all never have a problem knowing where to find me. Same thing now. If you've got something that needs to be said, we the ones it needs saying to." There was a scattering of *Yes sirs* and *We surely will do just that* and, perhaps because they were in a church basement, more *Amens*. Weldon asked if Reverend Charleston would lead them in a prayer before he read the official statement that the precinct had prepared. He wished, though, that the pastor had been closer to the front of the hall because during the time it took him to make his way through the crowd, the opportunity to do exactly what Weldon had clearly said would not be the format for the evening presented itself.

Officer Thomas! I hear they left a ten-page-long kidnap letter in the carriage.

Fool! Ain't nobody got time to write ten pages about no kidnap.

You right. Don't need to write anything more than "Hand over the money—all in twenties." That's alls it needs to say.

Or hunnerts. This the time to go for the big bucks.

Who got any big bucks up in Harlem other than them runners? An anybody could tell you they ain't got time to mess with nobody's baby.

True enough. Ain't nobody I know gonna kidnap somebody for a bunch of twenty-dollar bills.

And how you be knowing anything about a kidnap at all is what I want to know. A woman's sharp voice promised an argument for somebody's household, but it would happen later.

Weldon didn't respond except to ask if people would put themselves into a posture of prayer and bow their heads.

It didn't make the minister move any more quickly. Reverend Charleston was a portly man, and the aisles were crowded with folks who had not been able to get a seat.

They gonna get the Investigation Bureau down here just like they done for Colonel Lindbergh? There was a scattering of approving applause.

How about that, Big T? They gonna do for us like they done for the white folks when that flying baby went missing? In that brief moment, the

144

decorum and control shifted aside for the kinds of questions and commentary that a community meeting was ordinarily designed to encourage.

Voices flew from anonymous spaces, calls met responses, gruff tones, whines, stalwart declarations, shushes, and even some sobbing scattered across the room with no one waiting for or perhaps even expecting an answer. Speaking them aloud seemed to satisfy a need.

Kidnapped, you mean! a man from the side of the room indignantly shouted. *Lindbergh baby was kidnapped just like ours was. Them 'nappers took the boy out the window with a ladder. Ain't no flying in, about, or around it.*

But still an all, Hoover got to do right by us like he done for them. He done set the Feds loose and put the National Guard on alert.

We ain't no kinda like them. And it's President Hoover. Give the president his due respects.

*I did exactly that. Like I said, "*Hoover *got to do right by us."* There was a bit of scattered laughter.

You right. You right. They opened up Fort Knox money for Lucky.

Y'all know-nothings don't know nothing at all. Lindbergh didn't need a blessed dime from the U.S. of A. He richer than Fort Knox twice over.

So where we gonna get our ransom money from? We ain't got that kinda coin, voiced a high-pitched, worried-sounding woman.

Ain't no coins in the Knox. It's gold bars. The real deal. And stacks of 'em. Up to the ceiling high. And you can bet enough guards to make you rethink even coming anywheres close up to them. Building don't even have no windows. Not a one. The sun don't shine in there, but you can bet those bars be shining with every wall covered up with 'em. One woman said that it sounded like he knew a bit too much to believe it. But then another interrupted with a more serious question.

How much they asking is what I want to know. How much they want to bring a colored baby back to the mother and father?

Ain't no daddy is what I heard.

Uh-oh. Price drop . . . Scattered chuckles were quickly shut down by women who *tsk*ed their disapproval—either of the statement or the fact of the matter.

Weldon let the talk die down on its own. Later, when the cop and his cadet compared notes and reviewed the meeting, Weldon explained to LT that sometimes we just need the space to say it. Just watch and let it be.

It didn't take long for people to notice that he wasn't trying to answer any of these questions shouted back and forth and that he wasn't going to say a thing until they finished. Finally someone said: "All y'all hush now. That's disrespectful. Let's listen to what Officer Thomas has to say."

After a pause Weldon turned to see if the Reverend had caught his breath, and then asked for a prayer.

"Now that's right," an elderly voice declared. "Now we got the right somebodies in charge. First things is first. Praise the Lord." She raised her hands upwards. Others followed her example, but more just bowed their heads. Caps were snatched off the few who had forgotten their respects.

The crowd went silent and Reverend Orage Charleston's deep baritone blanketed the room and brought everyone to the moment: "May we bow our heads?" Weldon hoped it would be a long prayer. The official report was short and would do nothing to stem the speculation that people wanted to engage in. He could only tell them that before Selma Mosby broke down, she was able to say that she left the baby in the carriage outside of the store. She wasn't gone more than five minutes because it took her some time to find a case quarter she had at the bottom of the bag, and she didn't want to waste time counting out nickels and pennies she'd found in the change purse. And when she was finished, she came right back outside, reached into the pram to put the apples in it, and that was when she saw that her baby was gone. Mr. Chasen's report was that he knew the folks who were in the store, and it was his wife who had cried out, "Somebody took the baby." Now she was home, feeling quite unwell. Doris Gayles—who commended Weldon for his request for prayer—was the one who went with Cadet Mitchell to accompany the family back home. Her report to them only verified that the girl had kept to the silence that fell over her in the grocery. The baby, Chloe Antonia Mosby, was born August 18th at Harlem Hospital. No, there was no kidnap note. Yes, the baby's mother was Miss Selma Mosby, who was the daughter of Mrs. Lilah Mosby, who up until recently worked uptown at the Thayer mansion on Manhattan's Upper East Side. Yes, that would be the real estate family. The hotel people. But moving back to the relevant facts of the case, by way of identification, Chloe Antonia Mosby has a full head of wavy hair—more lightish than dark—and a small strawberry-colored splotch on the outside of her left ankle. Her last recorded weight was her birth weight: 5 pounds, 11 ounces. Yes. A small baby. Yes, the police had printed notices for everybody with that description. There were plenty to go round. Weldon nodded to LT, who waved a stack of them over his head. No, they did not have a picture of the baby. No, there was no ransom note at this moment in time. And in conclusion would the members of the press please continue to be respectful to family and get updated information from the precinct's public officer.

While the crowd was leaving, some gathered around an elderly woman with silver-blue braids and a book sack. She certainly had another name at some point, but everybody grew up knowing her as Lady Professor. In fact, "Ladee" was her given Christian name, but there was nobody still living who could have known that fact. Rumor had it that she used to teach at one of the colored colleges down south until she didn't. And whatever reason that was made her ubiquitous, and seemingly a time-bending presence in Harlem. Old Harlem folks talked about how their mamas had known her, and they described her no differently than she looked and acted today. She kept a back table spread with books and papers over at the branch library and used it like it was her office. As reliable as the seasons, she sat there every day the library was open. She'd commandeered one of the Windsor chairs that lined the long oak tables, available for any patron's reading or research, but pulled it up to the short edge of the long table. It made it look as if it were a desk, and patrons generally gave her the entire length, unless the reading room was crowded, and then folks would only sit at the far end, respecting the space she'd cleared. She kept a stack of books, spine out, ready to consult as if they were her own personal shelf. Her box of pencils—pens were forbidden because they might carelessly leave marks in a book—was always available. She liberally used the library's atlas. Folks heard her whispering under her breath sometimes. *We live in a world. Harlem's a world.* Generally she pulled books about the Negro—fiction to her left, and nonfiction on her right. She kept a clear space in the center so that she could glare down to the other end of the table to any readers daring enough to sit there and waiting for the question they inevitably had.

Lady Professor was bone thin and once had been light-skinned, but mottled liver spots threatened to cover her face and hands. Or it may have been that she was dark-skinned and was having some breakthrough. She could recite stories about streets and families and stores and schools from any era in Harlem's history—even telling you about families that came and went since way before Harlem went colored. Sometimes schoolchildren stopped in to see if she could help them on some research assigned by a teacher who wanted them to know about their own people. Some of them remembered her from their youth. But that kind of teacher ran few and far between. Most of them wanted you to learn about anything in the U.S. of A. and not particularly New York and certainly not Harlem. It was their home, not their history. They did have to learn the names of all the presidents. After that, it was Tudors and the Magna Carta, Constantinople and the Holy Roman Empire, that focused their studies. And anyway, most children used their free time to select candies from Chasen's rather than listen to Lady Professor's recitations. But because they went to the library with their teachers once a month on a Tuesday afternoon, they came to know her ways despite their inclinations. Some complained. Why would they make their way to the very last table in the room to hear what some old lady with braids as thick as dust mops have to say? When the fifth graders had their section on Greek mythology, someone brash enough would inevitably and loudly compare her braids to the Medusa. Others were quite reasonably drawn to her enigmatic bearing.

But this night, feeling the queerness of seeing her outside of her ordinary seat at the library table, some folks did stop to listen because they were still in need of something or somebody to help them understand how one of theirs could be so vulnerable and especially because on that night she felt like the one with the longest understanding and most compassionate attention to Harlem. *She should know,* somebody said as they passed by—with as much hope as speculation.

You right about that. She been here forever.

And a day . . .

"As I have heretofore informally extemporized," the Lady Professor explained to the small clutch of people who stopped on their way out of the church hall to listen to her assessment of the events, "it is then as it is now. Harlem lives as Harlem evolves. This sad circumstance will be neither definitive nor emblematic. It is but a season. Rest assured, ye who are heavy laden. By the spring solstice, the landscape will make its way toward our meridian. The arboreal horizon will leaf out green and fresh, and each of you will struggle mightily to recall anything different than that effulgent display of nature's promise. Sweet spring zephyrs will dispense any lingering chill, and all matter of things will find their correct place. You'll see. Consider the question and rest assured: *Quem quaeritis?* Nothing stays gone forever." She always finished her monologues with something Latin. For flourish. Or truth. It signaled that her oration had come to its formal conclusion. And of course, she did not entertain questions.

"What do that mean?" asked a youngster who'd come with her mother and stopped to listen to Lady Professor while she pulled on her galoshes.

"Does." The girl's mother corrected her daughter while she tugged her coat sleeves and noticed her wrists were longer than the sleeve. "What *does* that mean?" She reached down to fasten the top button of her jacket. "I'm not altogether sure. But something like, don't worry. Time will tell." The girl tucked her mittened hand into her mother's, even though she ordinarily thought herself too grown to still be holding her mother's hand. But today had unsettled anything ordinary. Together they climbed the stairs up from the basement and walked hand in hand, until the mother and daughter tenderly blended into the night.

19

All the Dark Things

IT WAS THANKSGIVING MORNING AND THE THAYERS RETURNED TO their Hamptons cottage to close it for the year and to host the holiday meal—the last time they would gather until spring and the day when decisions about leadership would be formally accomplished. The two eldest cousins—Edward Jr. and Cole—met at the edge of the cove, where Cole urged Edward to join him in a canoe ride. "We can talk out there. No distractions. Just us guys doing what we were born to do, take matters into our hands. Be the men they expect us to be. They'll watch us row out and probably still be watching when we turn the bend. Then when we're out of sight, they'll slap each other on the back and say, 'The boys can handle it. We raised them for this. They'll work things out.'" Cole grabbed Edward's shoulders. "Let's live up to their expectations. Come on, guy! I'll take the oars."

Edward didn't stop to consider how conveniently this excursion developed. But the fact was that Cole had planned every facet of the day. That it turned into a tragedy may or may not have been a part of his plan. Perhaps it was somewhere in his subconscious. However, as the police retrieved the details and interviewed family members, it seemed quite reasonable that everything he did seemed designed for a conversation rather than a drowning. Up to the drowning, Cole's planning had been exquisitely managed. He handled the matter of the potential heir by dispatching Raddice to make sure there was no baby. All reports from

Harlem indicated his success in that assignment. He talked with and had notes from his conversations with families whose daughters his cousin had traumatized. He overcame their objections and worry assuring them their confidentiality agreements and settlements with Thayer Corporation would never be breached—him being a Thayer himself. He had testimony to prove his cousin was not a mere playboy (as Aunt Phee would have it), but that he was brutal and vicious. Later, while trying *not* to remember what had happened out on the lake, Cole wondered how much his own anger over what he'd learned might be some measure of explanation for his inaction. Of course, he wanted the corporation's leadership. But wasn't he also acting out of some sense of responsibility to what he'd learned?

Cole placed the boat at the water's edge the evening before and lured his cousin there under the premise of their talking through strategy for the meeting that afternoon when the family would name the new executive vice president, a position that was effectively CEO-in-waiting for when the head of the clan turned seventy-two and his term contractually concluded. Whomever they named would become the Thayer Corporation's next in line. Cole had two lists in his pocket. One that speculated how the votes would align, whose vote was certain, and who might need to be persuaded, and another that annotated each indiscretion Edward had been involved with—at least the ones he knew about—since they were kids. That was Adelaide's idea. She suggested some of the elders might need reminding before the votes were cast, and he planned to assist their recollection by showing them the paper. He didn't even need to say anything, just unfold the sheet and tell them, "Of course, there are these matters which might become as much a pattern for the future as they have been in the past." He would assure the family that he would be of assistance, whatever they decided. But the phrasing he practiced was key. "I'll do whatever I can to protect the family from anything that might harm us." That would be enough, Adelaide assured him. So he brought the paper along to show his cousin in case it could help with the decision he hoped Edward would make on his own, without unnecessary persuasion. Most of the "situations" were unknown to the board, and he was sure Edward would want to keep it that way. Especially the ones with the grade-school girls. And the boys. The stray animals he tortured or mutilated could be explained away with the too frequently used, and not frequently enough interrogated, "boys will be boys." He was going to promise to sink the list (he brought a stone and some twine and planned how he would dramatically wrap it around the rock, tie it, and then give it to his cousin to toss overboard). But first he'd get Edward's assurance to voluntarily step aside and allow Cole's name to be the only one put forward as the executive vice president. There were no confidential votes on the board, so everyone's choice would be apparent. Especially because Aunt Phee was swayed by the tradition attached to the line of succession (she thought it bespoke a model of European stability), it was important for Cole to demonstrate how following that tradition might not lead to the kind of stability she imagined. It would be even better if Edward Jr. explained that he backed the appointment of his cousin.

Cole's plan worked only because Edward was concerned enough about the outcome of the vote to agree to his cousin's proposal to talk. But this was the last place he wanted to be. Unlike the rest of the clan, he hated being on the water. There was too little control, and he liked his ground stable and fixed. But his cousin's interest in a conversation betrayed what he thought was some lack of surety in the outcome he wanted. So in fact, he was as anxious as Cole about the vote scheduled for late that afternoon. Edward reasoned that a public performance of his good nature couldn't hurt. He looked back toward the house. Cole was right. A group was gathered at the railing. More were inside, at the long row of windows that looked out toward the water. Cole noticed as well. "See? They're right there, eyes glued on us." He gave his family a friendly wave. "Hah," he said to Edward. "Pleased as punch to see us arm in arm, behaving like cousins should even when the stakes are high for both of us. It will work to our advantage—you'll see. Our conduct will give them confidence that we are planning to behave in the best traditions of kin. Mark my word! Being buddies just before the vote will bode well for the outcome." Of course, each had a different outcome in mind; but that fixed it. Edward was already practiced in manipulating his family's perceptions of him. This would be an ideal time for theater.

The vote would go for one of the two of them. And the outcome was not certain. No one was aware enough of Edward's dark side, and nobody held something as inconsequential as a dalliance with the colored help over him. In fact, they were used to exercising their ability to attend to matters that could tarnish the family's reputation. The family ledgers attested to the appropriate management of the most recent situation, and the pattern of their wealth being used to maintain the family's stature was a given.

On the other hand, Cole was respected but eager. He was clearly more settled than his cousin. Adelaide's new baby was the center of attention, and his maturity was demonstrably more developed than Edward's. But it also could be suggested that there was something slightly unbecoming in his eagerness. He was sometimes overly solicitous. And although, as Aunt Phee indicated, Edward Jr. was "so much more incautious," she fondly admitted that his "unpredictable shenanigans" sometimes left her a bit unsettled.

"He makes his mother wonder if we'll ever get to be elderly," Edward Sr. replied. "Or at least, reach the kind of dignity that keeps you the beauty of the family."

"Hah! I know flattery when I hear it. And it becomes you!" Aunt Ophelia patted his hand. "It becomes you and it shall become that young son of yours."

"From your lips, dearest Phee . . . from your lips."

THE LAST ANYONE SAW BOTH COUSINS WAS AS THE CANOE TURNED east just outside of the cove. Cole manned the oars, and it was noted how splendidly the two modeled the conduct the family cherished. It was a great show.

The dark, cold water stretched out before them, and the morning fog had not quite lifted from the still surface. A loon's long limber cry stretched out across the bay. Unnerved, Edward nearly backed out, but Cole reminded him of the kin watching from the veranda. Their cousins pointed and waved, remarking that they were glad to be inside even though the lake looked perfectly beguiling. He rowed steady and straight until they were well past the bend. Once the show was no longer necessary, he was content to let the boat drift while the two ignored the silence that had settled around them. They really had nothing much in common and little to say to each other. The trip was merely for display, and Cole was trying to decide how to introduce the subject neither of them thought was an open discussion. Edward grew preoccupied and fidgety. He missed those youthful days with Cole when the two of them would just take off for some adventure without telling anyone where they were headed. The challenge of making their way back to the summerhouse just before daybreak, with him most often too drunk to remember their nighttime antics, was good fun. Edward didn't recall how frequently those were times when Cole had to save him from some folly that would turn out to be harmful to the family. And he never guessed that Cole had been keeping track and even had a list of the worst of those moments. When they were very young, it was small things, like tugging a sack that held a just-whelped pup from his cousin's hands before he dropped it into the stream that ran behind their house. It got more serious when they were older. He'd nearly beaten a classmate unconscious when their lacrosse team lost the finals. His cousin pulled him off the kid before he finished the beat-down. Edward felt safe with Cole—he not only protected him, but he felt as if he could maintain better control over himself when his cousin was around. Cole was a check on his going too far. He wanted those days back. Especially because his dark moods came with more frequency, and sometimes he didn't even remember what he had done, or to whom. If Cole were around more often, he'd feel safer. He longed for that feeling again. While he slowly regained some sense of the present, he also noticed they had drifted into deep waters. Something was off.

The canoe glided silently toward the middle of the lake, where it was too deep for the water lilies that had hugged the shore or the bulrushes that pierced through the dark foliage. Edward tried to shrug away his sense of discomfiture. But then his cousin—in his own moment of reverie and noticing a slight eddying off to their right, remembered a game from their youth. Cole whispered—which made it seem more threatening and ominous—"Hey! Look there! Is that the creature?"

It was a local legend. Every summer camper knew to look for it, and more than one giggling canoe of screaming campers fell overboard during each camp session, buoyed by life jackets and boys counting on a quick grab of shrieking girls whom they rushed to rescue. The seniors waited until they were at the lake's center before they rehearsed the legendary story of the creature said to be lurking at its depths. They all knew it was a fabrication designed as a part of the relentless hazing that camp first-years endured. As soon as the story was told, somebody pointed and someone else screamed and inevitably the canoe tipped. It was a ritual.

Until that moment, both cousins were preoccupied with the afternoon's deliberations and the performance they were enacting for their elders. Edward had forgotten the legend. He'd long ago repressed the terror of his own dumping into the lake and how his fear and panic—even though he had on the requisite camp life jacket—was overpowering. He stayed away from the lake the rest of that summer and never returned to camp.

But Cole's playful (maybe) whisper brought the panic from his youth back with extraordinary intensity. Edward instinctively and incautiously jumped up from his seat. Of course this sudden movement unsteadied the boat, and this time there was no life preserver wrapped across his chest. The canoe tipped. They both tumbled overboard, dumped into the deepest part of Greenwood Lake. Cole, who was an expert swimmer, easily made his way back to the canoe and held on to the side opposite from his cousin's desperate flailing. Edward was still several feet away from the boat's overturned edge pitifully wailing for his cousin's help. From the shore, it sounded no different from a loon's early morning cry. But Cole was on the other side of the canoe, and somehow—perhaps because of the panic and trauma of the moment, but perhaps not—found himself pulling it away from his cousin even while he called Edward's name. Later, remembering the sequence of events, he had no recollection that he was at all deliberate in the way he pulled the canoe away rather than toward Edward's panicked thrashing.

Cole called his cousin's name. But very quickly he was already too far away from where Edward gurgled and gulped, trying desperately but ultimately unsuccessfully to keep his head above water. He slipped beneath the surface. And when the waters closed quietly over the place where he'd fought desperately to stay aloft, Cole's plaintive cry lingered until a distant bird called across the lake and one echo was like the other until they faded into the void.

Cole broke down telling and retelling the story. He explained how the oars slipped away. How he tried to hold on to his cousin and swim toward shore but how Edward panicked and nearly pulled them both down. At least it might have happened that way if he'd at least attempted to make it to where Edward thrashed at the water in his useless struggle to stay afloat.

He shuddered and gulped the brandy that Hobart handed to him. Even his man's usual composure was shaken by the tragedy. His parents, cousins, uncles, and aunts clustered around him. The downstairs help came up and gathered outside the morning room, wiping tears with tea towels and the edges of their aprons. Adelaide sobbed into her husband's shoulder, and Enid and Edward Sr. clutched each other with a relief they didn't dare voice. But later each would say to the other, *Well, it's over.*

Their worries about the next phone call, the next visitor, the next accusation, had come to an end. They would recover their son's body and then bury him and let him find a peace that was nowhere near the destiny that was more likely had he lived. Without this tragedy they would have spent their days waiting for word of whatever terror would eventually and inevitably come to their door. So for those who kept a record (but no one did), Chloe Antonia Mosby's father drowned before the end of her first year.

MOTHERS DO BIRTHS AND, QUIET AS IT'S KEPT, MOTHERS DO THE BURIALS as well. So Enid Thayer planned a service that would be intimate and understated. There was no stifled mourning at the church, no exquisitely bejeweled urns swinging from the Right Reverend's hands and threading trails of holy smoke down the aisle. There was no ceremonial sitting, praying, standing, and sitting again. She had had enough. Hers had been a ritual of worry—when he wasn't home, when there was a delivery, when one of the cars went missing, when the help asked to talk with her privately about an issue concerning the young master. Their parish priest presided over the graveside service rather than the bishop, who had, with ceremonial insistence given the family's social standing and wealth, generously "suggested" his availability. But only close family attended. Its quiet intimacy would be the counterweight to her son's complicated life. There had been enough excess attached to her beautiful boy. The one who grasped her fingers and then didn't. The one who fell into her arms giggling or whimpering and then the one who avoided her embrace and her lingering mother-eye. Her beloved boy had gone missing long before this moment. It frightened her to have seen his eyes emptied out when he spoke to her. There had already been enough, and certainly too much. The fear that displaced his embrace fell away to grief. But this was a grief that was knowable and, perhaps, might even—eventually—be managed. Perhaps.

She was grateful when the priest spoke his full name. *"Edward Sanders Thayer Jr."*; and then when he said, *"Beloved son of Edward Sanders Sr. and Enid Barfield Thayer."* She nearly expected someone to object when he said "beloved," as if someone knew the fear and hurt she lived with and refused or was unable to see that he was loved. But he was. And despite the other truths, there were no objections. The words were soothing. They placed her child into a ritual and lifted him into a ceremony

156

that, goodness knows, may have been enough to give her some peace and maybe him as well. How tortured he must have been living with the threat of himself. Whenever the spirit of the child she had loved and nurtured and found her joy in might have surfaced—as it could have at any point in the midst of his cycle of destruction—whenever it looked out from her son's eyes and wondered at the evil he had wrought, what grief it must have borne to discover the boy he had been replaced by a man who was hurtful and dangerous and empty-eyed.

"We are offered the sure and certain hope of resurrection." His mother sighed. "And the fullness and awareness of the beauty and presence of God." Her eyes filled. She wanted this promise of rest for herself and her boy. The priest's assurance that "neither death, nor life, nor angels, nor rulers, nor things to come, nor powers, nor height, nor depth, nor anything else in all creation will be able to separate us . . ." would be enough, Enid thought. *Come for him now,* she dared. *Say what he did, tell what he planned, share whatever you want of what he imagined. Unveil all the dark things.* She looked up defiantly, as if someone spoke back. *It is finished.* She nearly wanted to thank Cole for not saving him, but that would seem peculiar. "In your mercy defend us from all perils and dangers of this night." It was exactly the shield she needed. She was certain the words were directed only to her. The rest of the family, gathered round her, faded away. Even though the priest's head was bowed over the mahogany casket of her son and even though there was now some quiet weeping amongst the family—including Cole, who looked dazed (or was he drunk?)—the priest's words belonged to her. She gazed around the circle of family, and her gaze settled on the shrouded, gaunt figure of Aunt Phee. *Why, this must be what grief-stricken looks like,* she thought. *Do I look this way? Should I?* Edward had been Ophelia's favorite. *Poor Phee,* she thought. *This is like losing a child.* She heard her thoughts and almost laughed aloud with the irony. *This was a child! Hers. And now here I am having lost him.* People heard her stifling her laugh and thought she was overcome. Her husband took her hand in his and grasped it tightly. Despite her sharp grief, Enid discovered how loss could be a saving grace.

After a suitable period passed, to respect the family's loss, there was sufficient notice, in both the business pages and the society columns (at Adelaide Thayer's urging), of Cole Thayer's appointment as executive vice president of the Thayer Corporation.

20

How We Doin?

AS IF IT WERE A DYING, WHICH AT FIRST REACHED WIDE AND DEEP WITH the grievous unfairness of it all but eventually and inevitably settled back into familiar and even anticipated sorrows, little Chloe Mosby's disappearing found its place among the quotidian. The police filed away the kidnapping as unsolved, and Harlem's days ambled on with their complications and requisites, workaday complaints, and back-and-forth banter. Clothes were squeezed, shaken, and with just a sliver of sun hung out on lines that ran from window to window, tracing webs of kin and necessity. Children stopped at Chasen's for candy, their mothers stayed awhile looking over dry goods and finding community. Church bells called some, warned others. Preachers shared the word, morticians presided over rites both posh and ordinary, and Harlem went on about its days leaving the mystery of the missing child to those most concerned. After a while, in fact, after not too long at all, those numbers—once swollen with the curious, the empathetic, those who stood in need of a project or who could offer some rationed relief—slowly fell away, their own necessities taking precedence. The ones who cared most about little Chloe found private ways to grieve her absence. Building neighbors left an occasional prayer card or a pie, but mostly found themselves waiting to hear Mrs. Mosby shut her door, counting on her absence from the stairwell before they ventured in or out. It was awkward to run into her and difficult to hear as well as to ask.

Any news?

No. No news.

Okay, then. Y'all have a good day now.

She never asked how that was supposed to happen given what she'd said. But DeLilah was good at not expecting or wanting more. And too, she had a new job with one of the uplift ladies up in Hamilton Heights who took her on as their household help. Vera Scott and Earlene Kinsdale commended her to the group, and noted that her having worked for uptown white folks was enough in way of commendation and that employment clearly mitigated her family situation. Almost nobody saw Selma anymore. The last time they had, right after Chloe went missing, she wasn't fit company for anybody, not even herself.

Lilah ought to send that girl away.

Somebody else need to be taking care of that kind of tilted.

She need to find the Lord.

No. What she need is to find her baby girl. That will go a long ways to fixing her spirit.

She was broke before . . .

Hush! Here come the mama.

Which?

Some said that the family had already lost one, two if you count her boy June Bug.

Only so much leave-taking folks can manage 'fore they take leave of they own selves.

Even the news reporters went away. In fact, they were the first to leave, followed by the downtown detectives, then the church clubs and social welfare ladies whose calendars were already packed with uplift activities decided on earlier in the season. Eventually the only one who kept track of the case was Officer Weldon Thomas, who knew personally how easily Harlem's troubles fell away from the police investigation docket unless somebody did something to the white folks who populated Harlem at night, wandering in and out, usually looking for something exotic, something illegal, or both.

Doris sat with Lilah Mosby on the day that the baby's daddy died and read about the boating accident in the news. "This one any kin to your Manhattan white folks, Lilah?"—she asked, when she read the headlines. EDWARD THAYER, DEAD AT AGE 26, HEIR OF REAL ESTATE MAGNATES.

"Ummm-hmm. Sure could be. Shame." She shook her head and went back to her sewing. The fact was that she thought very little about them. And the same was true for the family who had put both Mosby women out of their minds fully dedicated now to the complex grief they experienced in mourning their son. Selma seemed to have forgotten she ever had had a baby to begin with. Out of sight, out of mind.

"She full gone?"

"Not full," Lilah replied. "But it do seem like she put up some kinda curtain that lays between her and anything that hurt." Lilah meant that she was included in that, but did not say so.

"You right. It seems she might have got herself too much hurt for love to stand like it should."

Lilah patted her friend's hands. "But I thanks you for asking. Sometimes feels like Selma not the only one who put my grandbaby out their minds."

"Girl, it ain't for want of wanting to care. Sometimes caring feels like a threat instead of a thoughtfulness. You got to be forgiving of folks." Doris's caution was right but it rubbed.

"Seems like I spend my days making ways for forgiving." A long harsh cough interrupted and instead of finishing she held the teacup—the one with violets twisted across the rim. Today, with the wear across the rim, it looked more like thorns or knotted twigs instead of a gracefully braided vine. She hoped its warmth would take on her chill.

While others unkindly dropped any association with the family, worried that the Mosbys' misfortunes would cross some kind of unspoken barrier and infect their own, others simply decided that they just weren't appropriately exemplary of the uplift doctrine that was so vital to their new Negro lives.

But Doris was different. She had been Lilah's friend since the Mosbys first came to Harlem. She was resourceful, and single, so there were no family obligations that stood in the way of her being available to anyone with need. When she first came to Harlem, she'd had a lady friend who also died with the flu. It made her understanding of the progress of Iredell's illness and its potential; but it also left her vulnerable to gossip about exactly what kind of friend the lady had been. Lilah never had time for any nonsense about people loving each other, and when she saw Nella's picture in Doris's apartment, she offered her condolences and remarked as to how beautiful she was. It was one of those sepia photographs where just the cheeks and lips were colored with a matte blush. The way she was turned, slightly to the side and looking back over her shoulder—like a good-bye, Doris always thought. Because her hair was pulled back in a smooth chignon, her eyes and smile were more prominent. The day that Lilah said she looked like "loving kindness," after coming to understand that the two had been very special friends, made Doris tear up and it settled their friendship.

Doris knew the city's seasons. She had weathered them and learned their patterns. She knew to brace for the cold and wind, how to stuff windowsills with newspaper, and even to anticipate the in-between of sleet and spring's maddening delay. Still, there were days when she plain forgot the sun and the way its brilliance left its glow, even when her days would attach to nothing but sorrow. When it came, slipping through the last of winter's dim chill, she reached for its warmth like the rest of folks who came from down home and who needed the light. She was young when she rode up from Richmond and totally alone except for the company of the knowledge she had that made her as vulnerable as it made her special. The girl she left back home went on and got married and took herself away from the temptation of their meetings, the gentle exploration of each other, skin to skin, brown girl to brown girl, short breaths and deep sighs. She had no idea except that she wanted more. When they were discovered, Doris was given terms of when and how quickly to get gone. Even her own parents would not save her from the threat. In fact, they were a party to it, as embarrassed and outdone by the wicked peculiarity of their child as the church elders. They had boy children to think of and protect. Their girl was expendable. So when Doris boarded the train north, she knew little more than her difference was as much about desire as it was desperation. She was saved from the hatefulness that surrounded her leave-taking because after she arrived, and for a brief season before the influenza and then the consumption ravaged the city, there was Nella, an older woman who took her in and helped her to know that exact "loving kindness" Lilah guessed at looking at the picture she left on the mantel. Doris's resolve and understanding and that spring and summer and part of an autumn with Nella gave her a way to know and then protect herself that was vital. She watched others get claimed into all sorts of missions and ministries, causes and collaborations. But Nella taught her to focus on her own intentions and that she deserved as much as anyone to be safe and cared for. Too many were left with doubts. She got left with clarity. So, in ways that helped the Mosbys, Doris was experienced enough with love and loss and making do to show the new family how to navigate the city, how to find work, and how to find a way to make a home in the tiny kitchenette. She walked DeLilah and her boy down to where the five-and-dime was, showed them where to leave the waste, how to arrange a bed near the stove. ("It's a pallet, roll it up and stuff it behind the coal bin during the day, and roll it back out at night for your boy.") She knew to expect the iceman in summer and the coal wagon in winter, and told Lilah to have Percy out there to catch stray pieces of coal when the horse pulled away, and which vendor to buy from and which to pass on. She told them the Chasens were good people and that Jesus didn't save everyone quite the same way and which church— if that was your intent—would cater to your spirit more than earn you a call from ladies working their way through the uplift registry. Doris was there when Iredell got sick and when he died—and when Lilah's morning sickness became apparent, she knew how to mix the sassafras root into a tea, where to find Lady Professor, who would know the right salve to rub across her belly, and how to tell her new friend: "It's a girl. You carrying high." Doris brought home to Harlem all the things her Gran'mam would have been able to notice if they had never left Sedalia. Lilah nestled easily into her available care.

Lilah named the baby girl Selma Althea and raised her with a deliberate caution. June Bug had already found a life in the streets, doing God knows what, and she was determined Selma would be safe from whatever risks were so appealing to her brother.

After Chloe went missing, and after the rest of the neighbors left her to their gossip rather than their generosity, and the church folks got more to talking about her wrongs than her rights, Doris continued to come by, sit at the kitchenette table, pour tea, and listen. She told Doris what her daughter had done with the white cloth, again, as if retelling that moment might be some explanation. Doris listened patiently, as she did each time Lilah said how she remembered that day she "come home to the white." And over and over again, Doris put her arms around her and asked what it was she could do to help. "Ain't nothing nobody can do. I got to keep on and my girl has got to find her own way back." Doris declared she would wait with her, and she tried to keep her promise.

That November morning, she asked what she'd heard from Officer Thomas about the progress of the search.

"Search?"

"For Chloe, for heaven's sake! For your grandbaby!"

Lilah twisted her teacup around so the faded violets on the edge faced outwards.

"You been down there, haven't you? You been down to ask what they have done and where they have looked and who's on the list of suspicious? Remember that white man they said was hanging around? They found him yet?"

Lilah asked her if she wanted more hot water for her tea.

"How about the baby's daddy? That whole family ought to be up under investigation if you ask me. Could it be some kinda way that they wanted the baby?"

Lilah folded the newspaper with the column reporting Edward Thayer's death and funeral services until it was letter-sized. She placed it in the tea tin alongside Percy's letters and offered to fry up some bologna for a sandwich if Doris was feeling peckish.

"Girl. What I want to know is where is your own mind?" Doris demanded. Lilah's silence seemed too deliberate and its weight was unsettling. "You gotta care about this way more than anybody else. Your Selma done lost her sense, common or otherwise (bless her broken heart and Lord have mercy), so, sweetheart, it's you what's got to pull yourself together!" Lilah placed her hands inside her apron pockets and dug into her thighs with the needles that were embedded in the seams. She slipped one out under her skirt and pressed it her into her skin, knowing there would be stains.

"Doris," she whispered back to her friend. Her voice was slow and deliberate, and she shook her head with a practiced weariness. "Doris, what you think it is I've been doing? I got more than my share of things tryin to pull me to pieces. What I'm planning is how to keep me together." Doris reached across the table and patted her arm while Lilah pressed harder into her thighs. She shook her head. "And then I get home not sure at all what it is is going to be here." She looked over to the shadow on the wall and thought it shifted.

Doris reached across the table. "I know, sweetheart," she said with a *sorry* buried in her voice. "I do know. I'm just trying to help in some kinda way." She looked across the room and tried to change the subject. "Tell me what the club ladies up to this season?" Just at that moment, Selma

163

opened the door from her mother's bedroom. The women could see her sitting quietly on the bed. She didn't come into the kitchen, and Doris's "How do, Miss Selma?" went unanswered. Almost too eagerly, and to make up for the silence Selma offered, Lilah took up Doris's query about work.

"Well, they planning a winter tea in order to choose the one to get a scholarship down to one of the colored women's colleges." Lilah shook her head thinking how all the planning the club put into the affair ended up being more work for her and the rest of the help. In fact and in some ways, working for her own people up in the Heights was more stress than her white folks were downtown.

"We got to serve the tea for the meeting where they make the choice."

"Choose how?" Doris asked.

"Well, they invite all the girls that is eligible to this tea party. The girls think it's just a 'how do' kinda affair, where folks get to know them. But for real it's a kinda test where they watch their manners and how they speak. They even add up points on everything from whether they put their napkins in their laps and which fork they use for the tea cake. I been serving the planning meetings and I know exactly how the whole thing is a setup. After dessert they gonna dismiss the girls to home, then the real meeting gets started and that's when they will add up points and vote."

"Sounds complicated."

"Well, it would be if that was the only plan." Lilah set her teacup back in the saucer. "Fact is, anyone of them can shift the numbers they come up with by adding some comment or another about any girl they choose. Some of them already got their favorites, and some others don't have a chance even though they coming to the tea thinking they do." She sucked her teeth in. "Far as I'm concerned it's just another extra workday for me. All the auxiliary ladies bring in their help to do the service."

"All y'all?"

"Every one of us that works outside of the kitchens."

"Well, I guess if that's their way." Doris was quiet for a moment, then said, "Work makes life sweet."

"Yeah, I done heard that too. And sometimes it do. Other times . . ." Lilah pulled her hands out of her pocket, the distraction having helped some, opened her palms, and gestured outwards, and Doris flinched with the thoughtlessness that seemed to edge every potential conversation.

"Well, still and all, whatever happens up in the Heights, it's this I been coming home to." She gestured over to the open door. Selma sat quietly on her mother's bed, rocking back and forth and humming the same melody over and over. Sometimes she sang it.

You know she's waiting, just anticipating . . . it makes it easier to bear . . .

Doris nodded her head with a pitiful understanding of the vigil her friend endured. She dropped her voice to a whisper.

"She stopped going out on her own?"

"Yeah. You see her out sitting the stoop sometimes." Doris nodded that she had. "And walking over by the churchyard and down the block some."

"Uh-huh."

"Well, that's about all."

"She ask after Chloe?"

"She never say much." But she thought, *. . . less after I hurt her.* "It's like nothing never happened. Not having the baby, not losing it. Nothing."

Doris tried to shift the subject back, away from their obvious grief. "Tell me about the scholarship candidates. Do I know any of them?" Lilah sighed and shook her head. She got up to turn the gas back on under the teakettle.

"Well, one, she the daughter of the minister, you know, the one that took over the Episcopal church. They doing some mighty social striving in that family."

"Episcopal? They already strived away from us Baptists. Seems like they woulda been a shoo-in for the e-light bunch."

"Yeah, but that's just it exactly. It's a cross the family have to bear."

"What is?" Doris asked. Lilah stroked the back of her hand.

"She brown," Lilah explained. "Deep brown. Prettiest girl you ever seen. Sweet speaking and lovely acting. Always 'please' and 'thank you' when I see her. Calls me Mrs. Mosby. Proper and bright as a button. Straight A's in school all the time up from grade school."

"That do sound impressive," Doris admitted. "But you already said what it is that's going to count. She brown-skinded, and with that bunch of ladies, it's gonna be what counts. It's like they worried some of it could rub off on them. If they has two candidates just the same but one look like this"—she rubbed the top of her hand—"then they gonna choose the one closer to this"—she turned her hand over and pointed at her palm. "You mark my words. Those ladies been done made up their minds. They just going through the act because it's on their social calendar. If you're bright . . ."

Lilah finished it for her. "You all right."

"Honey, hush."

Both of them looked over to the rocking girl.

As the room settled into its silence, Doris mouthed a *Lord have mercy* and meant it to cover everything that could possibly need His mercy in this family.

Lilah's silence was focused too. She was thinking about how near her daughter had come to having a chance at that scholarship. She had been smart in school, was well-spoken, was more on the cinnamon side of brown, and she would've given the clubwomen a chance to exhibit their charity. They were looking for an opportunity to prove that they had the ability to lift the race by selecting a girl who had the potential to become more like them. She'd reared Selma to be that girl. But none of it made a difference now. Her daughter didn't have the mind to know right from wrong much less what she had missed, or who was gone missing, or how she got to be gone. Doris took her leave and left DeLilah at the table sipping from a cooling cup of tea. Selma closed the bedroom door.

HOW WE DOIN?

The sunlight shifted to a slant and the shadows played with possibilities. These days she didn't even look up. She needed him so intensely that staying away from his light actually gave her more assurance than engaging it and then having to watch it fade away from her.

"All right. I'm thinking on sending Baby Girl home. She seem all right to travel sometime soon. She quiet. Not so skittish. And too, this ain't no kind of place to be with folks still waitin for news."

Home? That's what you lookin for?

"Always has been about home."

Well, you best get on with it. You don't got all the time there is.

"Don't I know it." Her cough was punctuation and evidence. "Where you goin to be is what I don't know."

Yes you do, sweetness. I'm not the puzzle. I'm the promise.

166

21

The Kidnap Book

WELDON AND LT MITCHELL SAT DOWN AND CLEARED A SPACE ON THE sofa table. Books were stacked everywhere around them. Some were on the floor—but even these were deliberately organized and carefully positioned. They lined up against the walls two rows deep—ordered from nonfiction, then how-to, and finally reference. Instruction manuals, dictionaries, and an incomplete set of encyclopedias were stacked spine out and covers down flat. Travel books took up the places on kitchen shelves where stored groceries or a stack of plates or jelly glasses might have been. He kept the necessities—a dish, a couple of mugs, the coffeepot, and a fry pan—inside the oven for the few times when he needed to cook up some rice on the stove top, or maybe fry an egg; but his rooms in Zenobia's came with plated breakfast and dinner, so he didn't spend too much time thinking about cooking for himself. The small icebox held all he needed in foodstuff—milk for his coffee, a few eggs (never more than a half dozen), a loaf of bread, and a bottle of hot sauce, in case he wanted a snack. Most of the time, he sat in Zenobia's dining room and took his meals with the other boarders and the few who managed a case quarter for dinner when there was an empty seat at her table. Which was rare.

A seat at Zenobia's was worth more than the quarter, and the few folks who'd been foolish enough to try to sell their seat for a profit learned that the permanent ban from her parlor wasn't worth the extra nickel or dime. She never changed her mind once she threw somebody out. When she figured out there were some shenanigans, she'd pull the offender into her kitchen, set him down at the table where the cobbler was cooling and where she was transferring the stew meat on top of the rice and buttering the tops of rolls, and explain to him that she knew what was up and he wasn't welcome at her table anymore. Then she'd open the back door and put them out. Invariably they stood at the window, looking plaintively at the table and fingering the extra nickel or dime they'd made by selling their seat. Didn't make any difference how long or pitifully they stood there. Nothing they could say would earn them entry again to one of the few seats available after her boarders sat down to their meals.

Since Weldon had no cause to use his rooms as a kitchen, he made it his library. When he ran out of vertical space, he piled his books on top of each other, still somehow managing to make the display look orderly and intentional. When he ran out of room there, he built shelves onto the walls. These held the more important books, as well as his boxes of files. The boxes held every detail—notes, diagrams, interviews, and sometimes photographs of each of the cases he worked through the years. Even though he was still just a beat cop and had no official reason to keep files, his notebooks were composed with absolute attention and care. Each arrest, its circumstance, the people in the crowd, the kids hanging around—at least the ones he knew (which was more than likely to be most or all of them)—what folks had said, the weather, whatever stories went alongside the event. The day somebody took the barbershop cigar boxes. Both of them—the one with the money and the one with the cigars. Or how it was the flu epidemic took the daddy and sister and that was why the mother opened herself a home for women to make their money by their own means. How she or he had been done wrong by folks at the social agency. How the husband had a woman he saw down to the boardinghouse before he came home and laid subway-muddied shoes at his family's stoop even after he had already taken them off (and everything else he wore) for her and how that was the reason a bottle got broken when the wife smacked it upside his head. Left a good size cut too. When he had time to think of it, Weldon sometimes worried that he might run out of room for his books. In the meantime, he depended on his habit of orderliness. He kept the ones on loan from the library in his

168

mother's china cabinet. He dusted them and wiped their spines as if they were as fine as the china teacups that once held precious places on the shelves. His Aunt Beulah had them now that his mother had passed. She had more memory in them than he did. He kept his bought and paid-for books (as opposed to those he simply found) on his handmade shelves—the ones with the fancy bookends that looked like globes.

Weldon was bookish, he knew it, and some time ago he embraced the appellation rather than bristled against it. The truth was that it never did him any harm and more than once gave him a way to think about things that he wouldn't have come up with on his own. So when he and LT sat down to start reviewing the case from the start, opening the boxes, pulling down his notebooks, essentially opening the full file, it looked like a mess, but he knew what every stack and pile and box was for. LT had learned enough about and from Weldon to respect his ways, and even to emulate them. Although books were never going to be his thing, he understood that this was the way his mentor worked best. Surrounded by words. In their profession, talking was important. So was listening. But reading made you special. And knowing how to extrapolate a good thought from a book was exceptional.

The rest of the force, the detectives, the special investigation and units directed to the Mosby case closed down long ago. Harlem baby missing. Unsolved case. Move along. He'd even heard folks talking about just one more juvie they wouldn't have to worry about later. Or that the mother wasn't even married—like that mattered. While he was working his beat, Weldon moved on along with them, focusing on other cases, attending to the docket and maintaining his presence in the neighborhood. But none of that meant he let this one go. He watched out in Harlem for her. And he checked in with Mrs. Mosby and Selma as often as he could. Not that either one bothered him about it. Selma stayed to herself. And Mrs. Mosby kept busy caring for her daughter (who mostly didn't require much) and her new family up in the Heights. It was clear that her body carried the weight of it. She was slow, deflated, and not given much to conversation. But still it seemed like she refused a full-on sorrow. She went to work every weekday but Thursdays, and carried on.

There was no way for Weldon to influence the precinct to be more aggressive with the investigation or even to keep it on the detective's open case files. And there was no likelihood that he would ever be on the detective force himself, or even in line for that kind of promotion. There would be another "first colored" to reach that distinction, but he knew full well that it wouldn't be him. He'd made his impact by just getting into one of the New York Police Department uniforms. And his being a successful experimental first colored cop meant there would be others. But that didn't mean the community's expectations of him could be unattended. Or that a mother's grief could go unresolved.

So he recorded Harlem's "situations" as he called them, the ones where he had been on duty and the ones where he was sought out because he knew there was a rest of the story, some shadow or subtlety, some explanation or addition that didn't seem official enough for a record but that mattered to somebody. Some were vicious crimes and killings. But there were petty thefts and suspicious fires as well. Arguments that went further than was safe. Zip gun shootings and switchblade fights. Gangs loosely formed or tightly regimented, and youngsters looking for unclassified trouble. Missing husbands, brothers, sons—some who wanted to be found, and others that didn't. Not babies though. Sure there were ones found on the steps of the colored orphanage or abandoned in alleys newborn and even earlier. Discarded, unwanted, or unable. However small or large the situation, if he was there or asked to look into it because he could get to the insides of the matter, given his "connects," Weldon recorded the details in one of the black-and-white composition books that lined the shelves he'd made for the back of his front door. With the door closed, it almost seemed as if there was nothing in his world but words and the books that held them.

Even as Harlem shaped itself into an enclave where color was both complex and simple, there was a way to know this community better than what the newspapers wrote or police files contained or agency records documented. Weldon heard his mother's voice in his head finishing his thought "you shall know them." *By their deeds,* Susan Thomas would have said. Her voice stayed in his head, and the lessons she taught echoed when he recorded the deeds with storied explanations. His own reading told him that how you shaped the words mattered, and he was determined to give a shape to Harlem that would be different from official records kept in anybody's files. Instead, as he composed them, they became stories. How else would someone know the complexities behind their names? That the Scotts were musical and how the Nunleys made sure everybody knew something about science. How the DeBerry, Childers, and Stallings families stayed busy with school. How the Warrens, Shockleys, and Washingtons sent their children down to Birmingham every summer and shared a Green Book between them for the road trip. The aspirations of the Armstrongs, Bennetts, and Johnsons. And how being a storefront preacher narrowed the potential of the Baldwins and limited the congregation to an upper room for the Howards. The Knights (the name not the brotherhood) and the Wards and Strasners were the ones who stayed looking for work, and when ice covered the girders, they went underground, blasting their way through the city, making ways and means for the trains. The Wallaces and Currys governed Harlem's churches, and some established themselves first as its undertakers before the profession grew more established. They became morticians and funeral directors, men with suits and titles that matched the evolving pageantry. Nearly everybody— official or not—had a listing in the index of Harlem that Weldon kept filed. It included baptisms and first Communions. Those funeralized from the parlor on St. Nicholas or on the program to recite Easter or children's day poems at the church. Suspended from school or placed on its honor rolls. Selected to become an NWA debutante or being on the list to get in line at the soup kitchen. But Weldon's notebooks did not merely collect this information as if it was data. His books composed their stories. How there was a great Aunt Sis or Uncle Son who could step in and might could take over when a household fell apart. Which families might have extra resources and who had none. His records told the precipitating event, from school-yard thefts to parade-route accidents, and what would soon be the second Harlem riot. The streets were already feeling the tensions that would explode into that moment. And the fact was, most folks had never fully recovered from the emotions that led to the 1935 riot. Officer Thomas filled in the in-between, the gaps as to who they were and how they came to be and where they had people down home that might be called in to take a straying youngster or be the address where they sent the body that wanted to be buried back home. What relations were claimed and which ones ought to be. His composition books were neatly indexed with a catalogue of cards that rivaled the library's stacks. He took down the subject cards as often as he used the last-name file. So when his cadet got settled and had his notebook ready, Weldon pulled out a fresh composition book. He'd already written "The Kidnap Book" on the place where it said "name" and "subject." He laid it open in front of them. "Where you want to start?" he asked LT.

"It's New Year's. So let's start like it's a new beginning. Everything fresh."

"Makes sense to me. And if that's what we going to do, I'ma need some fresh coffee." Weldon pulled the scoop from the Maxwell can and leveled several into the basket. He struck a match to light the gas under the percolator, and LT started with the first book. Weldon waited for him to take the lead.

22

Let the Dead Bury Their Dead

THE TWO MEN THUMBED THROUGH THE BOOKS, STACKING SOME TO THE side, leaving others open to particular pages. LT finally broke their silence. "The daddy. I think we might should look at the baby's daddy. You always be saying these things turn out closer to the family than folks like to think. But then ..."

"Then what?" Weldon asked as he flipped through the pages.

"Let me go to the other hand. So, on the other hand ... if we was to try that, there wasn't no daddy to speak on. Selma never told. And nobody never stepped up to say he's the one."

"But why would it help us to know?" Weldon was teaching as much as he was rethinking the whole case himself. How could knowing about the daddy help? He was wondering the same thing, but maybe the boy had an angle he couldn't figure out.

"Because what if it's not about money? Then what we would be thinking on is who would do a kidnapping of a baby in a family with no money when they didn't have no plan to charge for getting it back. What's the motive?"

"Sounds like you taking your 'motive' direction from that chapter in the po-lice manual." Weldon had been encouraged until he asked the question that way. Manuals usually produced the kinds of answers the manuals had already considered. LT's shoulders slumped. He'd been eager to contribute to Weldon's investigations and felt special being included. Weldon noticed his disappointment. He hadn't intended to dampen his enthusiasm as much as encourage him to be a more independent thinker, so he tried to smooth over his critique. "But . . . Well, that's okay. Long as you understand that sometimes you got to go outside a book. Tell me what the daddy would . . . ?"

"Man, I don't know. But it got me thinking about why it is that nobody never sent a note. In the community meeting, that's the first thing folks asked after. Lindbergh, he got a note. So . . ."

"We ain't folks, son. We the police. That meeting was as much for them to get their feelings out so they wouldn't fester . . ."

"Say what?"

"*Fester.* Look it up. Dictionary on the top of that stack to the right of the radiator. Or in this book of poems. One of our Harlem poets got a poem about it: 'Fester like a sore—and then run?'"

"Oh, that's nasty." LT went for the dictionary. But then he paused and said, "You got poetry books up in here?" Before Weldon could point him to that section where he kept poetry and long fiction (he wasn't much for drama), he was off on another track. "But . . . but I take your point." He had the dictionary but hadn't opened it yet. "See, what it makes me think of is who would've wanted a baby instead of who was after a bundle of bills like that what was dropped off for the Lindbergh baby. So maybe we think about a daddy because the motive, ummm . . . I mean whatever reasons there might be that could go into a baby snatching could change. Maybe we didn't never see a note because this is about a daddy that wanted his baby and so he took it. No charge. And the daddy, being as he just wanted his baby, there wasn't never a need for a Lindbergh note."

Weldon cautioned his protégé. "You keep on attaching another case into this one. We're sitting here trying to start clean. You can't start with these two things connected. If you do that kind of thinking, we never get to examine them independently. It has to come together organically . . ." He anticipated LT's quizzical look. "Which means, if they come together natural, it's the circumstance that leads one toward the other. But we can't put them together without reason to do so. Got to be some evidence that makes us go one way rather than another."

LT put the dictionary aside, but left a sheet of notepaper on the page with the guide words "fervid" and "feud." He thumbed through Weldon's stack of papers and leafed through the notebooks that carried the family stories. A photograph of Selma fell out. "This evidence?" he asked.

Weldon reached for the image, remembering the day back in the fall when he took it. He had the camera because he'd been assigned to take pictures of the store window that was smashed up the night before. Harlem was tense and oddly aggravated. Folks couldn't tell an important event from happenstance, and the precinct, wary of the mood, wanted to make sure they documented everything. He turned the pictures he took over to the precinct but kept the photograph of Selma Mosby for his own files. She was sitting on a bench at the edge of the park. The newspaper with the Lindbergh story on the front page was spread out on her lap, and she was bent over it, her finger tracing across the image of the Lindbergh family. Given that she looked to be reading a newspaper from nearly six months back—and what kind of sense did that make?—Weldon snapped the picture to remind him of how it looked as if Miss Selma was separated from whatever day or season it was. He'd kept his own copy of the *Times'* story that Selma was reading. But it wasn't until he filed the two—the newspaper's front-page story and his photograph—that he noticed how Selma was dressed as near to exactly like Mrs. Lindbergh as she could be. The circle of plastic pearlescent snap-it beads around her neck resembled the pearls that Mrs. Lindbergh wore. A patterned scarf tied in a loose bow draped in gentle folds that matched the modest neckline of Mrs. Lindbergh's dress. Selma wore a scarf as well, but hers just fell loosely from her neck and could have easily fallen off since one edge was hanging way lower than the other. Selma's scarf was obviously too small (it was more like a handkerchief than a scarf) to form the carefully managed accessory Mrs. Lindbergh wore. However, her effort did look enough like the photograph to invite a comparison. The dead giveaway that she was trying to look like Mrs. Lindbergh was Selma's hat. The newspaper photo showed the baby's mother wearing a small cloche. Delicate white blossoms trailed from her hat's brim. The clutch of flowers pinned to Selma's felt hat were wilted and looked as if they'd come from somebody's garden and missed being there. In any case, they were a gross caricature of the perfectly shaped florets that garnished Mrs. Lindbergh's headpiece. Weldon folded his copy of the Lindbergh news article and clipped it to the back of his photograph so that he'd have a reminder of how Selma had gone and dressed herself to look like Mrs. Lindbergh. He flipped it from one side to the other, looking first at the article and then the photograph. Finally, he asked LT what he thought.

Neither knew that Selma carried a worn copy of the very same newspaper photograph of Mrs. Lindbergh, the babies' grandmothers, and the missing baby. She'd kept the article in her purse, meticulously folded over so many times over that the creases threatened to tear the edges. It was the front page from the news that appeared the day that Selma realized she was pregnant and the newsboy in front of Chasen's shouted out the breaking story. But it wasn't the announced kidnapping that captured Selma's imagination. It was the generational circling of mothers around the baby. Mrs. Lindbergh seemed to be sitting on the edge of a chair as she reached down to hold on to her baby's hand. A woman who looked very much like her but was obviously more mature than the young mother stood beside her daughter and looked over the shoulder of a distinguished, gray-haired woman—likely the baby's great-grandmother—who held the laughing baby on her lap. It was their implicit protection and attention that Selma kept folded into her purse. It was their caring embrace that she slid down into its inside pocket.

LT unclipped the newspaper from the photograph and laid them out on the table, side by side. After a while he said: "Look like she copying off a woman whose baby is dead." Weldon looked over at LT with some puzzlement. He would've said the first part about copying himself, but when LT added the "whose baby is dead," the association gave him pause.

"Excuse me?"

"Well, she gone and put herself in this Lindbergh lady's situation even though that lady's baby is dead. Damn! That's the last connection I'd be wanting! Feels creepy. Back then, and even now, everybody be hoping that there was some kinda way that Baby Chloe gonna turn up. And there she go dressing up to look like a baby widow."

"Well, not widow. Far as I know there's no kinda word for a mother whose baby died. Or a daddy for that matter. But you right. Most folks in that kind of circumstance would want to be hopeful. And this picture, at least given how things turned out . . ." Weldon shook his head remembering. "This picture seems to look like she's in mourning. Only difference is that Mrs. Lindy got on this flower-print dress and here's Selma all done up in black. And far as we know, that could be a difference she went on and chose to make." LT nodded his head in agreement. "But, then again . . ." He opened his notebook and readied himself to take down Weldon's thoughts. It was clear they were still in formation. "Well, then again . . ." He took the picture and turned it back from the newspaper side to the side with the photograph of Selma. "Seems like we might want to consider that even though we say she's looking like Mrs. Lindbergh, it could be that Miss Selma's already clear on what happened. Like what you said—she's looking like a mother whose baby is dead. She's taking after that lady for a reason. And if so, we might want to know what it was that could lead her to one conclusion rather than another?"

"You mean whether her baby be missing or is her baby dead like the Lindbergh baby?"

"Well, without the comparison. But yes."

"Damn," the younger cop said, blowing over the rim of his hot coffee. "We already knew she kinda tilted. But if she know that, seem like the next step is if she knows what happened to her little girl and we don't, then we got to consider has she done something to her own baby?"

"Well, the least it can do is take us back to the inside of the family instead of going outside it." He tapped his finger on Selma's photograph. "Miss Selma's always been our principal, and maybe she's always been our problem as well."

"How's that?"

"Well, as to the principal, she's still our primary connection to the baby. But being like she is, we can't depend on her word being any more steady than her behavior."

"Except . . ."

"Except what?" Weldon was still flipping the photograph back and forth, from the newsprint image of Mrs. Lindbergh to Selma Mosby. LT focused him otherwise.

"Well, look right here." LT reached for the book that recorded notes from their interviews. He pointed to a line in the notebook. "See right here where I asked her whether she had put Chloe into one of those little dresses she got when the baby was born? Remember I interviewed her right after I got them back home. You was still at the store. So this from my notes. I got what she said right here." LT read from the page he'd smoothed down. "She said: 'Mama did. Mama put her clothes on her that morning.'"

"Okay . . . ?"

"Well, how come she said that instead of answering what I asked her? I was just trying to get a detail that might help in the search. Seems like an easy-enough question to answer straight on. But she didn't. And . . ."

"Write that down. You're right. It's clearly a deflection."

"A what?"

"Just write it down." The two spent the rest of the evening plowing through their notes, reading over the early interrogations, and matching up what they thought then to what they were beginning to understand.

IF OFFICER THOMAS HAD STAYED A BIT LONGER WITH HIS "WITNESS Interviews" section of his composition book, perhaps he and LT would have focused more on the white man, Ned Raddice. Both of them had taken notice he was there. LT saw him in the room at the community meeting, and Weldon noted him as being outside of the grocer's on the morning of the baby's disappearance. But there was nothing in the notes that indicated either of them had made that connection—that the "white man" outside the grocery was the same person with his hat on in the community meeting. If they had discussed it, they surely would have figured out the connection—the descriptions were close enough. And although that could have been an important connection, frankly, even their failure to put the two together wouldn't have done any good. The only talking Raddice ever did was to Thayer, when he assured the new chief executive-in-waiting that the matter had been handled, as requested, and he received the promised hefty sum for making the issue disappear. Easiest bucks he'd ever earned, Raddice later told his wife. If any of the police had bothered to track him down, there could have been more of an interrogation than the "asked and answered" he faced from Cole Thayer. But since the man never wanted to know more than necessary, Raddice never had a reason to explain why he didn't even need to snatch the baby and take her to Buffalo, because there was no baby in the perambulator ready for him to snatch. He'd certainly tried when the girl went into the store. He was fully ready to carry out the heist. Except when he crossed the street to take the kid and reached down into the buggy, it was empty. At first, Raddice just stood there puzzled. But then the baby's mother and the shopkeeper's wife came out to look inside the carriage, and when all hell broke out, he joined the crowd that formed and, like everyone else, waited around hoping to get some idea of what happened.

One thing was certain. She'd never be sheltered in Mount St. Joe's like he and Juanita had planned. He simply shrugged when Juanita asked where was the baby, hoping he hadn't messed it up again. *At that point, it just wasn't in my interests no more. After they put it down in the station house as "kidnapped and not recovered," Mr. Cole took it like all that was my doing. At least he paid me like it was. But I didn't even get near the baby that second time. She wasn't never in the buggy when the mother went into the store. I know that for sure. I was watching the whole time. She walked up to Chasen's with that thing already empty. Which to my mind means she's way past finding alive. Shame. But . . . you never know with these folks.*

As far as his thoughts on the matter, the girl did away with her own kid, likely leaving it in one of those fresh graves she had so much fondness for in the church cemetery. By the time anybody found her, it would be an almost certainty that she'd be in no better shape than the Lindbergh baby, although this one probably got more buried than Lindbergh's kid, given that Selma had a habit of digging around the churchyard flowers and poking in the dirt. And if she was that demented to do in her own kid, it just proved what folks said about the coloreds. No values. Like it says in the good book: *Let the dead bury their dead . . .*

INSTEAD OF FOCUSING ON THE LIST OF PEOPLE WHO GATHERED AT Chasen's and then at the community meeting, or the white man who'd showed up in both places, Weldon pulled his chair back from the table, went over to the stovetop, and pulled the percolator basket out of the coffeepot. He laid it in the sink and replaced the top, adjusting the small glass knob on top so it wouldn't topple into the cup. He poured fresh coffee into the mugs that were already leaving circled brown stains on the table. Which didn't matter, as long as his books and notebooks stayed pristine. He was still thinking about what Selma said to LT. Something about it nagged at him. LT spoke first.

"Well, how about this. When I asked her what the baby was wearing and she answered that her mama dressed her. You always say that what folks answer can be more important than what they got asked."

"And? Your point being . . . ?"

179

"Well, how come she didn't just tell me what the baby was wearing. She coulda said that as easy as she said the other thing. But she didn't."

"I already said that was a deflection."

"Yup. Looked it up. So now we need to know how come she deflected? She all up in her feelings that day 'cause her baby gone, but she's got sense enough to . . ." He looked down at the dictionary to find the root word. "Sense enough to deflect?" This time, LT interrupted Weldon's attempted response. He held up his hand. "Man, that was rhetorical. I mean, That was rhetorical . . . sir." Weldon couldn't help but smile. The boy had come a long way in being able to think through the implications of a question. Even his own. "What I'm trying to say is what if she couldn't answer it? What if her response was addled rather than strategic or something like that. What if it just sounds like it makes sense. You always saying, 'You can't make sense from nonsense so . . .'" Weldon got up so abruptly he nearly knocked over the coffee mug. LT reached out quickly to steady the cup, and Weldon moved his books over to a side table. "What if . . . what if she was already too far gone to care what happened to her own baby?"

"That's possible. But that isn't what I just thought."

"Which is . . . ?"

Weldon replied reluctantly despite the fact that his was a reasonable deduction. "What if she didn't answer because she didn't know? Look here." He pointed to his witness notes of the folks who helped to describe little Chloe. *Pink cheeks. Big dark eyes. Light hair. Look a little red-bone.* And then he flipped back and forth several pages, skimming them with his fingers. "There's nobody who described her on that day. Nobody who said they saw her from the time she left the house till she got to Chasen's. Nobody who stopped on the street to get a peep at the new baby. And you know how people are around a new baby."

"Yeah, like Mrs. Chasen, who followed her out the store to get a look."

"Exactly. But look here." He turned to the next page where his notes were about the perambulator. How it didn't fit in the door. How it was mighty sleek and fancy for a family living in a kitchenette. The speculation that it came from Mrs. Mosby's white folks. "There's a gap. And right there is what we want. We looking for exactly that. A space."

LT eyed the open notebook. "It looks to me like you filled up every line on every page." He flipped the pages. "I'm not seeing no gaps."

"Not a literal gap. A figurative one. Gaps is where the stories are." LT went quiet and Weldon started thinking about the other thing that had been bothering him. He didn't share it out loud; but it had been nagging at him for some time.

Usually when something went wrong, or was about to go wrong, he got a nudge. Like somebody or something was brushing up against him. Sometimes it could even feel like a full-on shove. As if somebody was telling him to "pay attention" without saying it aloud. The first time was when his daddy died. Sometimes it came in time for him to help keep a disaster from happening. Or a warning that one was impending. Like when Miss Olivia Frelon went out the window at the Hotel Theresa. But good outcome or not, when things like this happened, he'd ordinarily get some kind of heads-up by way of whatever this nudge was. He'd already realized—but pushed the thought aside—that he never felt a nudge around the time Chloe Mosby went missing. It worried him, but he hadn't focused on it. But there'd been no mental shove, no disquiet, nothing. No forewarning. Perhaps his premonitions had simply run their course. Maybe he'd just outgrown them. But it bothered him that something so serious had happened that, with just some kind of shove, he might could've helped before things got to where they were now. Or at least anticipated an aftermath.

LT interrupted Weldon's silence. "Go back to the time when you said she didn't know. What you mean? Didn't know like she didn't pay much attention or didn't know because . . ." Weldon had to recall what he'd been saying before he went down the road of trying to understand why he didn't feel any premonition when Chloe was taken.

"Ask me again, son, I was distracted."

"I said, What do you mean that she didn't know what the baby was wearing?"

"Oh. That. Well, one unusual, but nonetheless not unreasonable possibility is because Chloe never was in her baby buggy to begin with."

"Excuse me?"

"Miss Selma took an empty carriage to Chasen's."

"She that tilted?"

"Or that deliberate."

They both sat back to take in where their discussion had led them. Neither quite knew the next question to ask, or what statement to make. Weldon quoted aloud from his favorite detective, Conan Doyle's Sherlock

Holmes: "The little things are infinitely the most important." He was trying not to think of how his lack of premonition could be a little thing, or it could be nothing at all.

"Infinitely?"

"Like endlessly and always. Like no matter what else." He tossed the dictionary onto the sofa.

"You mean how this thing always takes us back to Lindbergh."

Weldon looked away for a moment, and then snatched the newspaper article up from the table. "Exactly! That's it exactly!"

"The Lindberghs?"

"No. Not the Lindberghs. They're the problem!" He explained how their thinking could well have been tainted by the Lindbergh event. "We may have operated under a coupling of influence that, had it not been attached, would have liberated us to direct our inquiry in different ways." LT was glazing over. "In other words, whose story are we investigating? Harlem's Lindbergh matter or little Chloe Mosby's disappearance?"

"Ummm, the second one?"

"That's correct, but I'm not sure it's evident."

"I get it. You mean if it hadn't been for Lindbergh, we might could have come up with some other ideas about what happened."

"Exactly so."

LT was wondering why he didn't just say it plain like that, but he knew that wasn't Officer Thomas's way, and he also knew it was entirely possible, even probable, that by the time he got himself through all that vocabulary, that that was how Weldon figured out what it was he wanted to say. It was sort of like the first ten minutes of a sermon by Reverend Charleston. It wasn't until a good fifteen or twenty minutes in till the pastor got the rhythm and the message together.

"You right. You right, Officer T. Folks started talking kidnapping from jump and all of us still talking kidnapping, even though we don't have nothing at all that tells us what exactly happened. The Lindbergh story ain't necessarily our story."

"Exactly, son. That's exactly right." LT looked pleased with himself and put his feet up on the table in front of him. He was careful of the coffee.

"So lemme say it plain. The mother thought the baby was dead. And stepping back from that, she was thinking that way because Miss Selma done killed her own baby."

"Boy, I took you back to a beginning, and here you went and done jumped to the end of the story. Weren't you listening to anything I said?"

"Well, okay. But if it's not been kidnapped, and if our principal didn't take out her own kid, then where's the baby?"

"Let's spend some time at the beginning. Back yourself up. If we've really separated out the Lindberghs, we're left with the family. Selma and her baby."

"Well, Miss Selma, she don't talk."

"You can back up in more ways than one. Selma's story doesn't begin with her. She's got a mother too."

"Mrs. Mosby? Nawww, man. Ain't nothing wrong with Mrs. Mosby. Sure, she's seriously particular about things. I went to school with her boy Percy when he was still around. She was always one to try and keep him home and stay with his lesson, but he wouldn't have none of it. He didn't like being left with his baby sister. And he didn't like being tied down. He was kind of peculiar in his own way."

"Put him on the list of family worth talking about."

"But Percy been gone."

"We're focused on that family. He's still her brother and his mother's son. Start a Percy page." LT turned the notebook to a clean sheet. "But you right in one sense. It's still correct to be placing the mother before the boy. It's her I want us to consider now. We'll get to Miss Selma directly. But let's spend some time with Mama Lil." Weldon began stacking the composition books he'd pulled from the shelves. "It's because of what you said earlier."

"Me? I said something usable?"

"Absolutely you did. You got me thinking when you read back the question Miss Selma answered by saying, 'Mama did.' Maybe what she said doesn't turn our attention to her, but to . . .'"

"Man! You saying we need to look at Mrs. Mosby. At Mama Lil."

"That's exactly what I'm saying."

"Well, hot damn."

"Consider this. Consider why Mrs. Mosby isn't down to the station every day asking what we found out about her grandbaby. Why isn't she pulling us aside when we see her on her way to work and going up and coming back down from her family up in the Heights she working for and we tip our hats and say 'Good evening' to her, why the next thing out of her mouth isn't why we haven't found her grandbaby? What could be more important than that?"

"But we been keeping her informed and she, the both of them, the mother and the daughter—I mean the grandmother and mother—the baby's mother, they traumatized." LT paused and looked at the older policeman for verification. "I say that right?"

"Yup. And it certainly seems so. But you tell me when how the way we police organize and proceed with our investigations is ever good enough for a family that wants results yesterday if not the day before?"

LT nodded his agreement. "But then, maybe she don't ask because she trusts you and me to keep looking for her grandbaby?" He made it more a question than an answer.

"I think she does trust us. But I also know that grief has a way of getting in the middle of anybody's good sense. It has its own time."

"Which means what? I thought we was here to come up with a plan."

"Boy, haven't you been listening at all?" Weldon cuffed him upside his head. "It's a plan all right. Let's get on outta here. You brought us to exactly where we want to be. Or at least to where we need to get to."

"I did?" LT asked, grabbing for his cap and following Weldon out of Zenobia's and back toward 129th Street. "Where's that? Where we goin?" he shouted. Weldon's long strides already outpaced his.

THE FIRST OF THE YEAR IN THE CITY WAS BRIGHT AND BRITTLE COLD. There was sun but it didn't warm anything. And there was plenty of light. But it didn't make anything feel hopeful or happy. It was a winter's day. The chill won out over the sun, and the brisk wind from the East River swept through the streets and made sure there was nothing that would break through the icy grip that would hold on to the city until spring. But neither the cold nor the chill stopped the two policemen or slowed them down at all. They walked with determination and focus until they got to the stairway leading up to the Mosbys' apartment.

"You want I should ring their bell?" LT asked.

"Whose bell?"

"Mrs. Mosby. The grandmother. We gonna question her right?"

"Wrong."

"Then why we here?" LT was flustered.

"We've got questions all right," Weldon replied. "But not for Mrs. Mosby. For her."

"Who?"

"Her." He nodded over to where a soft edge of Leona Griffin's lace curtain had just dropped back into place.

Of course, Leona Griffin was more than eager to have guests and to assure them there was good reason for them to come in and have a seat while they talked. And perhaps they would want some coffee and cake? A cup of tea? She could add a little taste to take the chill off if they wished. Both of them quickly demurred and almost before they got settled in her small living room, both of them sharing the sofa, Mrs. Griffin held court, sitting forward in a regal brocaded chair with winged edges. She was happy and eager to tell them about that day. She wished they had asked before. Especially because she remembered every detail of how tragic it had been to notify the grandmother of her grandchild's kidnapping. She used her cloth napkin to tap at the tears forming in the corners of her eyes while she recalled how Lilah Mosby had to lean on the railing to catch her breath because she had just come from up the street and how the shocking news unsettled her.

"Did she come from up the street or down?" Weldon asked.

"Down." Leona pointed. "Mrs. Mosby came from that way—down by the five-and-dime and past the stone church. She got off the trolley from down there."

"You're certain?"

"She still had the transfer ticket gripped in her hand when we talked. Hadn't even put it in her bag."

"Ma'am?"

"Her bag. Not the carpetbag that she was toting when she left, those things are just too unwieldy. And she didn't even have it with her on the way back. But she most certainly could've put the ticket in her fold-over cloth purse. I remember clearly that she had her green one with her. Or she might could've easily slipped it into the outside pocket. Of course, one might also consider the pockets of her outerwear. Putting things in pockets simply stretches out the fabric and makes whatever you're wearing quite unsightly. Eventually. I've always held that pockets are purely decorative. Usually. Unless an apron pocket . . ." She almost began to wander, but brought herself back to the subject of the ticket. "Nevertheless, she should've used her purse. That's what I always do." Leona paused to pour her tea, and she did add a splash from her flask. Just because the officers didn't want any did not mean she'd fail to use the moment in a way that would allow her to report how Harlem's two policemen had been to her home for tea. And she'd used the cloth napkins with the lace edges. And her best china tea set—the one she kept dusted and polished for a moment just like this. Being prepared was always first-order conduct. She was pleased with their attention, so she made sure to give as much detail as she could. "As to what I was explaining, I saw the ticket so I knew she'd been on the trolley. And she wore her tweed coat that day—the one with the oversize collar. Perfectly appropriate given the early morning chill, but still, there was no reason I could fathom for her to pick up that green cloth purse. It didn't match. She has a darker-colored one. I've seen it." She shook her head back and forth and waited for one of the officers to speak. Since neither did, she thought she might have been a bit too critical—given the circumstance. So with somewhat more consideration of the unhappy situation of the Mosbys, she attempted to shift her tone. "But then again." She laughed lightly, hoping that it might push aside any negative thoughts the policemen might be having about her. "Well, gracious. Who knows? For heaven's sake, I might've tried to stick it up under my arm too!" She was still met with their silence. So before either of her visitors had the chance to infer anything about her overabundance of interest in what Mrs. Mosby carried with her, or whether her accessories matched her clothing, she rushed an explanation. "You must understand, officers. It was pure happenstance that I was at my window when she departed so early—so very early, in fact—that morning. I'd just wanted to open it a bit, in case there was a morning breeze; but certainly not wide enough to let in a chill. I was seated right over there"—she pointed to a cane chair with a small side table next to it, positioned by her front window so she could easily look outside. "I saw her leave, and then when she came back down, I saw how she was holding on to that ticket like she expected somebody to try to snatch it from her—which, given the kind of news it was my unhappy duty to share—was especially pitiful."

23

How Long You Got?

WHEN THEY LEFT MRS. GRIFFIN'S, WELDON TOLD LT THAT HE WAS going to wait around and interview Mrs. Mosby by himself. He needed to keep it simple. The two of them being there could be a distraction. He'd get back up with LT afterwards and then they could sit down together to figure out where they were. No judgments until they had all the information they could gather under this new "not a kidnap" perspective that could change old information and reorient anything new they learned.

DeLilah Mosby was headed back to her flat. Her breath rose in puffy clouds punctuating the rhythm of her steps and the verse in her head. *Keep step. Keep step* . . . She thought it cruel the way their shared and playful ritual religiously echoed whenever she headed home. Especially today. Sometimes no memories were better than the ones that came unsummoned. *You've got it! Now keep it!* But there was nothing left to keep. Her son left. The baby. Her daughter gone. What was the point? She'd made the plan, made it work, and here she was walking home remembering when things were full and their days were not long enough for the busyness they called for. When they were needy and she could fix it with a cuddle and hug or a trip around the block or one more story at bedtime. When there was trouble, but how—even in their extraordinary neediness and capacious hurt—they would be too full for this kind of anguish to take root. *Don't lose it* . . . Too much had already slipped away. Lilah turned the corner fully prepared to see Mrs. Griffin's curtain drop back into place. She was less prepared for Officer Thomas to be sitting on the inside stairwell.

"Morning, Mama Lil." Weldon took off his cap. He was in his work uniform.

"Good morning, son. I mean, Officer. Didn't expect to see you here first thing and all. But as always, if you're here for me, it comes with my appreciation of your every attention."

"Yes, ma'am. But I haven't been here long at all. Except long enough to run into your mailman, Mr. Childers. He's like clockwork with his route. I told him I was waiting to see you and he said since it's Friday . . ."

She finished it for him and smiled with the expectation. "If it's Friday I likely got mail from home. Percy keeps to his schedule. Writes me right after church first and third Sunday, and sure as thunder follows the lightning I get his post the following Friday. He's a good son." She pulled the envelope from her mail slot and ran her fingers across the carefully executed script as if she could clasp his hand while his pen pressed the letters carefully into the envelope. *Mrs. Lilah Harrison Mosby.* You comin up?" she asked.

"Yes, ma'am, if you'll have me." She leaned into Weldon as they took the stairs up to her flat.

It almost felt as if he could make a difference in what weighed her down. Before she sat at the table, she pulled the last tin from a stacked row of Lipton tea cans, pulled the lid from the top, and took out a packet of letters, tied together with a blue string. "I'll read this new one later when I take my afternoon tea," she said to Weldon, as much as to herself. She placed the stack on the table between them. "Percy do keep up with his correspondence."

"That's good to hear. I know you must miss him." She didn't respond so he commented how her son's penmanship looked like those green alphabet cards they keep over the schoolroom blackboards.

"Palmer," she said. "Percy always got the Palmer script better than anybody. See for yourself." She pushed a stack toward him, and Weldon fanned them through. He looked up, letting his eyes follow the shelf of tea tins, some with envelopes edging out from the tops. "I see you've got a whole bunch of these cans for your letters. But Mr. Childers told me you stuff your mail in a blue carpetbag satchel your mama made. That sometimes you wait for him with the satchel ready for the mail."

"Well, I never stuffed them. I placed his letters inside there. With especial care for the edges. They do fray, you know. But Mr. C right. I used to keep them like that. He been delivering our mail since we moved up here so he would know. Seems like I can remember how some times back we had a set-to as to whose mama stitched the best bag. His mama made up a green one. But that was way back when." She paused and looked around, as if expecting to see it. "That satchel ain't here no more." She sighed deeply. "So I put his letters in these. Not cans. Tea tins. Much Lipton as I drink, might as well use the empties for something."

Weldon read aloud from the stack she slid across the table. "*Mrs. Lilah Harrison Mosby and Miss Selma Mosby.* I like how he makes his *L*'s and *M*'s," he said. More letters to *Mrs. Lilah Harrison Mosby and Miss Selma Mosby.* Then one to *Mrs. Lilah Harrison Mosby and Miss Selma Mosby and Baby Girl Chloe Mosby.* Each was in order according to the date sent. "He always write everybody's name on here?"

She smiled in response. "Even when he found out we had that cat back before Chloe was born he would write '*Mrs. Lilah Harrison Mosby, Miss Selma Mosby, and Cat.*'" Her soft giggle was stifled but surfaced. Weldon was glad to hear it. But something nagged, and he reminded himself to remember the feeling even if he couldn't yet figure out the thing. Something about the last letter, the one that came today, addressed to *Mrs. Lilah Harrison Mosby.*

"Nothing new?" she asked, but not like she was hoping or thought there might be.

"No, ma'am. I'm sorry to say there's nothing new. But I'm here in part to say again that even though the station might've put it aside, I'm still here for you. Cadet Mitchell and me, we're working on it. My file stays open even if the department has moved theirs from the active desk. We're not going to let it go."

"I wouldn't have expected different from you, son. Nothing different at all. Wish I could be more help." She moved the whistling kettle from the fire and poured steaming water into two cups.

"Yes, ma'am." He looked around. "How's Miss Selma doing?" he asked. "I've been wondering after her."

"She 'bout to be gettin better. Much better, indeed."

"That so? Glad to hear it. She could use some ease. Both of you could." Then he asked, "'Bout to be ...?"

"I thank you for the kindness in that thought, son. And since you going to detect it out, I may as well be the one to tell you now that just this week I've sent Selma down to her brother. Percy and 'em picked her up at the Raleigh station and carried her back to Sedalia. This letter here likely gon let me know how she got on." She laid her hand across the letters that she'd placed back into a neat stack, the most recent on the top of the pile. "I'ma miss her, but she gonna get to be more stable. And too, whilst I was taking her to the train, she finally got to conversating a bit. Even making some sense. Talking about the sun. Up here we going to have to wait past April for some good and steady sun. But her being home means she can take up the garden she says she wants. An help out Percy and his missus." Weldon wanted to ask more about Selma, but he waited for her to direct the conversation. He did express that he wished they had had a chance to talk before she left. But not much more than that. He kept his questions simple and waited for her to fill in the gaps.

"Percy married?"

"He is." Weldon didn't say anything else and after a while, as he'd anticipated, Lilah volunteered what he was wondering. "He married the undertaker's daughter what lived in Greensboro, and he done took over the funeral home. His letters always full of how he keeps the figures— what's owed, what's paid for—he calls them the books. But they ledgers really. You know the kind. Rows and columns. Red ink and black."

"Yes, ma'am. He always did have a head for numbers."

"He did. And he liked to see them placed right. And about now I finally have got some ease that he done found himself a way to make a life from that and that he safe."

"I'm happy to hear that, for him as much as for you, Mama Lil."

"Thank you, son. His missus seems to be good for him. You can tell in the way he hasn't stopped at all with writing to his mama. Just like clockwork he writes asking after us and telling us about how the business is going and how the family getting on and all about what his plans be. My June Bug always was orderly about how he do things."

"And how you think Miss Selma going to get on?"

Lilah looked over to the kitchen window where a bit of morning sun was beginning to creep across the sill. She spoke toward the window rather than directly back to Weldon.

"Well." She took a long sip of her tea and wrapped her hands around the violets circling the rim of her cup. So Weldon drank some of his as well. "Well, Percy got a room in the house built on especially for her. It's a big house too. Funeral home in front, family home in the back. And now a room behind that one for his sister. And outside that room, it's a garden. He drawed out the whole thing just for me. Measurements and everything." She unrolled one of the papers from a letter that was some ways back in the stack and showed Weldon the house plans. It looked like an architectural rendering. The numbers—lengths and widths—fell between lines and arrows. Windows broke thick lines of outside walls. He saw a garden plot so meticulously sketched that the landscaping was accounted for. There were gaps for doors and each room was labeled. In the front of the house were *Reception. Office. Sitting Room. Slumber Room A. Slumber Room B. Toilet. Preparation Room. Closet. Hall.* At the back the labels signaled a family home. *Kitchen. Bedroom 1. Nursery. Sitting Room. Closet. Bath.* And off the back porch an addition: *Bedroom 2. Sitting Room.* It looked mighty fine, he thought. Then he said it. "It looks mighty fine. Mighty fine, indeed. He married well." He fingered the sketches she'd shared. "This must have cost a pretty penny."

"He did," she said, answering his first question but avoiding the implied question in what he said after that. But it was important for him to know that things weren't at all haphazard. She had had a role in their safety and the way they could go ahead and plan. "I did my share though. I helped him out." Lilah paused a moment and slipped her hands into her pockets and pressed them hard against her thighs. "I helped with what I managed to do." She meant to say "managed to save" but "managed to do" was at least accurate. She tugged the conversation back toward her son.

"But don't be mistaking that he got more than he gived. That funeral home family got them a young man who can keep them in business. He said they mighta had a business but they books was a mess and things headed straight downhill until he brought some order to the way things were done. Her people are mighty grateful for the skills he brought to the establishment and to the marriage. Mighty grateful, indeed. My Percy loyal." She let that sink it, because it was important for Officer Thomas, and anybody he might talk to about this news, to have the right information about her boy.

"And too," she said, because it might have gone unmentioned, "he making product. He does woodwork and makes some of the best caskets around, and they sell them direct from outta the establishment. Here"— she pointed to the diagram where a fourteen-by-fourteen room was labeled: *Display Room.* When she turned the paper over, Weldon nearly gasped. It was a drawing of a casket. Even though it was all in pencil, he could see a delicate woodwork joinery. Each piece fit into the next like a puzzle, with a slant or an edge or an arrow that slid into a gap. Some were long and slender. Others were thick and intricate. They slid into each other like veins looking for their next unfolding. They were squared and thick, then delicately spiraled. Their edges were an intricate puzzle of ladderlike slats, composing a web of woodwork suitable for a forest primeval. The penciled drawing was so intricately wrought that he could tell the difference in finishes. There were short strokes, corrugated lines, graded tones, slants, crosshatching, and some pieces that looked more like pebbles and waves. Each wood slat seemed different in color and grain—oak, walnut, mahogany, birch, cherry, pine, chestnut, and cedar—but each seamlessly and meticulously aligned into the unmistakable shape of a casket. He let out a long, low whistle, and Lilah shook her head, understanding and appreciating his admiration. "Once folks down there see my Percy's work, they don't even want that pretend velvet flock cloth they paste on those old-timey cardboard boxes. His work done got so recognizable that he got back orders from folks still living. They say they gonna wait to die till he finishes their piece."

"They are beautiful, Mama Lil." He lingered over the drawing. "Your boy got found right here."

"Yes. Yes he has." She paused a moment. "And for Selma, too. She going to be better with some sun and . . ." She wandered for a moment, fingering the blue thread that bound the letters. He prompted her to finish . . .

"And?"

"You wants some more hot water for your tea, son?"

"No, ma'am. Thank you kindly. I got to be going. I just wanted to come by today being it's getting near that time of month when Baby Chloe went missing. I know these times might be harder than other days. It's coming up to three months now. Maybe even crawling already."

"Rolling over."

"Ma'am?"

AFTER WELDON LEFT, SHE CAREFULLY OPENED AND READ HER SON'S most recent letter and sighed. She slipped it back into the envelope, placed it atop the stack of his most recent letters—all organized by date, as Percy would have done—and slid them back into the tea tin. She folded her hands and sat quietly at the table. Waiting. She'd done almost all she could.

YOU DID, SWEETNESS. YOU DID ALLA THAT AND MORE. YOU PLANNED. YOU TOOK care. You brought your best self and gived it to our children just like I knew you would. But DeLilah had moved past memory to grieving. And she was angry to be left with its residue.

"Yeah? You knew? You knew? So I suppose you also knew I'd be left up here by myownself too?" He shimmered.

Girl, how long you gonna let hurt hold on to you?

"How long you got, Iredell?" She looked over to his shadow. The thin winter sun teased the morning air as if it were light or warm. But of course it was neither. There was barely enough light for his shadow to take up an edge and slip through its filter. Whatever shine there was was dim. He slanted into the light as easily as he slipped into the room's dusky corner. She knew he had whatever time it would take, and when she moved away from her grief, she could feel at the edges the ease in his promise of rest. They were quiet together.

24

A Common Denominator

WELDON AND LT MET UP AT THE HARLEM BRANCH LIBRARY. WELDON brought the Kidnap Book, and LT brought his spiral notebooks. Weldon explained the plan.

"We're starting from jump and going in sequence. Starting with the day the baby went missing. And what we're looking for is a common denominator."

"Excuse me? We doing math?"

"Boy, cut it out! You know by now words can have different meanings in different contexts. We're looking for something shared that we didn't see when we were focused on thinking about this thing as a kidnap."

"So why not start by telling me about your meeting with Mama Lil so I can know what you know? Then we go to the first-day sequence."

"That's the last thing we want LT. I mean, yeah. We want to know things together; but first we go one at a time in order to give what both of us have to say due consideration." He paused, remembering the conversation and letting LT suss out the compliment that his information has value. "And too, I need for you to let me let my talk with Mrs. Mosby out on its own time. I know you interested, but it needs to settle. I'ma keep thinking on it while we get on to other things. But I'll say this now. I think I learned a lot. But I don't know that I'm sure of what it is yet. I'm still trying to piece it together in my head." He thought of the slices of wood that Percy drew to design his caskets. But it wasn't the piecework that was necessary. It was the joinery. The story did not need a shove. It should slide into its place.

They respected the quiet of the library reading room, whispering when necessary and turning pages with an effort to shush the rustling. They reviewed their notes, then exchanged them with the other to get the benefit of what Weldon called "fresh eyes." When the two took a break sitting outside on the long stone steps that led to the library's arched doors, Weldon told LT about the letters and how Mama Lil had sent Selma back home almost a week ago.

"What! Selma gone? And you just now telling me this?" He gave a long, slow whistle and was just about to complain further about how he could've started with that information. But Weldon explained how it wasn't as much her being gone as it was how Mrs. Mosby's telling felt as if there was something missing. That gave LT pause. "So it's two new things I learned talking with her. One—Selma back home. Two—Percy writing his mama."

"How Percy's letters figure into this? Everybody with any good sense at all gonna write home when they away. Especially if it's to their mama."

"It's not about sense. Remember? We could be dealing with nonsense. I've got to discern the difference. What I know is the feeling of puzzlement I had sitting with Mrs. Mosby and looking at the stacks of letters from Percy. In fact, Mr. C. brought her mail while I was there settin on the stoop waiting for her. Seems like Percy wrote his mama right after Selma got home."

"And . . . ?"

Weldon paused and pushed himself up from the steps where they were seated and paced back and forth under one of the tall arched windows at the front of the library. He folded his arms and stood there trying to figure it out. He knew something was asking for its place in the puzzle. The two returned to the reading room where they had left their papers and notes. The librarian, a young woman who had just graduated from Howard University's library science school, nodded to acknowledge their return. When they were seated, he quietly told LT that he knew what it was that had given him this pause. "When I talked to her, I saw almost all the letters from her boy on her table. She let me flip through them. She was proud how he kept up with her. I even saw the one she got the day after Chloe went missing. It was addressed to Mrs. Lilah Harrison Mosby and Miss Selma Mosby."

"Okay, so?" The two spoke quietly, but soon one thought followed the other, developing the organic sequence Weldon had anticipated.

"So, the point is, why didn't the letter she got the day after Chloe went missing have the baby's name on it? Baby Chloe was kidnapped on Thursday. His mama said he wrote on first and third Sundays, right after church. And Mr. Childers says mail from him came in regular as clock-work every other Friday. So how come, before the kidnap even happen, he's writing to just his mama and his sister and not to Baby Chloe?"

"Ummm . . . Well, maybe . . ."

"Hold on a minute. That's the first time I got the question out the way I wanted. I need to think on it a bit." Weldon got back up and let his hands rest on the back of the Windsor chair. Finally he turned to LT and asked, "Okay, what is it that *you* think?"

"Well, what I think hurts to say. But these Mosbys, at least Mama Lil and her son, they write back and forth. Regular. And if she's like my own mother, Mama Lil writes about what is going on with the family. And he do too. So I think we have to consider that she wrote him and told him something that let him know there was no reason to put the baby's name on the letter."

"Nope." Weldon didn't even entertain that LT could be partially right. "Uh-uh," he said, shaking his head to emphasize the point. "Can't happen like that."

"But it seems like from what you saw at Mama Lil's that Percy coulda known there was no baby in the house."

"That's reasonable, except the baby didn't go missing till Thursday. This a Friday letter. The day after." LT put his head between his hands and said he didn't know what to think anymore. "Well, focus on this question then. It's more about now than then. Why did Mrs. Mosby send Selma back to Sedalia by herownself?"

"Yeah. Yeah." LT nodded in agreement. "How come Mama Lil didn't go too? Nothing keeping her here."

"I asked her that exact thing. That's where I got a problem I can't quite figure what to do with. She said it wouldn't be right with the baby gone missing and the investigation and all for them both to leave. She said, 'Somebody has to keep up with things.'"

"What she mean by that? 'Keep up with things'?" The fact is, we the onliest ones trying to let them know what's going on. That doesn't fit with how they been acting."

"You got that right." Weldon picked up one of the notebooks and thumbed through it. "And I thought the same thing. So that conversation is one of the things I'm trying to find a space for. And now that Selma is down home with her brother, I need to figure out whether this puzzle is about the mail or if it's about something else."

"Maybe just figure out what we do know and then see what's missing?"

The librarian's look was a warning, so they turned away from her desk and faced a shelf of encyclopedias. "First is Selma going back home by herself. Then second, how Mama Lil been communicating with Percy in some way that suggests he knew the baby would go missing before she went missing." He paused and closed his eyes. Eventually LT prompted him.

"Is there a three?"

"Three is how come that carpetbag is missing."

"How'd a carpetbag get to be on our list?"

"That's from our conversation with Mrs. Griffin put together with what I just heard from Mama Lil. Didn't you notice what Mrs. Griffin had to say about the bag?"

"That it didn't match?"

"No. That was her purse. She said that she had the bag when she left and didn't have it when she came back. She went on and on about the purse, but it's the carpetbag caught my attention."

"Oh yeah. I didn't even . . ."

"That's all right. When it come up again when I talked with Mama Lil, it moved up to the front of what I was paying attention to myownself. What we know is the mailman said she kept her letters in it. Mrs. Griffin said she toted it out of the building and told us directly she didn't have it coming back. Then Mama Lil told me today that it was gone."

"Should I write this down?"

"Nope. Just listen. I need to talk it out. It's something that's not sitting well with me on this. A carpetbag, that's . . . that's home. And now I'm thinking about how they usually a certain size. And shape. And about why would she leave with it and not come back with something she done held on to since her first days in Harlem? That she brought up from home when she and Percy and Iredell Mosby come to the city."

"You think she went and got rid of all of Percy's letters? How come?"

197

"Nope. Not at all. I saw the letters in a bunch of tea tins in her kitchen. By the number of cans lined up on her wall shelf, she held on to every single one."

"So she carried off an empty bag?"

Weldon paused long enough to be sure. Then he replied with a sadness that was evident. "No son. That's not what I think." LT just stared at him. "Not. At. All." He said each word with a decided emphasis. The boy put his head down on the table and then raised his hands up to cover his ears as if what he was hearing was too painful.

"Awww, man, no! Naw! Can't be! You think it's a baby was in there, don't you? You think Baby Chloe was in the carpetbag." The look and loud shush from the young librarian was enough to cause the two to gather up their notes and head outside. They sat together on the stone steps—each holding his head in his hands, and neither one wanting to be the first to engage LT's lingering question. Weldon finally did; but without repeating the question. It was still too hard to say aloud and again.

"Let me say this. What you have implied is indeed within the realm of unhappy possibilities. But that's not the end of it. Wish it was. But the question that now goes alongside is as relevant."

"Which is?"

"Which is: 'A live baby, or a dead one?'"

"Damn." LT shook his head and asked, "How'd we get to this being the question?"

"Because of what's in *my* notes about that day." Weldon opened the page from his composition books to his own interviews. And the words he underlined in red pencil because more than one person said it when talking about Selma: "addled," "tilted," "daft," "peculiar," "tetched." "When I put my notes and your notes together with what I heard today, and then when I put all that together with how come we at three months missing and it's me and you going down to see Mrs. Mosby instead of her harassing the heck outta us about where her grandbaby is. That's just ass backwards from how this ought to be playing out." He slapped his hands down on his knees with a resigned finality. "Lord knows these folks had more trouble than anybody deserves. But a missing grandbaby calls for a certain kind of energy. And it's not the kind that takes me down to their place more 'n they ever been down to the station to ask about progress on a search."

"So we back to what you say we always s'posed do first. Look to the family."

"We are. And when we put our notes together, and when we add this carpetbag that goes out of the house the same day the baby did . . ." He unfolded his bifocals and looked down to his notes. And then today she's telling me 'that satchel ain't here no more.'"

"So 'where is it?' is our question?"

"Not so much that as 'what was in it?'"

"Like I said. Damn."

25

Some Things Stay

AFTER SHE LEFT THE TRAIN STATION THAT LAST THURSDAY IN OCTOBER, DeLilah Mosby made her way home, reversing her morning's route. She took the streetcar then walked the last few blocks. She was slower than she had been starting out even though the baby's weight no longer pulled on her shoulder. The deed carried its own heft and she was nearly disabled by the sorrow of it all. Her chest heaved along with her steps—*Keep step . . . Keep step.* She hated it when something like that, something so light and promising and full of a different kind of memory pushed forward and took up room in a day when it was the last kind of re-memory that she needed. On reflection, those early days with the children that seemed so cluttered and so hard were actually the ones that were weightless. She wished she had treated them that way instead of with the intensity and shrill she recalled. Now, even the late morning light struggled to make its way to the streets through the tangles of gnarled chestnut branches. Everything seemed to join her unbearable duty.

She knew Selma favored the churchyard. Lilah appreciated its appeal as well. The gardens kept a serenity about them that felt unreal, even though it was only a gate and some shrubbery merely a short ways away from the city's streets and sidewalks. It was a quieter block, but still that didn't take it out of Harlem. The church had only been there since the first decade of the 1800s. But it looked older and its grounds matched its

Gothic aspiration. The gardens and graveyard were carefully tended and mirrored the quiet elegance of the sanctuary.

When Selma took to escaping to the churchyard's silences along with Baby Chloe, nobody was there to try to make her speak, to ask what she had seen or who had done what, and there was no one to remark about how "pretty her light-skinded baby girl look" or to try to touch her silky curls. She felt safe there, in the promise of an unassuming quiet. It was a bearable landscape. Even her mother noticed her calm after she came in from walking the baby. DeLilah briefly thought that her daughter was finding her way back, but then she came home to the day that Selma made it clear how the panic that feathered in her daughter's mind had crystallized into a menace.

That day in their kitchenette, when her mother's eyes finally focused and took in the storm of white, Lilah saw the furious emptiness that enveloped her daughter. It was chilled like windswept spring blossoms and was brittle like dry flurries of a first snowfall. Its residue blanketed their tiny room in a way that made plain there was no escape from her daughter's loss.

She'd already sent all the money she'd managed to gain from that morning of bargaining and accusation at the Thayers' down to Percy in Sedalia to help him prepare for the family's return. Her plan had always been home. Step by cautious step. *Keep step.* And it included Percy too, who joined in, fully ready to manage their transition and eager to make up for his youthful missteps. They would be together back where she and Iredell had started out. It was the right and only thing to do. Memories of kin.

And in fact, everything about her plan was working just fine until the man who (now that she thought about it) had probably been looking for her boy since the day he left, showed up again across the street from their building. He wasn't even trying to be discreet; he just took up the same position at the streetlamp he'd had back in the day. Once again he was a sentinel, watching folks' coming and going with a stoic and threatening vigilance. DeLilah was as irritated with his persistence as she was frightened by it. Despite the years that had passed, she was certain that he was still looking for Percy just like he did in those weeks after she sent her son back home—away from the danger he'd encouraged. It wasn't hard at all to notice a lingering white man, and too, she remembered his hat. This one seemed better made but it was still brown and still pulled slightly down over his forehead and it still shadowed a pale and gaunt-looking face. Looking closer, she couldn't mistake the chin—long and pointy. More form than flesh. And then there was his gait. He had a limp that gave him an uneven step that was so memorable that when he moved from the post to the corner, and then back again, she could almost count the steps before he'd shift his weight and take a skip and a hop instead of place his foot firm and flat down onto the pavement. His pocket watch looked to be the same, or at least that he treated it the same, pulling it out of his vest, looking at it, then toward the clock in the pharmacy window. It was a pattern that was too familiar, and the fear it held came back with a knifelike thrust that carried all the dread she'd felt when she watched him on the lookout for Percy years ago. Back then she knew her son was already far away and safe. After a couple of weeks of his hanging around, he'd finally disappeared, giving up on hurting her boy like she was sure he planned to do. *Silencing him* she heard it was called. Lilah was determined that her son would not be silenced. And that he would be safe.

When Lilah saw him again, it was just after she'd written Percy and told him to come on up right away and get the baby because Selma had lost her mind and he and his wife—she was sure she would be a fine mother to little Chloe—they could raise Selma's baby like she was their own given they had lost one like he said in his last letter. Here was this little one, which—given it was his sister's baby—would be his own kin. She needed a better and safer place than she could give them. And there was the added feature that his wife, being the daughter of a funeral director, was light-skinned. Their tiny wedding photograph was stuck inside her dresser mirror, right next to the one of Iredell holding his son on his knee and her around her waist. This was a fine-looking girl Percy had married. Little Chloe could grow up just like she was their baby girl. She'd seen the touch of nutmeg lining the lobe of her granddaughter's ear, and knew she had some color yet to come in. Just enough so that if she had to, she could pass for Percy's daughter if that was what they wanted to do. It didn't matter and after a while, she was sure people would forget if they wanted to tell her that. Percy should get him a ticket on the Tuesday train and he could get up here and take the baby on Thursday. In fact, the plan had it so that he would come down the street that very day ready to greet his mother and sister and meet the little one she was going to turn over to his care and keeping.

She had it all figured out what she would say to Selma. First, how they would all reunite, and then how she would promise Selma—if she was at all attentive to her brother's return, which she couldn't promise would happen—that as soon as she was well, she could go home too. That Percy was making a house for them. He'd sent drawings that sketched out the plans he was making to build a funeral home with the family house at the back. It would have room enough for all of them. It might be difficult for a bit, not knowing how Selma would take to it and because he could not stay around and wait till she adjusted. The adjustment his sister needed to make was no sure thing. Selma would just have to trust that her mother cared enough to make a plan and that her brother June Bug had grown up responsible and found himself a place, and could take care of them all because he had figured out a way to be in the world. Just like she told him when he left.

And up to that moment, everything was fine until Lilah looked out over the stoop and saw Ned Raddice back on their block. Of course DeLilah had no idea that Raddice was on a different mission entirely. That he was there because the Thayers were going to make certain they had no unknown heirs and had directed him to assure there would be no future kinship claims. She was correct in that it was her family he was after. But it was not her boy. He was there to take her granddaughter.

The truth was, Raddice hadn't even made the connection between the boy who used to be his accountant and the work that used to occupy him before he started up with the Thayers. He knew the street corner and the building, sure. But he knew a lot about Harlem's tenements. He was focused on this job, not the one Lilah remembered from years back when he just wanted to be sure the boy wouldn't talk. Back then, when he didn't see him around, he figured the kid was smart enough to get lost. That was the end of his thinking about it. But not Lilah's. Her imagination took off. She thought of how Percy would soon be getting off the train and how, unbeknownst to him, he was heading straight for an old and obstinate trouble. She knew as soon as she saw Raddice malingering across the street that he was the same one as before. There was no way her boy could come anywhere near where they stayed. But she had no way to warn him away. Percy's train was already close, probably just outside the state, heading north like it was promise not peril. The only thing she could do that would still save Chloe from Selma's disarray and Percy from his past was to take the baby down to the station and meet her son there. She could be there when the train arrived and send them both back without Percy even having to leave the station and risk that man's deadly intentions. And she could still save her grandbaby from her mother.

After DeLilah decided that was for sure who it was, she wasted no time in preparing the baby to leave. She laid her sweet grandbaby gently inside the blue carpetbag and swaddled her in as many of her blankets and little layette things she had bought for her with the Thayer money. She stuffed some bottles in one corner and buttressed them with bunting. Then she slung the strap across her shoulder, cradling the bag in her arms and carried the unwieldy load down the stairs and out of her building. Mrs. Griffin's curtain fluttered when she turned in the direction of the trolley stop three blocks down, just past the churchyard.

It went exactly like she planned. Lilah met Percy on the platform where the Southern Sky moved slowly into the station. She held him as long as she possibly could, then pushed the baby into his arms and told him about the man. "The porters, they'll help you with Chloe. Look out for some colored ladies to help. You won't have no trouble with the baby being she's just past two months, and the way the train rocks back and forth—I still remember that rhythm—that for sure will help her sleep nearly all the way home. Plus I put a little taste in her bottle for when or if she get too fussy. But you got to go, boy. You got to go now." It wasn't the reunion she'd planned or needed. There was no lingering in his long arms, no listening for his warm voice, no holding his face in her hands and looking deep into his eyes to make sure he was all there and all right. There was only time for her to tell him that man was back and looking out for him and to say what she'd said those many years ago. "You got to go. Take this baby and get back on this train straightaway and head directly back home. Go on now. Get gone."

LILAH KNEW SHE HAD DONE RIGHT WHEN SHE SAW THE MAN AGAIN later that morning across from Chasen's. His fedora and pale white features stood out in the panicked crowd of warm brown faces. He must've thought Percy would come down there. Still trying to get at my June Bug, she figured. Lilah already knew from Leona Griffin that folks thought the baby was kidnapped. She couldn't quite reckon out the whole thing from listening to Leona, so she made her way down to the grocery as soon as she could get away from her neighbor's prattling in order to get the story straight and her daughter back to where she belonged. She could at least take some relief that Chloe was safe on the train with her Uncle (or Daddy) Percy. She'd stayed at the station until the Southern Sky took off and headed for home.

But when she got down to Chasen's, an impossible crowd had gathered around the store, and there was no place anywhere for her to make room for a sane or sensible explanation. It was pure chaos. People were shouting and making declarations that "this one here just like the Lindbergh."

She turned her head to try to keep track of the pale threat across the street even while she looked past the crowd to see through the store window where her Selma was settled in the back of the store being coddled and soothed by the women who explained to DeLilah that her granddaughter was kidnapped right out the perambulator. *Right in the broad and bold light of day.* Like they knew it and had seen it happen. Before she could explain that Selma probably did push the perambulator to the store, but there wasn't a baby to be taken in it, somebody asked, *Where the daddy?* clear and loud enough in order to be helpful, or heard.

Ain't no daddy. A large woman with a burlap satchel declared as a matter-of-fact as she stood to the side to allow Lilah to push her way to the back with an authority that undercut the foolishness of the woman's question. As prepared as she was to break through the nonsense, there was an almost furious level of necessity and a fierce appeal in this kidnapping story. It was being shaped like freshly cut cloth ready for embroidery with a fine and fanciful stitchery that might make them all more important than they were. It began to be as beguiling as it was obligatory to imagine Harlem's very own version of the Lindbergh affair. Lilah was sick with fear. The chaos had its effect on her and dampened the assurance of safety she'd balanced against her fear of the white man's interests. He was outside the store. She was certain his interest was as fresh as the day she helped Percy escape the first time. So there was no way she was going to tell anybody where her boy was, and that meant she certainly couldn't say a word of explanation about how there was no baby in the buggy because the baby was with her son. And too, it wasn't like anybody asked her what had happened. Folks were snatching at her arm, and hollering over each other, and telling her for a fact that Chloe was kidnapped. So she said nothing at all, and it became easier to say nothing later. It was the only way she could protect her children and the plan.

"*Hush!*" she told her daughter when it looked like Selma might have something to say. "*Just hush!*"

Eventually, after questions and prodding and sobbing and shushing, Officer Thomas's cadet—the young Mitchell boy—and her sweet neighbor Doris Gayles got them all back home, and before she knew it, she was full-on the other side of being able to explain anything to anybody.

THE CHURCHYARD WAS BATHED IN JUST-BEFORE-DAYBREAK SHADOWS. There was enough duskiness and early morning fog to make her path unsure, to make the difference between a piling of earth, a mound of granite, and a tree stump inscrutable. Given how the morning had gone with the sheer weight of her panic and its urgency, it seemed right to take the time to pause and slow down. She needed to get back before Selma woke up so she could tell her what had happened and be gentle-like and slow. She needed to hear it in a way she could take it in. But she knew she needed a moment to gather herownself before she went back home for whatever that telling would be like.

Before she got well into the gardens, she already knew Iredell was there. Not there in the earth—his place was still that dusty mound out on Hart Island. But she could feel how he was waiting in the light that splayed across the stones in the back corner. Of course she would have loved for him to have a space there. Something fine and chiseled and solid. But this was just a visiting place for people like her and Selma. It was not for their burials. But perhaps it could be a place of rest. She sat on a bench and watched the sun brighten the east row of church windows. The early rays caught the stained glass, and the morning light sparkled.

This it?

"If you mean is this the best I can do, no. Is it what I can do? Yes. This be it."

You sure, sweetness, that this the way to do this thing?

"You didn't see the petals."

Petals?

"Or snowflakes, feathers, whatever. Cloth. Pieces of cloth. Scattered and torn. Some cut thick and full. Like she done made her own blizzard and plopped herself down in the middle of it. And the baby . . ."

Baby girl there too?

"Lying there squalling like all get out. It's a good thing she was wearing that marigold-yellow nightie 'cause if she had had on the white one, Selma would've likely cut all over her too trying to get some cloth to make her dress she was sewing. Didn't matter where the cloth came from. Long as it was white. And what was on her was pitiful. But then I found Baby Girl had scissors up under her. Open. Ready to cut. Like Selma put them down and then laid Chloe down right on top of them when she got to stitching. So that was it. There was too much. Chloe had to go in order to live. That was the onliest thing clear about what I saw on that day."

She finished spilling it out and then turned to look at the shadow, trying not to think of how different it was from when he was in their kitchen door. This sun shaft of light from a church window was something fresh and nearly dangerous in its untethering. Their kitchenette kept him housed in a way that was familiar and even sure. Here, out here in the air—he had a freedom that frightened her. She felt he was tentative, pulled away from her rather than close and captive in the rooms they had shared. So she was managing a caution born of her need to keep him there with her instead of his surrendering to the fresh and tranquil freedom of the morning air. Which seemed fully possible, and even desirable.

"I had to do something. Just didn't know it was going to happen like this. Didn't know that I'd have to move this quick. Which is why I needed to sit here and be still right now. It's been a lot."

Might get to be more.

She didn't respond to that because she couldn't imagine more. "Once I started, once I got her and Chloe her Thayer money, once I sent it all down to June Bug so's he could get started on getting things ready for us, well, all of it but what I spent on that pram. I had to have that Gimbel's pram for her, I wasn't going to have a baby everybody looking at in anything old and broke down. I wanted her to have something fine that didn't shout out that we was still in need. Or pitiful. I wrote to Percy and gived him the money to start getting ready for her. Then after what had happened with all the cutting I wrote again to tell him how he had to make his way back home quick and take the baby. And then, and then . . . well, I hadn't yet finished my figuring on what would come after . . ." She coughed, as if to indicate the context of her decision-making. He glistened. Did that mean he understood the complexity of everything? How one act led to another? How just making the one decision that would fix things simply led to another and then another? Or was it judgment that shifted his light?

It feels different out here. The air be moving. Me too . . .

"You goin now? Now while I'm tryin to tell you what it was that had happened?" His shadow had taken on a dim luster of early morning. She felt envious and threatened. He seemed warm and it invited the kind of memories she ordinarily resisted.

"I miss you."

I'm here.

"You say that like it's someplace. I don't know nothing about your 'here.' Your being there is the onliest thing I can feel. You being there with your pale and shimmer and trails of dust spiraling out. You got all and everything I know. And what I know for sure is what I want is you." She said it again. "I miss you."

This here ain't forever.

"Which 'this' you talkin 'bout, Iredell? Mine or yours? Where's this 'here' that you say like it's ours? 'Cause that would make a world of difference to me."

Nothing here is forever. Not a thing. Nothing but what matters. Love. Love is the forever. This here, this ain't nobody's forever.

She bent down and picked up a chestnut pod that had nestled in the grass near the bench where she sat. She sliced her thumbnails through the ridge that showed the fruit and broke it open. The spines pricked her fingers, but the deep brown nut, shiny and new, still slick with the protective caul that clung to its skin, was there for her plucking. She nudged and pulled it from the skin and then held it between her palms. "I love you, Iredell. I do. It's been a long, hard love. Lonely. Tiresome. But this here, if this is what you been calling a plan, this kind of love needs somebody braver than me to . . ."

You is brave. But that's not what we have here. What you did, what you going to have to do, brave ain't what's called for. You and me, we always needed more than brave. When we sat in the dirt and waited for the train, when you had me laid out there on the island and tucked that blue string into the dirt . . .

"You saw? You saw that?"

He lifted his hand from his pocket. The sleeve fell down over his wrist, but he rubbed his arm against his side and that showed some . . . some skin? But mostly she saw the blue string bracelet, the knots she'd tightened with her teeth. The threads from her mother's carpetbag. The one she had nudged into the graveyard soil where she left him buried.

Some things stay. They find where they supposed to be and they keep to their place. Love does that. That's all you got to know.

The sun rose higher and the churchyard felt less private. She could hear the city's waking. It was time for her to leave. She looked toward the stone-stacked corner. Its glimmer was fading. Now it was dewy and wet. Nothing else. Nothing left of him but what she had known. She clutched her bag and picked up the trolley transfer ticket so as not to leave anything there that didn't belong. She made her way back down the stone path toward the street. When she got to the fence, she traced the iron pickets with her hand then reached down for the latch, lifted it from the clasp, and closed the iron gate behind her. She headed home, where Leona Griffin was perched on the stoop, waiting to tell her that just like the Lindbergh baby, her grandbaby Chloe was gone missing and been kidnapped.

26

A Ways and a Means

WELDON AND LT GATHERED UP THEIR PAPERS FROM THE STEPS AND headed back into the library. They needed its orderliness and form for whatever was working its way out from their conversation and detailed reviews. As they settled back in, they were well aware and respectful of the librarian's guarded oversight. Weldon looked over at LT. The boy was nearly buried in composition notebooks. Loose papers and raggedy-edged sheets from his spiral notes scattered across the width of the long library table. After a long and uncomfortable silence, all Weldon could do was sigh and say. "Awww damn. I got this. I *got* this. Mrs. Mosby she told me. It was me that wasn't attending to her words like I should have been."

"Huh?" LT asked. "What you mean she told you?" At the other end of the table, the professor looked up. She was stacking her own books, returning the fiction to one side, the nonfiction to the other. As was her habit, the atlas was open right at the middle of the table, so she could pull it toward her whenever necessary. It stayed on the page with the southern states of the United States. She pulled the atlas forward as Weldon spoke and tapped her finger on North Carolina's Piedmont region and nodded her small gray head. Weldon acknowledged her blessing.

"What I don't know for sure is why. But I'ma find out now. You stay here and straighten up. I'll be back." He left LT at the library puzzling over whatever clue it was that he must've missed. Before long Officer Thomas was sitting with Mrs. Mosby at the kitchenette's table.

"I didn't expect to see you again so soon. But I'm glad you're here like always."

"Yes, ma'am," Weldon replied, trying to figure out how to start. Then he just said it plain. "So Baby Chloe turning over all by herownself now." It was a statement, not a question. Lilah turned her head silently to look directly at him. She was relieved but not without worry. Without her interruption, which he took as an unspoken affirmation, he kept going. "She all right too. Been staying with Percy and his missus since back in the autumn?" She shook her head and for a moment slipped her hands into her pockets. He clasped his together and leaned in toward her. "Ma'am. What it is I don't know though is why not tell me, Miss Lilah? Why not just say you sent the baby off?" For a moment she fingered the needle in the inside seam of the pocket but then she stopped. Maybe it was his gentle questioning. Maybe it was simply time to stop. She pulled her hands out and held on to the violet-laced teacup. She kept her head down while she told Weldon how the white man came back.

It was in the library when Weldon remembered how Mama Lil said the baby was turning over by itself. That was the piece that shifted the puzzle's shape. It didn't make any sense as to how she could know what the baby was doing unless she knew where the baby was. And that didn't make sense unless she had something to do with it. And too, he had never felt his nudge, his premonition that something terrible was going to happen on that day. He didn't feel it because nothing terrible did happen. Another Harlem mother just did what she could to keep her family safe. She just lost her way in the doing. How could Mrs. Mosby be called to make sense of nonsense? She was focused on saving a life instead of losing one. Weldon needed to get clear as to why she didn't say it all in the beginning and so she told him why, and how. She couldn't put her Percy at risk again. She'd written her son and explained how he had to come back and take his sister's baby before something more terrible happened to her. It was left to her to make sure Chloe, at least, would be safe. And if she'd told anybody where the baby was, given that all Harlem was talking about their own kidnapped-like-Lindbergh baby,

211

it would only make it easier for that man to track down her June Bug. Weldon felt her helplessness. He nodded as her story slipped everything into place. He took her hands and held them.

Much later that evening, Lilah finally looked. Before it was always touch. Her fingers would follow the tracery of her cutting as reassurance and proof. Evidence that this had all been a labor. But it wasn't until that night when she finally lifted her skirts and maneuvered herself under the lamp bulb and dared to look long and without turning away at what she'd done. She gasped at the intricacy of it all. It could have been stitchery or tatting. It was lacy but not light. Ridged scars poked through her smooth brown thighs in whorls and lumps that only because DeLilah knew stitchery made her cuts seem more like lacework than injury. Still, there was no solace in the patterns. Instead, the weave of wounds seemed more like a terrible consequence trying to find its way, even if it was dim and private. She sighed while forcing her finger to try to follow some kind of route, but it was more like a maze. She'd find it came back to some origin near her knees or too close to the inside folds of her most private parts. There were no decipherable shapes, nothing like orderliness. Her cuttings were so embedded in her mourning that any starting place could well have been a destination. Lilah's tears fell into the few spaces between where the intricate detail seemed deliberate rather than haphazard. The lamplight or moonlight or the shimmering trace of her tears left a glow that was finally proof enough of her loss and her longing. She pressed her hands flat into her bare skin and let them stay until their warmth seeped into each cut and every seam. She knew then, when the throbbing stopped and the ridges even seemed to recede some, that she could stop her record keeping. She pulled off her dark slip, gave it a good washing, and hung it from the window with everything else. Looking for sun, finding air.

LATER THE STORY GOT ADDED TO THE KIDNAP BOOK, THE END OF IT, THE reason for it, and what happened to them all. He didn't share it with the official record; he shelved it behind his door. He told LT, explaining how what they knew fit into what Lilah had done and how Percy went home and did what his mother told him to in the beginning. He was glad the boy didn't ask about bringing what they knew to their higher-ups. It was like he already figured out how there was more than one way to do Harlem's policing. And if the colored police couldn't keep their people safe in all the ways that their safety was different, and difficult, and especially challenging for these streets, he wasn't going to be much help to anybody. Much less his own folks. So instead of asking about protocol, LT helped Weldon shelve the books, return the photographs and ephemera of the case to the shoeboxes, and put things back into the kind of order that could keep them ready for the next time they'd need to do some outside-the-station-house detecting.

The next week, both cops helped Miss Lilah pack up what she wanted from her small household—mostly the pictures and the letters. And of course the teacup with the garland of faded violets edging its border, and the baby's perambulator, which would go in the luggage car. LT brought over a deep red-and-brown brocaded carpetbag. "You send it back whenever, Mama Lil. Or not. It was my mama's. She would have wanted you to have it for a trip like this one. Home calls for a certain kind of remembering." She looked up at the men and cupped both their faces with her hands. One at a time. She didn't say thank you. She didn't have to. It was a slight space of grace—and they were appreciative, the three of them, to have the moment together.

DELILAH MOSBY'S TRIP BACK HOME TO SEDALIA WAS NEARLY AS BRIEF AS the time she spent there. Just long enough to touch whom she needed to, and to understand and appreciate the artistry in her son's woodwork. When he heard his mother's cough in the train station, Percy recognized its rattle. He got busy with shaving and sanding the carefully curated pieces of wood, a spray of chips and dust falling around him, sliding their beveled railings, each meticulously edged by the gentle undulations of his adze blade, first onto the basket and then onto the fitted lid that would shape her resting place. He made house and home for the now and the then. She had time to draw her fingers across the grain and appreciate the artistry of her son's gift. DeLilah sat in the outside garden, beside the furious flowering of hollyhocks, listening to his plane shape the edges with a soothing, even rhythm and watching for the sun's setting.

AFTERWARDS, THE TWO LINGERED TOGETHER AT THE EDGE OF SELMA'S garden and took pride in how their girl had a way with growing things. Their Percy was quiet but held a measured calm and a certainty. And most important, he was loving with his family. All of them. Chloe's color came in a golden bronze and she was indeed crawling already, chasing bright and dusty shafts of sunlight that crisscrossed the floor in her nursery.

Where the jasmine and ivy climbed the garden fence, his light moved into hers. Where the branches and blossoms met, her shadow slipped into his. The dusk-dark caught an evening breeze filled with honeysuckle and a whisper. *This the promise. This is. That everything gone missing might find a ways and a means. Home.*

Author's Note

I HAVE ALTERED THE DATES OF THE LINDBERGH KIDNAPPING, MOVING IT forward in time in a way that may be noticeable to some readers, but the seasons remain intact and the telling does not stray from the facts of that infamous episode in United States cultural history. Additionally, it may be important to note that the great influenza of 1918 had several waves. Iredell Mosby died after the last wave of the epidemic, in one of the annual grim returns of the deadly virus's most virulent years.

I am deeply grateful for Trevor Perri's attentive and thoughtful reading, his many helpful suggestions, Erin DeWitt's careful and discerning copyediting, and all at Northwestern University Press who supported and encouraged this second book of my "In Harlem" series. The company of a university press community—its rigorous processes, its creativity, its equity, and its hallmark professionalism—is one I have learned to cherish. I urge our shared celebration and support of the academy's necessary institution.

Finally, I have had nothing less than sheer good fortune to be folded into and embraced by colleagues, friends, the indefatigable Friday Night Women's bookclub (circa 1986)—many of whom have kindly lent me their names for this fiction—and of course my precious family, who are not only ideal readers but who have been constant and selfless in their generous support. Fixed at the center of the loving circle they constitute—with necessary, encouraging, full faith and kindness—are my devoted husband, Russell; my sister, Leslie Ellen; my children, Ayana and Javier; and my sweet grandboy, Jacobo Xavier. They are steadfast and certain in their absolute love. I am because they are.

CPSIA information can be obtained
at www.ICGtesting.com
Printed in the USA
FSHW012050050521
81163FS